Advance Praise

"Spisak's delightful fiction debut is a compelling tale of lost-and-found and enlightenment. Clues dropped like breadcrumbs take two sisters to the exotic land of their ancestors who hold secrets. *The Baba Yaga Mask* unfolds much like Baba Vira's childhood nesting dolls—a captivating story within a story within a story. The result is part mystery and part fairytale but all gratifying."

—**Leah Weiss**, best-selling author of *If The Creek Don't Rise* and *All The Little Hopes*

"*The Baba Yaga Mask* is a fascinating journey that twists and turns through the streets of contemporary Eastern Europe as it traces lines back into a shrouded and difficult past. In the process, the characters pull back the masks of former traumas and disconnection to discover the true faces of friendship, family, and sisterhood. *The Baba Yaga Mask* is a wild ride through a legacy of love."

—**Laisha Rosnau**, author of *Little Fortress* and *Our Familiar Hunger*

"In the skillful hands of the author, the granddaughters' search across Europe intersects with the historical timeline of Baba Vira experiencing young womanhood under the cruel and crushing weight first of the Soviet Union and then of the German Nazis during World War II. Profound love collides with mystery and magic."

—**Solveig Eggerz**, author of *Seal Woman* and *Sigga of Reykjavik*

"*The Baba Yaga Mask* is all heart and soul. A tender and thought-provoking story that demonstrates the countless ways that a woman can be strong. A timeless tale that will touch readers across generations and around the globe."

 —**Sadeqa Johnson**, International best-selling author
 of *Yellow Wife*

"In her novel, Spisak lyrically interweaves elements from Ukrainian culture, such as traditional dance, matryoshka nesting dolls, and tales. Each motif illuminates Vira's character, as with the dolls hidden within one another, speaking to her lifesaving abilities in disguise, deceit, and concealment. A complex, poetic tale, strongly linking past and present through folk art's rich traditions."

 —*KIRKUS REVIEWS*

"With hints of the fantastical, *The Baba Yaga Mask* is a multigenerational story of endurance and survival."

 —*March/April 2022 issue FOREWORD MAGAZINE*

THE
BABA
YAGA
MASK

THE
BABA
YAGA
MASK

KRIS SPISAK

Wyatt-MacKenzie Publishing
DEADWOOD, OREGON

The Baba Yaga Mask
Kris Spisak

ISBN: 978-1-954332-31-7
Library of Congress Control Number on file.

Cover illustration by Wyatt Cleary

Wyatt-MacKenzie Publishing
DEADWOOD, OREGON

www.WyattMacKenzie.com

Dedication

For my mother

1

Larissa

The sidewalks of her neighborhood held strollers and casually mascaraed moms, eyebrows shaped and clothes the perfect combination of shabby chic couture. Flowers in hand, Larissa wore her perfect-mommy face too, even if she wanted to run home from her stop at the florist, muscle memory making up for the misfortune of others.

But she forced herself to slow. Heel, toe, heel, toe. She was okay. The party would be fine. She was a master at this. The choreography of her blood simmered under her skin but remained hidden in her simple, well-postured stroll. Just a stroll. She had never been as excited as Ira about the Ukrainian dance classes they had taken as children, but she'd been good. She'd turned heads. She had danced, and her worries flew away off the tips of the ribbons cascading behind her—at least until she realized that Ukrainian dance was weird to the other kids at school.

Heel, toe, heel, toe. Larissa relaxed the wrinkles forming on her forehead.

The English garden scene she'd created in their backyard looked lovely from the sidewalk approaching her house. Very Beatrix Potter—though didn't Beatrix Potter hate kids? She needed to think of a better comparison. She needed to take pictures before guests arrived.

With two hours until her daughter's party and five hours until Baba Vira needed to be at the airport, Larissa straightened the birthday cake flag by their front door before walking inside.

Baba Vira's thin boney legs were propped up on the ottoman, the skin of her fingers stained a splattered red from making borsht. Larissa's two children sat on the floor by her side.

"I told them I was German citizen. I said, 'Heil Hitler' and raised hand."

"You lied?" Anna wrung her hands with their freshly painted pixie-dust pink fingernails.

"If they knew truth, I'd disappear. No one would know what happened to me."

"Like magic, Baba?" Alex hugged his knobby, four-year-old knees in front of him.

Larissa raised her eyebrows, willing her grandmother to turn her way. She didn't.

"*Tak*, like magic," Baba Vira agreed solemnly, putting her veined hand on the little boy's head.

"I don't want someone to disappear me."

"Then be good liar."

Both children looked to their mom at these words. They'd, of course, heard her come in, keys jangling in her hands.

"No one will make you disappear, little bug." Alex had outgrown the nickname, but Larissa couldn't help herself sometimes. She set her rosebuds and baby's breath on the kitchen counter next to the eight naked grapevine wreaths they would decorate for Anna's guests in lieu of party hats.

"But Baba knows how to disappear." The boy stood, awe for his great-grandmother in the clenching and unclenching of his little fists. "We played hide and seek. We couldn't find her!"

Larissa knew the feeling. Her grandmother had played the same way when Larissa was a child, making doors creak then moving in the opposite direction.

"We always find her, though, don't we?"

Baba Vira's plane tickets sat out on the counter. Larissa's doubts about the sanity of her grandmother's trip to Warsaw, Poland for the International Folkdance Exhibition was something she didn't have time for right now. Prep. Party. Flight.

She picked up the tickets, tucking them into her purse.

"Knowing how to hide can save life too." Baba Vira whistled like a bird deep in the forest, such a familiar sound in their home. "I told you about soldiers after me. Two big men. Hairy giants. One had mole size of dime on forehead."

Baba Vira raised an imaginary gun across the room with her red-stained fingers.

"Baba, please..." Larissa swept up her grandmother's medications in their crowded pill box and tucked them into the front pocket of the luggage packed and hidden in the hall closet, making a mental note to doublecheck—triple-check?—her communications on medications. "Who wants to get ready for a party?"

Baba Vira leaned back into the chair, closing her eyes. Her white-blond hair lay wiry and untamed against the pillows. The children rushed to their mother, and Larissa hugged them tightly, checking their faces to see if she could read any childhood trauma in their souls. There were surely worse babysitters. But where was Ira? Her sister said she'd be here two hours ago. Ira's relationship with time was the same as her relationship with men—loose and unpredictable.

Anna ran her small fingers against the delicate rose petals. Alex pinched off a few blooms of baby's breath before Larissa guided his hand away, directing the children outside, each with armfuls of decorations.

"Good lies can save world," Baba Vira added, eyes still closed. Larissa stopped in the threshold. The back-patio door was open, and both children had already thankfully walked out. "Remember this, Lyalya."

2

Ira

The sign said, "Don't pick the wildflowers," but she could have easily not seen it. She wasn't one to rob bees of their life-source or drivers of their scenic route beauty and all that, but a seven-year-old niece's birthday sometimes came before all things.

Ira adjusted the neckline of her shirt. She hadn't realized until she slipped on her shoes how revealing this new top could be when she leaned over. She had to keep aware of that, she knew. No "bad influence Ira," not today.

The rumble-strip on the side of the highway made her car vibrate like a carnival ride before it came to a stop—a slightly pathetic carnival ride, but still.

The road's shoulder was wide, but Ira pulled up her feet and climbed across the front passenger seat to exit her car on the right all the same. An eighteen-wheeler blew its horn at her as she clambered out the side window—that door always did stick—and she waved back like the driver was the best of her friends.

She didn't know who sprinkled the wildflower seeds along this stretch of roadside, whether it was an annual gardening effort she could join or just some little old lady with a passion for pollinators. Maybe the county government handled it, which was far less fascinating, but she would find a way to thank them. Deep red corn poppies, blush pink African daisies, tall tapering purple spikes of lupine, and orange bunches of Siberian wall-flowers stretched as far as she could see. If she lay down, she would be completely hidden, like a rabbit or a field mouse. Or maybe like a dead body dumped on the side of the road. No, she wouldn't lie down. Anyway, Ira needed to collect flowers for Anna, but only the very best ones.

After a few steps down the slight hill, her fingertips trailed the tops of the blooms at the edge of the wildflower bed. What was Anna's favorite color? Pink? Orange? Rainbow? That was it. God bless any child who thought "rainbow" was a color.

Traffic sped by, kicking up dust and wind. The smell of gasoline overpowered the light scent of the wildflowers. She forgot to lock her car, but she just needed a deep breath of floral-scented air.

Ira nudged her foot into the tangle of stems, pointing an exploratory toe into their depths. A grasshopper jumped into the air, a little superman of insects, able to leap buildings a thousand times its size—or something like that. She'd discuss it with Alex later. He'd likely know.

The grasshopper leapt again—this time surely just for fun, not from fear of mortal danger—and Ira saw exactly what she was looking for, a ready-made bouquet of blooms. The shasta daisies and black-eyed susans practically blinked at her. The flowering spikes of lupine were broader and longer than Anna's upstretched arms. And baby snapdragons. Dear god, she had a weakness for the bringers of eternal youth and beauty, whether the superstitions were true or not. Every color, every texture, every scent—she was simply an amazing aunt. That's all there was to it.

She waded through the flower patch, step by step, trying to disturb as few of the stems as possible—definitely disturbing what had to be a nest of grasshoppers. They launched in every direction around her, a celebration of her victory.

If only she had scissors. She hadn't thought of how she'd cut them. She could rip them out, but that would likely bend or break too many of the stems, jostling the beauty of the blooms. Traffic flew by on the road, which felt far away from her now, though she'd only wandered a little bit down the gently sloping shoulder—well, gentle in this part, rather steep close by.

Ira tried to breathe in the crayon blue sky, the flowers, the strangely persistent little grasshoppers that kept clinging to her legs like they were claiming her.

She had a Swiss army knife in her car. That would work for cutting the flowers. She was pretty sure a little pair of clippers was folded up transformer-style in there.

A car door slammed from the direction of the road. A man shielded his eyes from the sun, looking down on her, then looking to her car.

"Okay down there?" he called out when she turned his way.

Ira pulled at her neckline, brushing away a few grasshoppers like lint.

"Sure."

She moved up the hill slowly. She didn't know this dude. She wanted to be in sight of the busy road—or for drivers to be in sight of her. Just in case. Always good to be thinking. She imagined the grasshoppers still clinging to her, applauding her safety-conscious choices.

"Your car break down?" the man called to her, same volume, though she'd cut the short distance in half.

"No. I'm fine, thanks."

The angle of the sun haloed his entire body. She could barely make out anything more than the outline of his jacket and his short, shaggy hair. But he still moved toward her car. His beat-up truck behind him hid a passenger behind the glare of sunlight bouncing off the windshield.

"You left your keys on the seat?"

Did she? She didn't think she did, though where were her keys?

"No!" she answered quickly, not knowing what else to say, not knowing why running toward him at full speed seemed the most logical answer, not knowing why he swung open her car door when she was only a few steps away from the passenger side. He grabbed for the keys, and she grabbed handfuls of the grasshoppers clinging to her arms and legs, pelting him with them. And they hit their mark, his face, his body, his shoulders. Landing then hopping maniacally around her car, around him.

"What the...?"

His arms flew like high-speed windshield wipers while he leapt out of the car. Straight onto the highway.

Ira bolted around her car. The horn from the man's truck blared from its spot parked behind him. Whoever was in there was warning him. Trying to distract him from his grasshopper-induced dervishing on the interstate. He spun backward, into the space between their two vehicles, but still one foot on the road.

Another eighteen-wheeler barreled toward them, its own horn sounding, telling this fool to get out of the way.

The shoulder was wide. The man's distraction clear. Ira sprinted straight at him, grabbed one of his still flailing arms, yanking him with her whole-body weight before letting him go. She reached for her neckline, adjusting it quickly. No bad-influence Ira today. The man tripped and fell, but the hill sloped steeper here. His tumble turned into a roll. Ira couldn't help but worry for the grasshoppers. They'd likely hop away and be fine, though. Wow, he really hadn't liked those grasshoppers.

Looking down, she found one still clinging to her shoulder. Ira plucked it off, the insect apparently realizing her benevolence by stilling in her palm—the palm that had seen too many fortune-teller readings, crooked line of heart, frayed line of head, deep line of intuition, spliced line of destiny, and a life line far too short. She didn't know who had a lengthier future predicted, her or this bug. But she nestled it back onto her shoulder, a much cooler present than a bunch of wildflowers anyway. Rushing back to her car before the rolling man recovered, she grabbed her keys tight, twisted them in the ignition, and waited for one more big truck to pass her by, before pulling away.

3

Larissa

"It's so great you get to stay home and play with your kids all day. I don't think my wife could do it. She's the ambitious type, you know?"

The father stared at his phone instead of Larissa or his own daughter as he walked toward his car. Larissa bit the inside of her mouth, feeling her cheeks turning red.

"Yes, I will speak with granddaughter about lack of contribution to society." Larissa hadn't seen her grandmother step out onto the front porch beside her. Her hair had been pulled into a smooth braid that encircled her head. Her face had been powdered, but the red stains on her hands remained. "Did we give you correct child? Did you check?" The man put his phone in his pocket and did a subtle glance at his daughter's face, but kept walking away. He buckled his daughter in the backseat of the minivan before turning on a video and driving off. They lived two miles away.

"Parents who care make difference," continued Baba Vira.

"We all find our ways." Larissa looked back inside, hearing her children arguing over a forgotten floral crown.

"You need guts, Lyalya."

Anna ran out the front door and down the porch steps onto the manicured lawn. Her long white dress, floral wreath, and bare feet made her look something of a pixie. Alex followed a moment behind her with his light-up tennis shoes and orange dinosaur t-shirt, killing the image. He wore a damaged wreath crooked on his thick curls. His sister ignored him while he buzzed around her, a confused fly.

Larissa looked at her watch then back to Baba Vira. "Are you all packed? Is there anything we've forgotten?"

"Was packed three days ago."

The painful squeak of brakes at the stop sign down the street made both kids freeze. Ira had finally arrived, doing her make-up as she drove the final block.

"Glad you could make it," Larissa said to her sister when she stepped out of the car. Anna and Alex swarmed their aunt, who hugged them both just as excitedly in return, jumping as they jumped, giggling as they giggled.

"I'm so sorry I'm late," she said as she kissed Baba Vira then Larissa on the cheek.

"We are happy you are here, Irena." Baba Vira held Ira's hand in her own, not letting it go, tilting her head to the side at her appearance, plucking a grasshopper from her hair.

"I wouldn't miss it," said Ira.

Larissa rolled her eyes, a motion perfected somewhere in the past thirty-odd years.

Flower petals and ivy leaves had fallen across the lawn like springtime was envious of autumn's annual sloughing. She took a deep breath.

"All of this can wait." Both children had arms now outspread, twirling in the sunshine. "Kids, it's time to take Baba to the airport."

Frosting still graced Alex's lips and fingertips. Larissa stepped toward him first, wiping him clean.

"Let me just use your bathroom for a second." Ira darted in the door.

"Of course. Take your time. We're here for whatever you need."

Her sister didn't respond.

Getting everyone to the car took longer than the fifteen-minute ride to the airport. Ira squeezed into the space between Alex's car seat and Anna's booster. Baba Vira told the kids' favorite folktales on the ride—foxes from *Lys Mykyta* and Baba Yaga stories. Ira listened as entranced by the tales as she had been in her childhood. Larissa pulled toward the departures' drop-off zone, following the direction of her grandmother's ringed finger.

"Are you sure you don't need me to come in with you?" She eyed her overloaded mom purse tucked perfectly between the seats and then the kids squirming and poking each other. Ira poked them both too, whispering something about superhero grasshoppers. Baba Vira shook her head.

The red and black geometric pattern on the blouse she wore for the trip was bold and old-fashioned. How different her childhood and her great-grandchildren's were: Ukrainian dance and song for every celebration of life versus a quaint foreign tradition put on as on occasional show.

As a child, Larissa hated when her grandmother made folk costumes for her. Only now did she appreciate their beauty and craftsmanship—the detailed design, the pom-pom tassels, the traditional patterns of her ancestry. They were social media shareworthy. But she couldn't imagine travelling that way herself. Anna, however, always begged her great-Baba to braid her hair "the Ukrainian way." The girl already had better cultural appreciation than Larissa had ever had. She took after Ira that way.

"Okay." Larissa again looked in her rear-view mirror at the kids.

"I'll walk you in, Baba," Ira interrupted, already shuffling through the backseat over and around the kids.

Baba Vira didn't check any luggage, though how she would manage her suitcase was beyond Larissa's grasp. She knew questioning such subtleties was pointless. She had called ahead for airport assistance, requested the airline keep an extra eye on her, and arranged an assistant from the airline to meet her at the Warsaw gate—but it wasn't enough.

"Please call me from your hotel."

"Eh, international connections—"

"They're fine these days."

"I will if I can." Baba Vira tapped on the backseat window, blowing kisses at the children, who blew them back, exaggerated and full of love. She put her red-stained hand over her heart and sighed before turning away.

"Be safe, Baba."

Her grandmother nodded. "Time to take on world, *tak*?"

4

Ira

A battery-powered airport assistance vehicle whirred by Ira and Baba Vira, yellow light flashing. They walked on slowly but walked all the same. Ira knew her grandmother would be offended if she suggested a ride to airport security and her gate. Old, sure, but not feeble. Larissa never picked up on this.

"So why are you really going to Poland, Baba?"

Her grandmother looked down to her blouse and smoothed it as if a single wrinkle had somehow appeared like a weed amidst the hand-stitched flowers.

"To see dancing, Irena. You know this."

Other passengers walked quickly by them—mostly businessmen in button-down shirts, laptop cases in hand.

"And that's the only reason?"

Baba Vira pressed her lips together, trapping her answer inside her mouth. Maybe Ira just had the Baba Yaga tales still on her mind.

"I am meeting Stefa and her dancers for folk dance exhibition. I will help girls, and...."

A loudspeaker called a missing person to his gate. Static clung between the voice's syllables.

"And find the good vodka?"

Baba Vira stopped her slow walk, resting a hand on a green metal trashcan by her side. Pink gum with gray fuzzy spots stuck to the lid inches from her finger.

Ira took up her hand, shifting it away and squeezing it in her own, feeling the thin bones within. She took the other for good measure. "Would you like to sit?"

Baba Vira shook her head and pressed on Ira's heart line with her fingertips. Her grandmother had been the one to teach her how to read palms. She'd learned it from travellers through her town when she was a child.

"You'll go through the security checkpoint just around that bend." Ira clung to Baba Vira's hands, struck for the first moment by how fragile this woman might be. Her age spots were highlighted under the strong lights in the terminal. Her thin neck looked built of wrinkles. "Would you like me to get—" Silenced by a glare, she didn't finish. Ira knew better than to offer shuttles or wheelchairs. Baba Vira's mouth flattened, still holding back whatever was inside. "Sorry." She squeezed her grandmother's hands, unable to find more than Baba Vira's fate line in her smooth palm. The groove felt deep. "I still think you're up to something," she added, trying to recover herself.

Just beyond them, people gathered at a collection of screens displaying arrivals and departures. Schedules. Delays. Cancellations. A nearby coffee vendor ground beans. Their warm scent mingled with the crisp conditioned air of the terminal.

"Always following your gut, Irena." Baba Vira met her granddaughter's eyes, shaking her head.

"You've always said I had good instincts."

"Gut is different from instincts. Your instincts are..." Baba Vira released her grasp from Ira's, teetering her borcht-stained hands back and forth. Dark veins lined them like maps.

"Can I go with you?"

Baba Vira frowned.

"What, you have passport?"

Ira tapped her purse hanging at her side.

"I'm ready to go."

"No luggage or clothes, my Irena. This isn't your journey."

"I have my toothbrush and an extra pair of underwear." Ira arched an eyebrow.

Another burst of static cut through the terminal as a flight began to board.

"*Proshu*, walk me to security."

"You're up to something."

"Up to nothing. Just take care of yourself. Lyalya too. She needs you."

"Yeah, right."

Another airport assistance vehicle passed by them. Its high-pitched electric motor hummed. Baba Vira did the same, the melody of the *Kolomyjka*, her favorite Ukrainian circle dance. Ira recognized it and took up her grandmother's hands again. She took a small step to the right, a cross-step, left foot in front of her right, and then a final step to the side. Ira's tight blue jeans stretched against her skin as she moved. She kicked out her right foot, tapped her heel on the floor, and repeated the motion to the left. Small steps. A circle of two, but the other dancer stood motionless. Baba Vira shifted only her outstretched hands as Ira moved to one side then the other, picking up her feet higher now. Baba Vira hummed louder, and Ira released her hands to sweep one arm out before her and place the other on her hip. She spun slowly and flirtatiously as Ukrainian girls had for generations, first one way, then another.

People had turned to watch them now, the humming old woman, the dancing girl. But Ira never minded an audience. A small child laughed and pointed before mimicking her slow spin. A businessman almost walked into a pillar.

Baba Vira continued the rapid melody, not clapping along with the rhythm, which she usually did. Instead, she blinked her watery eyes, lips still clenched together, watching her grand-daughter dance.

5

Vira (May 1941)

Vira thumbed through the magazine with dress designs straight from Paris while her sister looked over her shoulder. Wrought iron gates, street lanterns, gargoyles, and chic cafes stood out on nearly every page. The images were so distant from the thatch-covered roofs, goose ponds, and sunflower fields Vira knew so well. In France, the women probably walked straight out of this magazine. Wide collars, tiny polka dots, chunky heels, gloves with buttons tiny and white.

Her sister shifted behind her for a better view. Lesya had grown taller recently. Vira stood up straighter, but she knew it didn't do any good.

Before them, on the steps outside their home's front door, the dressmaker and her daughter pulled lengths of blue fabric from their oversized bag. Her mother would never dare to invite these women inside their Christian home, even though they were the best and every woman present knew it.

The exquisite material clashed with the hand-stitched flowers on her mother's blouse, but Vira had always clashed too. She flipped the magazine closed, to her sister's annoyance, stepping forward to hand it back to the dressmaker's daughter. She wanted to dive into the smooth, soft fabric before her, but instead she held her shoulders back, chin up, and hands clasped together. In a new dress of this blue with a row of five white ribbons down the front, she could win her first proposal. Or two. Was three too far-fetched? Vira could cross-stitch as well as her mother, but she couldn't make a creation that could take her away—not even with beautiful buttons from the blacksmith's son.

"*Proshu, Mama,*" her sister whispered. "May I pick a new dress too?"

"Not this time, Lyalya."

Vira positioned her back to her sister and studied the dressmaker's pencil-sketched designs presented to her.

Inside the house, in the parlor, Vira's brother tuned his viola. The long pulls of his bow across the taught strings reverberated when he began something in a minor key, something bold and dramatic, something the Lviv symphony must have been preparing for the season.

The dressmaker's daughter stood one step down from Vira, her long dark hair pinned back under a hand-stitched scarf. When no one had been looking, she and Vira had been occasional friends and playmates since they were young—one of the few girls Vira's age who she'd always been able to talk to about London, Paris, Budapest, and Vienna. The dressmaker's daughter talked about the beauty of the synagogues she'd always wanted to see. Vira talked about who they could be in a life of their own creation.

"A dress made for Paris," the dressmaker's daughter whispered to Vira. "Or Rome. Maybe Prague."

"What do you think, Panna Vira?" the dressmaker asked, turning to Vira now instead of her mother.

She stepped forward in the threshold, owning the authority and respect being given to her for the first time in her life, but she didn't know the word to answer. *Wunderbar.* Gorgeous. *Bellissimo.*

"*Magnifique.*" She let the new language roll around on her tongue, as soft and luxurious as an imagined chocolate-filled pastry.

"*Duzhe dobre,* very good," the dressmaker answered, her Ukrainian jarring against the French in Vira's mind and Ivan's viola in the next room. The vibrato of a minor chord resonated through the air, prickling her skin.

Vira's clasped hands released and fell to her sides.

"Dyakuyu." Her thanks tasted so flavorless in her mouth.

Voices rose out on the road beyond, though their massive linden tree blocked any view of the commotion from where they stood. Vira's father's voice boomed above any other. Inside, the strings screeched and came to a halt. Ivan's footsteps sounded, and he made his excuses as he pushed himself through the women at the door to take his place in whatever confrontation was ahead. The heavy, carved wooden door that he left open creaked as Vira leaned on it. She peered through the leafy branches, squinting as if that would help her see.

Behind her, Lesya took a step back into their long entry hall with its newly painted poppy bloom border, an indoor garden of lush red flowers, each with a tiny secret shadow at its core. Lesya reached for Vira's hand. A Russian truck had sat nearby on the street for days. Its dusty black metal had almost become a fixture in the landscape, but the yelling wasn't Russian. It was Ukrainian.

Their father's baritone amplified, with occasional bursts of Ivan's tenor now breaking in.

Vira's mother made her excuses to the dressmaker and rushed down the front stairs of their home. Vira followed, nudging Lesya's hand away. Her sister gracefully—if reluctantly—followed behind. Together, they wove beyond their flowerbeds toward the shade of the linden tree, where an old swing was still tied to one of the massive lower branches and a single white duck rested in the gnarled roots, as if escaping from the rowdiness of the geese at the pond.

When they came to a stop, Lesya clung to the swing's ropes as she had when she was a younger child, and Vira put a hand to the linden's gray-brown bark, tracing its rough contours and forcing herself to look toward the road now in view.

There, Vira's father and brother stood shoulder to shoulder with crossed arms and wide stances, yet the boy who stood before her father and brother wasn't a Russian soldier.

Vira brought a hand to the new buttons on the sleeve of her

blouse, cheeks reddening like she still stood by the heat of the blacksmith's forge. What was he doing here? She hadn't seen him since that day in town last week. She had just been on her way to look at ribbons. She'd only stopped to chat with Eugenia, who had the best voice in their church. She had answered a Russian soldier's greeting in Ukrainian, her mother tongue, as her Uncle Oleh trained her to do, always holding their eyes, never looking down, never speaking their language.

Vira's father's hands clapped together, the thwack punctuating his words and bringing Vira back to the moment. Nearby geese scattered, and he clearly intended for the boy to do the same. But the blacksmith's son held his ground. Dmytro's skin, normally blackened from exposure to coal smoke, had been wiped almost clean but for a smudge of smokey ash across his forearm that matched one on his pant legs.

He had pulled her away when the Russian had exhaled too close to her face, when her steps back had pressed her against a wall, when the soldier's grip had clasped her wrists.

Vira blinked, pressing her palms against the bark. Dmytro stood an inch or two taller than her brother, but Ivan swatted the air between them like he tried to rid their land of gadflies.

She darted out of the shade of the trees.

"Vira!" her mother called after her, but Vira pretended she didn't hear.

The men didn't turn as she approached, but they never did. Not even Dmytro's dark eyes shifted in her direction. He pointed toward a broken hinge on nearby gate as he spoke.

Vira forced herself not to run. She focused on her feet—heel, toe, heel, toe, a choreographed entrance. Her arms wanted to stray out into the warming breeze to continue the dance, to welcome the boy, to move into a twirl around him. Her body warmed but she shook off the unexpected emotion. She was grateful, nothing more. She owed him a rescue, though she knew this didn't quite compare.

Her father's presence loomed as solid as if he'd been cast in the blacksmith's forge himself.

"It wasn't broken yesterday." Ivan nearly spit as he spoke. "Did you break it yourself so you could stop by and offer to fix it for a higher fee?"

"I invited him here," Vira answered, approaching with perfectly paced footsteps, her rhythm always impeccable, wanting to look her father straight in the eyes as she said the lie but dropping her chin instead. She chastised herself for it.

Dmytro cocked his head to the side at her answer. Her father ground his teeth. He patted the leg of his pants, feeling for the familiar shapes of keys and coins inside.

"I saw some of his nice buttons ... last week," she continued, pushing a loose tendril of hair behind her ear, "when Lesya and I were sent to town for spices. Remember Marousha's nice ribs?" She'd almost forgotten Lesya had been there too, though she'd been at the art shop, talking with the owner for so long as she always did. Their cook's fall-off-the-bone ribs stewed in the best borscht she knew were the easiest distraction from the truth she could think of.

Her father nearly growled as Vira's mother joined them, though whether the sound came from his throat or stomach she didn't know.

"I knew the dressmaker would be here to plan my new dress," Vira continued, taking a single step forward. "New buttons would be a help." She attempted to make her voice meek and subservient, but it didn't quite work. She didn't know how her sister played that part so well. Vira toed the dirt by her foot, hoping that the blacksmith's son actually had his black case of buttons as he so often did in his coat pocket. Small five-petaled flowers, intricately woven metalwork spheres, sharp angled squares hatched and thatched like they were made of straw.

"Inside, Vira. Now." Her mother crossed her thin arms. Her face had reddened. She puffed out her cheeks ready to herd her daughter away, another stray goose to deal with.

But Vira didn't move.

Her mother put a hand on her shoulder.

"The buttons on my sleeves came from the blacksmith's son." When Vira extended her arms, showing the tiny perfect ovals, Dmytro took a step toward her, and Ivan stepped in front of his sister blocking his path.

Dmytro's eyebrows rose. The darkness of smoke lingered between the tiny hairs. His hazel green eyes were the color of sunflower stalks flecked with dust, swaying across their family's fields.

The pebble by her toe seemed a safer place for her attention. She kicked it aside, noticing something fall from Dmytro's hand to the ground. A stone had dropped behind his leg at an angle only she could see. A hole bore straight through its core, though something seemed to be wedged inside.

After it rolled to a stop, he cleared his throat.

"I didn't mean to offend." He rubbed at the smokey smear on his forearm, which he seemed to just have noticed, hiding in the defined muscle exposed below his rolled-up sleeves. "My father and I can help with this gate ... or with more buttons." Vira's cheeks reddened. "But you know where we are, and I'll bother you no further."

"I'll find someone who saw you break this gate," huffed Ivan.

"I give you my word it wasn't me," Dmytro said, looking Vira's brother straight in the eye, before turning to walk away, hand resting on the filth of his arm, as if he could hide it from view, as if it wasn't already too late for that. She needed to pick up the stone he'd dropped, but she couldn't do it with everyone right there.

Her mother's grip tightened, a bony baba yaga grasp guiding Vira back to the house. In the window, her sister stood alone, lips barely parted, having just corrected her agape mouth. The dressmaker and her daughter had slipped away.

But Vira didn't hang her head. She looked her mother in the eye. She stood taller now, slimmer, more beautiful. She'd retrieve that stone as soon as she could. No one else had seen it, she was sure.

When they were inside, the hard slap across her face didn't surprise her.

6

Larissa

When the phone rang, it was four a.m. Larissa's time, and unlike Ira who had passed out like an exhausted child, she had barely slept. If her grandmother had to go, why did she insist on trekking across the ocean by herself? Larissa should have pushed harder, maneuvered herself into the travel plan, or coerced Baba Vira into staying home. Some doctor in her social circle could have forbidden it if she had only tried. Meeting her mother's old friend, Panya Stefa, at the Warsaw airport wasn't good enough. She was a busy lady. She had no idea what she'd really signed on for. Baba Vira told stories about getting into so much trouble before the war—with her brother, her sisters, the neighbor's daughter who always had better gloves than her own ... who knew what she'd do when left on her own? Ira might have fallen for the allure of it all, but not Larissa.

Larissa grabbed at the ringing phone and darted into her bathroom before answering, past their new custom closets that gaped open like a mouth from a nightmare.

"Lyalya?" But the voice wasn't her grandmother's. Panya Stefa was the only other person left in the world outside of family who called her by the childhood nickname. She absolutely hated that nickname. *Lyalya*. Babydoll. Like some beautiful, dumb little thing.

"Are you with Baba?" Larissa bit her inner cheek, looking at her dim reflection in the bathroom mirror. She looked grayed and ghoulish, a chicken-bone neck, her nose almost mirroring her grandmother's bulbous one in the shadows. The only light in the room glowed from the pink owl nightlight Anna said she'd outgrown.

"You haven't had phone call from her?" The woman's accent alone always made her family. She'd first been pen-pals then later best friends with Larissa's mom. They'd bonded over Stefa's high school years in the States, when the friends had shared a bedroom and practically been sisters. Her offer to return the favor and open up her Warsaw apartment to Baba Vira had been the final detail that allowed Larissa to even dream of letting her grandmother go. "I hoped she had called you," Stefa added when Larissa didn't answer.

Larissa crinkled her nose, but its shadow only elongated.

"She hasn't called." Larissa didn't know how her whisper echoed against the bathroom walls.

Stefa would keep tabs on her, Larissa had been told. She'd been convinced. A school teacher was used to taking care of people, and Stefa had children in the classroom and dancers on the stage. But an old woman as unpredictable as the wind....

Baba Vira had bent her crooked back over backward to satisfy Larissa. Except that her grandmother could lie better than anyone Larissa had ever known.

"Her plane landed an hour and a half ago. I tracked it online." Larissa's oval face seemed disfigured by the darkness of the mirror. "Wasn't she supposed to meet you?"

"Maybe. I wasn't there."

"How were you not there?"

"My girls kept me at the dance exhibition. But I sent someone to meet her." Larissa stepped on a Matchbox car and fumbled her recovery between Stefa's words. She banged her elbow on the wall before kicking the tiny, oddly indestructible hot rod away. "Lyalya, are you still there?"

"Yes," she whispered, clutching at her foot.

Outside the bathroom door, her husband snored. Her two children slept silently down the hall. Ira probably drooled all over her pillow.

"I am so sorry. I will keep you updated."

"So sorry?" Larissa took rapid deep breaths. The clock ticked, reverberating off the bare walls.

"We'll find her, Lyalya."

"I'll call airport security."

"I did this. They told me she arrived in Warsaw. A flight attendant saw her with another older woman at baggage claim."

Larissa released her injured foot. The pink owl nightlight stared at her, wide-eyed and naïve.

"I will call back soon, when I find her," Stefa whispered. "*Pah-pah.*"

Larissa returned the goodbye and hung up, still gripping the phone tightly. She tip-toed past her sleeping husband, down the hallway to Baba Vira's room, where Ira now slept. Before her grandmother had moved in with them, they had planned on using the bedroom for a third child, another girl she had hoped. Larissa had wanted to name her Sonya, her mother's name, her mother who lived as the image of maternal perfection in her mind. A dead mother could do that. She tried to shake away the thought as she entered the small room and turned on the bedside lamp.

Ira groaned. Larissa ignored her, fumbling through the papers on her grandmother's dresser.

An icon of the Virgin Mary hung on the wall over the bed. Red rosary beads draped over the frame. Cross-stitched roses in deep red and pink decorated the walls. Bold Ukrainian embroidery ornamented the pillows on Baba Vira's plush easy-chair, the only surviving piece of furniture from her old house. Crosses for Christ. Wolves' teeth for strength. Lines of pine needles for eternal life.

Information covered the dresser: flight details, the address and phone number of Stefa's apartment, and the dance exhibition schedule.

"What are you doing, Lyalya? You're interrupting my beauty sleep." Ira rolled over with an arm over her eyes. Her makeup smeared across Baba Vira's white pillowcase.

"Baba's lost in Warsaw."

Ira groaned, peeking out from under her forearm.

"Call Stefa. They're probably having shots to each of the twelve apostles by now."

"Panya Stefa called me." She took a deep breath. Ira listened worse than the children. She tried to keep her voice measured, the way she spoke to Alex and Anna on a rough day... a legos-in-the-toilet, crayons-on-the-lampshade-to-make-rainbows kind of rough day. "She never showed up at Stefa's."

"She probably went straight to the dance exhibition."

Ira pushed herself up, spaghetti-strapped nightgown falling from her shoulder. Larissa rolled her eyes, hating that her sister raided her pajama drawer and picked out the slinkiest thing she owned. She didn't even remember the last time she'd worn that nightgown.

"Stefa called me from the dance exhibition."

The Virgin Mary stared down at her, palms clasped together in prayer. A golden halo surrounded her. Ira's feet swung off the bed, covers not bothering to conceal her. At least Greg still slept.

Larissa bit her lip and brushed her bed-messed hair out of her eyes.

A handmade lace runner ran across the length of the dresser under all of the notes. Picture frames and tiny figurines spread across it. Hand-painted nesting dolls. A photo of Baba Vira and her husband, their *dgidgo*, in post-World War II Canada. A picture of Larissa's mother as a child in Winnipeg. There were later pictures too. A portrait of Anna in traditional Ukrainian folk dress, a wide-sleeved peasant shirt with a neckline covered in flowers, a red beaded necklace, a long skirt perfect for twirling, and red leather boots. Alex's preschool photo sat beside it, where he sat on a pony in a cowboy hat. And underneath a framed picture of Larissa—a photo taken in high school, ponytailed and glowing with pride after a track meet—a small paper sat folded into a tiny triangle. Baba Vira's slanted, elegant hand peeked out.

Larissa's hands turned cold as she reached for it, as she

unfolded triangle after triangle like a game. When the paper was flat, she read her grandmother's words, ignoring Ira's pleas to see too.

Lyalya, I'm fine. I am being given surprise.

I have one too. I have not finished scaring the world into becoming a better place, you agree?

7

Ira

The first ring hadn't finished before Ira picked up the phone. Larissa had fallen asleep on Baba Vira's bed as the sisters lay together, the traditional cross motif of the extra pillow imprinting its design onto her cheek as she faced Ira. Baba Vira had given these pillows to Larissa so many years ago. The fact that the geometric Ukrainian designs didn't match her living room décor was so very Lyalya she couldn't stand it.

"Baba?"

"It's me, Lyalya." Stefa's voice sounded slow and heavy. Girls in the background intertwined Ukrainian folksong and tween excitement.

"It's Ira, Panya Stefa." Larissa stirred at her words, grabbing for the phone, but Ira shook her head and pushed her hand away. Her sister's surprisingly sexy nightgown slipped off her shoulder again, but she had more pressing concerns.

Over the girls, Stefa sounded beyond exhausted. "We don't know where she is. I think it's time to call police. You haven't heard—?"

"I'm coming," Ira said before she thought it through. Dawn seeped into the sky outside the window. She felt her sister's glare. "We're coming," Ira added, without hesitation.

Larissa nodded wearily at her.

"No need for that." Stefa's words were watered down with a jittery modulation.

"Just make sure your girls dance their little hearts out. We'll be there as soon as we can."

Ira hung up before handing over Larissa's phone.

"Do you have a valid passport?"

Larissa nodded, opening her eyes and staring up at the ceiling. Ira could practically see the lists of to-dos building upon one another in her brain, wrinkling her forehead while Ira's remained so smooth.

"When's the last time we went on a road trip?"

"I don't think we've ever been on a road trip, Ira."

"Then it's time."

"And I don't think international flights looking for a lost grandmother count as road trips." Larissa had grabbed for the papers on the dresser and scribbled notes on their backsides.

Ira shrugged.

"Maybe Baba planned it this way. You would never have gone otherwise."

On a bedside table, an old boombox stood next to a stack of cassette tapes. Ira reached out her hands to let her fingertips trace their rectangular plastic cases. She slipped one out from the middle.

Her grandmother had given Ira her first CD player. The first CD she'd ever bought was Jewel's *Pieces of You* album, and her elementary-school overjoyed heart had soared at the voice that emerged every time she pressed play. The cassette tape in her hands had been labelled by Baba Vira's hand in Cyrillic script she couldn't read. She slid it into the gaping cavern of the open cassette player, pressed it closed, then pushed down on the play button.

"What are you doing?" Larissa turned around at the barely audible click of the button before the music even played.

"Setting the mood for our trip."

A single bandura began first, filling the room with that mix of a harp and plucked guitar. Just as more banduras followed, Larissa reached over and stopped the tape.

"The kids are sleeping."

"Your kids sleep through anything. Remember Baba's last

birthday?" Ira plucked her fingers through the air like the sounds her sister hushed would arise again from her fingertips. "She liked the *medivka* I found her. She said she'd only made the honey liquor better once herself."

"Where did you find that stuff anyway?"

"This distillery in New Zealand has a great ecommerce site."

"New Zealand?"

"Ukrainians are everywhere." Ira stood, twirled, and did a curtsy in the small space between the bed and the dresser. The bedside lamp cast her shadow on the wall, all curves, grace, and wild curls that tossed about as she moved.

She flicked at the volume control before pushing the play button again. The music that filled the room was softer this time, incense rather than fire.

"Dance with me, Lyalya. Our adventure needs an opening number."

Larissa recoiled when Ira reached out for her, but Ira caught her hand and pulled her into the widest space of the bedroom, between the closet and the opposite side of the bed. The rug under their feet was a faded red, Baba Vira's favorite color.

On the cassette, clapping joined the bandura, followed by voices in song. With the sisters shoulder to shoulder, facing in opposite directions, Ira reached around to put a hand in front of Larissa's stomach and around her hip. She held her other hand high over her head and spun the two of them, as they had when they were girls. Her knees lifted high, and her toes pointed out as far as she could make them in the little space. Larissa flinched as Ira pulled her, and she kicked the bed's footboard.

"You've got to feel the music, Lyalya."

Larissa's body felt as easy to fling around as ever. She might have been the big sister, but she had humored Ira for so many childhood years, the movement must have been a muscle memory.

"We've got to figure out our plan." Larissa tried to stop, but Ira wouldn't let her.

"Please don't make this trip painful, Lyalya."

"This isn't a vacation. We've got to find Baba."

Ira threw her arms over her head and flung herself onto the bed. The headboard knocked into the wall with her motion, banging the corner of a hanging picture. It tilted, knocking into the frame beside it, jarring the Virgin Mary, and toppling the beads that hung over her. The red necklace knocked into the wooden headboard before crashing to the ground, the string broken, the red beads scattering in every direction.

"You broke Baba's rosary," Larissa whisper-growled.

Ira moved to all fours on the floor, reaching under the bed and crawling along the rug to pick up the stray red spheres.

"Those are her Ukrainian costume beads, not a rosary."

"They were hanging on the Virgin Mary."

"And she looks just fine in them." Ira shrugged. "Maybe they're both."

Her overflowing handful of collected beads looked like little red candies, cherry gumdrops or everlasting gobstoppers, something infused with her grandmother's sweetness and sourness and unexpectedly fierce longevity. She popped one into her mouth, holding it between her teeth and her cheek as she crawled along the rug to pick up more.

"I need to wake up Greg," Larissa whispered, but Ira wasn't sure if she was talking to herself or not. When she left the room, Ira sat up cross-legged. She moved the red bead across her mouth to her other cheek, wondering if its red dye had been hand-made from berries like the dyes Baba Vira used for Easter eggs as a child. The taste held more dust than fruit flavor. She balanced the bead on the tip of her tongue and swayed to the music, the gentle melody of the bandura. She imagined the sound of Baba Vira's warbling voice singing along.

8

Vira (May 1941)

Bees only flew in direct paths. They didn't get distracted. They didn't wander aimlessly, impassioned by shiny things again and again, like her brother. When Vira pressed her back against the wooden hive, her skin vibrated with the buzz echoing inside. The light of the moon seemed to settle on her home's heavy wooden front door. The stars winked in the glass of the windows. Their family had been the first in the village to have real glass panes, just like the city houses. But the house wasn't where she planned to go.

The buzz behind her didn't sleep like her family. Vira turned to press her chest and the side of her face to the wooden hive. The hum thundered through her entire body. She had declined Dmytro's invitations three times already, twice through messages hidden in bored-through stones and once face-to-face, when he had stopped only a few steps away from her in town to examine an old bench on the sidewalk, tightening its screws and sanding the rust off the underside. She guessed he'd invented the job. Just for that moment. Just to talk to her while Lesya lingered in the art store once again.

But she tired of declining.

Her skin prickled and buzzed. She had known the bees her whole life. They had surrounded her and given her honey. They had stung her and pollenated the most beautiful sunflowers on their land. Walking away from them was harder than walking away from her family—not that they'd know. Just until the dew formed, she told herself, the signal of the coming dawn.

The sweet vibration of the hive gave her wings. She ran across the grass, past the freshly painted bee boxes, past the rows of wooden structures tired and awaiting their turn. She wore a freshly woven floral crown in her hair. Its ribbons streamed behind her. The bees' crescendo of buzzing, their echoes and amplification of each other, pushed her onward. In a straight line. Not toward the emerging sunflowers but toward the cherry orchard far beyond, where she used to perch herself in the embrace of the low curving branches, counting the ripening fruit, snacking on cherries within arms' reach. Her tongue remembered the taste. The sweet smell so much a part of her childhood. But tonight, she didn't intend only childish things.

Ribbons tickled the skin on her neck as Vira slowed. The woods were the best shortcut to the orchard. She knew these woods, every path and every bramble. Or at least she used to. She still did, she told herself. She blew air out of her mouth as if drying the paint on the nesting doll Uncle Oleh had given her. Crickets chirped around her in every direction. One foot moved forward, then another. Movement in the fallen leaves nearby slowed her steps, surely just a mouse or a marten. Her own footfalls felt cacophonous in the absence of other sounds, only the wind through the leaves overhead, the crickets, the occasional call of an owl. The moonlight didn't reach through the tangles of branches overhead. She hadn't considered the darkness of her path.

A ribbon from her floral crown fell on her shoulder, and she flinched.

Ahead, two beech trees leaned against each other, their white bark just visible, shaping them like long crooked legs, the pedestals for baba yaga's hut to stand upon.

"Vira?"

She spun, more leaves stirring nearby. Other footfalls, no mouse, no martin. Crooked branches like fingers plucked at her sleeves.

"Vira."

A hand touched her shoulder where the ribbon had just been, and she yanked her body away. She stepped back, and a fallen tree caught her heel. She started to tumble, but the grasp on her became stronger.

"I've got you." The words made her entire body tense, but the voice wasn't an old, bony-necked woman with jagged teeth bared. "Vira, you're okay," Dmytro said in almost a whisper. His breath brushed against her cheek.

"It's you." Her arms threw themselves around his neck, but she loosened her grasp as soon as she noticed what she'd done. She hadn't meant to look so weak, so terrified. They weren't supposed to meet here. The plan was the orchard, full of its springtime blooms. But he circled his arms around her before she completely let him go. His hands rested on the small of her back, holding them close. She wasn't trapped. She was encircled. The buzzing began again inside her.

"I hoped you'd come."

The smell of smoke and ash rested on his skin. She'd never been so close to any man—not in a dance, not in a familial embrace. Their bodies still against each other, the rise and fall of their breathing fell into a steady rhythm. Her fingers linked themselves around his neck like the best of her stitches.

"I'm here."

The next morning, the smell of the small campfire Dmytro had made for them covered her like a blanket, even as she woke in her own bed. Across the room, Vira's sister fingered the floral wreath she had tossed aside on their shared dresser when she'd snuck back in. The blooms had wilted, curling into themselves. They surely smelled as smoky as she did.

"When did you make this?" Lesya whispered a moment after her sister's eyes cracked open. Her fingers traced the small yellow blooms before plucking a petal away and bringing it to her nose.

"Yesterday, as a surprise for you." Her voice cracked with dry-mouthed sleepiness. Vira sometimes worried that lying came too easily to her. Perhaps, deep down, she wasn't a good person. "I fashioned it near the bees when they were smoking the hives," she continued. "Sorry about the smell."

Lesya didn't respond. She plucked another yellow petal and tickled herself on the chin. Downstairs, voices became louder.

"Is Uncle Oleh here? He's back?" Vira sat up. She didn't know how she'd wash off the hint of smoke.

"*Tak.*" Lesya carefully weighed the crown in her hands before easing it onto her head. "He's been here since sunrise."

Vira traced her bare foot against the lines of grain in the wooden floor. She'd barely gotten home before dawn. Her sister mimed a conversation at her reflection in the glass windowpane of their bedroom.

"You were up at sunrise?"

"I've been up since you came home."

Vira's eyes widened, and Lesya's grin did too.

"I won't tell. I can lie like you."

The fourteen-year-old turned back to the window, re-adjusting her curls around the crown of flowers then shifting it forward to cover her eyes.

"No, be a better person than me, Lyalya."

The smoke from the campfire still filled her nostrils. Her body heat rose when she thought about the night, the boy, the kiss she allowed him to have under the shadow of the trees. The overhead branches seemed to bend around them. The roots and brambles formed a protective wall. Her lips were still warm, and she didn't want to wash them.

Downstairs, the men's voices rose again. Their father, their uncle, and their brother, Ivan. Ivan spent his days mostly in Lviv now, just like Uncle Oleh who was a poet at the University. Two years older than Vira, Ivan had been offered a spot with the symphony. Her father's brother rarely came to their house unless he had cryptic news to share, usually about the Organization of Ukrainian Nationalists.

"I don't want to go down there." Lesya whispered, eyes still covered with flower petals.

"Mama will worry if we don't soon." Vira stood, and in doing so, she released a cloud of gray dust. Flecks of ash sprinkled the wood grain at her feet. "It's already late."

Lesya nodded, removing the crown from her head. She slid it under her bed.

"You look..." She made a face, tightening her mouth and scrunching her eyebrows. "You look like you snuck out last night."

Vira didn't need to look at her reflection to believe it. She ran her fingers through her hair and found a tiny twig. Lesya handed her a brush. After weaving a fresh braid and fastening it around the crown of her head, Vira crossed the room to their washing bowl and splashed her face, rubbing the cool water into her temples and the corners of her eyes. She pulled a wet rag lathered with sweet French lavender soap across her neck, her arms, anywhere the tiny remnants of flame hid. But not her face, not where his hands had rested on her cheeks, nor where his lips had met her own. Vira blew out a breath and closed her eyes before raising her chin and readying herself for her family.

The sisters descended the stairs together hand-in-hand.

"They stand with us," Ivan said as the sisters entered the room.

"For the moment perhaps, but they aren't to be trusted, like the Soviets weren't to be trusted when they freed us from Poland," their uncle answered sharply.

The two men stood by their father's tall bookshelves, the bookshelves Vira, Lesya, and the twins weren't allowed to touch. Their father sat next to them in his favorite armchair—short and thickly upholstered with a button-tufted back. Dark green to match the sunflower leaves, their mother always said. She sat at the opposite side of the room, sipping coffee. Her eyes focused on a pink cross-stitched rose in its wooden embroidery hoop in her lap. Her fingers neatly pulled the thread taut, found a new hole for the needle, and slid the thread through, but her ear tilted toward the men. Her eldest daughters crossed over to her without a sound.

"The Germans understand what we want. They can help save us from the Communists," Ivan pressed, bringing a hand to his brow.

"Or they could do to us what they did to Poland."

Vira thought of the big Russian parked in his truck on the road by their sunflower field. His arms were as thick as hams, not so different from the Russian soldiers in town, like the one who had backed her between the buildings. Breath like sardines. A grip like a machine. She almost wanted to cross herself thinking of Dmytro saving her that day. Was that sacrilege? She took a seat next to her mother and picked up her own embroidery. Her body warmed at the thought of his grip around her instead. Definitely sacrilege.

Her mother nudged her toward the kitchen, toward the breakfast rolls, cheese, and thinly sliced meats she had already set out for the men, but Vira shook her head. Lesya tip-toed past them both, toward the promise of food.

"They could free us from another forced famine, like in the east. They could free us from the jailing and executions of anyone who dares to write or teach or paint the truth." Ivan tensed his fingers as if he held his viola.

"Why do we need liberators? We need to free ourselves. The OUN...."

Vira's mother stiffened and wrinkled her nose, turning to her daughter. Vira bit her lip and dedicated herself to her embroidery hoop. She worked on a new blouse. Its black and red cross-stitched design would match the poppies in her hair for her friend's wedding in the summer. But her mother's eyes didn't look away. They admonished her without a word, and Vira took the reprimand. She knew she deserved it, though for last night with Dmytro, she would take this one hundred times more. Her mother's disappointment didn't bother her as much as it used to.

When she met her mother's gaze, she wordlessly apologized

and waited for the stare to soften. Her mother had been so beautiful once, but at times, the woman looked little better than a baba yaga. There could be worse things, Vira supposed. There was power in being an old witch.

Vira's father cleared his throat.

"You both need to be careful," he said. "You're in positions that are very visible. The University is surely being watched. The lecture halls, the studios, the symphony players..." He had spent time in the city as a younger man himself, but the family bees had always called him back. He always said that words and song weren't as sweet as honey. "You need to keep your opinions to yourself."

"But, Tato, how can we not speak of it? It's what we're living every day." Ivan's index finger traced his brow like he tested the tautness of his instrument's strings.

"Then live silently."

"The Soviets are everywhere," Oleh conceded. He crossed to sit down near his brother.

"And be careful with your words as well, in print or at readings." Oleh nodded a reply, confidently, seriously, but not meeting his eyes. Vira's father grabbed his arm with his wide hand. "You're not writing anything nationalistic?"

"Nothing I'll share in wide circles."

"He's using a pen name for those poems. And he doesn't sign the OUN pamphlets. He's being safe," said Ivan. He paced. The strings at his brow weren't yet harmonious. He had been yelling at his uncle moments ago, but now he defended him to his father. Vira jabbed her finger with a needle.

Oleh swallowed and pressed the worn brown leather of his shoes into the floorboards.

"What are you doing?" Vira's father boomed.

"I wasn't going to mention that, brother, but it's true."

"You're endangering yourself." He pushed himself out of his chair and walked away from the others toward his treasured shelves. His wide shoulders lifted with his deep breaths. He patted his pockets, feeling for whatever lingered there this morning. "You're endangering all of us," he said in a lower voice, almost in a register Vira couldn't hear. She stuck her pierced finger in her mouth. The taste of smoke made her face flush.

"Only one side of things is the right side, Tato." Ivan lowered his hand from his frazzled eyebrows. He must have felt his sister's eyes on him, because he glared at her, quieting every thought of the prior night in her mind.

"The right side is the side of silence. We cannot trust those we don't know." Their father leaned forward. The big iron keys looped through his belt jangled against each other.

Vira's embroidery hoop seemed so dull. She withdrew her fingertip from her mouth. Such passions existed in the world—love and war and music and poetry. Lesya returned to the room and quietly sat beside her. She pulled a yellow flower petal out of her pocket and put it to her lips like a silent finger.

9

Larissa

Larissa shaded the ground beneath her sketched puppy, adding its long pink tongue and wag-lines around its tail. She wrote D-O-G next to it before putting down the pencil on her fourth completed sticky note. She didn't know how far ahead to plan, but Alex and Anna's lunchboxes would feel so empty without her notes. Greg wouldn't remember, and just last week Alex had come home ribbiting about the frog she'd drawn. She wasn't breaking her tradition, Baba Vira on the loose in Poland or not.

"Those are actually pretty good." Ira leaned over her shoulder, plucking a blue colored pencil from the counter beside her. "I'll help." She grabbed a sticky note and drew a cross-eyed cat opening its jaws for an unsuspecting goldfish.

"Did you find the flights?"

"Nothing direct." Ira added a small "o" for the fish's mouth, then eyelashes. "The fastest we can get to Warsaw is through a connection in Paris."

Greg sprawled across the living room couch, present for moral support. The kids wouldn't be awake for a few hours.

Larissa's long line of a whale's tail broke a hole in the paper. The note had almost been done. There were already waves in the water, a big blue splash spraying from the blowhole. She smoothed the page down. She reached for some scotch tape in the nearby junk drawer. There were still notes and notes to go. Desperate times called for desperate measures.

Ira slapped another note on the table. A voluptuous mermaid appearing to seduce the shark at its side.

"When's it leave?"

"Four hours."

Larissa nodded. She'd have time to hug the kids goodbye without having to wake them early. How would she tell them where she was going? That their great-baba was lost? That mommy would be gone for who knows how long?

Greg snored on the couch. She grimaced.

"He's a rock-star, Lyalya. He'll do great with the kids." Ira didn't look up from her latest sketch. Her arm blocked Larissa's view of it.

She hated how her sister always read her mind. Larissa pushed her hair out of her face and put a purple pencil to the paper. She was careful not to poke another hole. No one had time for that. She had done four for Alex and four for Anna now, plus Ira's three—they were almost there. They had to be.

The ice-maker in the freezer clanged behind them. Larissa turned toward the noise, drawn by the finger-painted master-pieces she knew every line of by heart. If something went wrong with the kids, she'd feel it even across the ocean—she knew she would. Ira claimed her instincts, but she didn't understand a mother's intuition.

Larissa took a deep breath. Where had her grandmother's irrational doggedness taken her?

"Baba's fine," Ira cut in. Larissa bit her lip. "And if you really want your lips red and swollen, I've got this great new cayenne pepper lipstick. It burns a bit, but the effect is pretty awesome." Larissa removed her teeth from her lip and loosened her jaw. "I'll make sure I pack it."

Larissa slammed down her pencil harder than she meant to.

"Oh my God. I didn't even think of you packing. You don't have time to get back to your place. What do you need to borrow?" She stood, and her barstool screeched on the newly installed hardwood floor. Greg opened his eyes, blinking in the bright light shining on him from the kitchen. "And your passport!"

"Calm down, Lyalya. I have my passport. If I could just borrow a few pairs of underwear, I'll be fine. You have something other than granny panties, right?"

Larissa groaned and retreated up the stairs to her bedroom, tiptoeing softly past the kids' rooms in the soft blue-white LED glow of the hallway nightlights.

In her bedroom, she paced around the mismatched furniture and old college prints. Matisse. Mondrian. Pollock. The room had been designed less with a nod to the nostalgia of her early years with Greg and more with an admission that no one but family saw this room. Blocky Ikea bedside lamps. Canvas storage boxes. An old, fraying blanket tossed on the rocker that had once been in Anna's and later Alex's room when they were babies. This room was perhaps the only thing in her life given permission to be imperfect.

She walked from her nightstand to her closet to their bathroom and back before settling on retrieving her own passport, paper-clipped to Greg's, from the tiny safe under their bed. The last time she'd used it was on a trip to the Bahamas before the kids were born. Taking it out by itself wasn't right somehow. Larissa didn't do things solo these days. She always had either a husband or kids in tow. Her hands sweated as she stared at the closed door of the safe.

Above the bed, the Pollock was a mess she wanted to clean up. She'd never thought that before, though she wondered when she really looked at it last. She'd loved Jackson Pollock in college.

Footsteps clomped down the hallway, and Larissa froze, listening for the sound of little voices waking from sleep. Ira charged into the room, and the house creaked. Ira crossed her arms and waited. Her eyebrows rose and not a wrinkle appeared on her forehead.

"Did I wake the little buggers?"

The house was nearly silent but for the air-conditioning clicking on. Far off, they could hear Greg snoring again downstairs. Larissa caught herself swaying side to side. She hadn't yet broken the subconscious constant rocking motion of early motherhood.

"I think they're still out."

"If they wake up, I'm blaming your husband. How do you sleep next to that?"

"I guess I'll have a few nights off from it."

"Where's your underwear drawer?"

Larissa pointed it out with her elbow as she lugged a suitcase onto the bed. She'd shared worse things with her sister over the years. Ira slid it open and held one item up at a time, nodding, grimacing, busting out into laughter. But today, Larissa didn't take the bait.

Clothes packed, she closed her suitcase. Ira left the room with Larissa's sexiest, rarely-worn-these-days underwear in her hands. She had a feeling that it all might not return to her.

Larissa sat down on the bed beside her bag, pulling her legs up and hugging them. Stefa said that they should take a taxi from the airport to the Palace of Culture and Science where the International Folkdance Exhibition would already be underway. Where they would look from there, she had no idea.

10

Ira

A male flight attendant covered the seats in coach. Ira craned her neck toward the open curtain directly behind their seats. Her first time flying first class wasn't impressing her yet. Beside her, Larissa gripped the arm-rest. She'd already covered herself with the thin airline blanket, settling in for hibernation. Only her rabbit eyes and her white knuckles gave her away. Ira wished she'd let her apply some concealer under her eyes. They would have done wonders for the dark bags there. She didn't know why her sister yelled at her about not wanting a make-over right now.

"Can I tell you a story?"

"I don't believe a word of your grasshopper superhero tale." Larissa closed her eyes. The engine rumbled to life underneath them. The lovely first-class flight attendant mimed the instructions of the safety manual underneath a tv screen that had lowered from the ceiling. The video was circa 1990-something. The dark red of the actress's lipstick, her stick-straight hair, and the lack of HD gave it away.

"Oh, it's true." Ira smiled. "But I was thinking of a different one, your favorite as a kid."

"What, Vasilisa?"

"Why not?"

The seatbelt light dinged and illuminated over their heads. Larissa's hands shifted under the blanket, and Ira's clicked her buckle into place

"Once upon a time, there was a girl named Vasilisa. Her

43

mother fell sick, but before she died, she gave her daughter a little wooden doll graced with a blessing. Whenever Vasilisa was in trouble, she was to give the doll food and drink and to tell it her troubles, and the doll would make them go away."

"Do you remember the wooden dolls we had as kids? What happened to those?"

"Shh... I have them. You're not listening to my story." The air vents burst to life above their heads, and Ira brushed aside the hair that blew into her face. "Anyhow," she continued, drawing out the word, "as the girl grew up, she was so enchanting that the townspeople all called her Vasilisa the Beautiful, much to the dismay of her hideous step-mother and fugly step-sisters."

Larissa's grip loosened on the arm-rests as Ira spoke.

"Fugly, huh?"

"So fugly. Unibrows and orange spray-tans."

The plane taxied to the runway. Ira reached up to turn off the vent and brushed her hair again out of her eyes.

"They were always giving Vasilisa near impossible chores to do, but with the help of the little wooden doll, she always made them happen. Until one day, they blew out their last candle and made Vasilisa go into the woods to ask Baba Yaga for more fire."

The male flight attendant walked by. His pants were tighter than they needed to be. Ira didn't mind. Larissa missed it with her eyes closed, but Ira knew it wasn't the time.

"Of course, Baba Yaga lived in a crazy-ass hut that stood on chicken legs inside a fence made of human bones. The locks were made of jaw bones and the gate was made of feet or something. And the hut stood up and turned around if someone other than the Baba Yaga approached it."

Outside, on the other side of Larissa, the land shrank underneath them, neighborhoods turning to collections of Monopoly houses. The view disappeared as they entered the clouds, and a new one appeared as they exited above them. Rays of the sun cut through the heavens.

"And?" Larissa prodded. She had kept her eyes closed. The plane leveled out.

"And when Vasilisa discovered the hut, she freaked, but she had to wait for Baba Yaga. At the end of the day, the witch appeared, flying in a mortar pushed with a pestle, and sweeping away her tracks with an old broom. The old woman knew Vasilisa was there because she smelled human flesh—Ukrainian flesh, which always smelled better than Russian."

The drink cart rattled through first-class, starting with their row, the last row.

"What kind of vodka do you have?" Ira said without hesitation. She made sure her voice had a measure of disappointment in it when they didn't have what she hoped. Her grandmother had shown her the better things in life. The good eastern European stuff was hard to beat. She understood why Baba Vira had distilled her own when she'd first come stateside. Wires and tubes coiling into a plugged-up claw-foot tub. Friends from the old country to enjoy it. Dancing. Singing. Ira wished she'd been alive for those parties.

Vodka mingled with tonic water and ice in her plastic cup. She waited for Larissa's chamomile tea to be in her sister's hands before continuing.

"Baba Yaga invited her in, and she told her she'd give Vasilisa fire if she could complete another crazy series of tasks—separating poppy seeds from dirt and making her huge dinners—and if Vasilisa failed, Baba Yaga would eat her."

Ira wanted to jump at her sister or grab her arm at least with her last words, but the hot tea made her behave herself. Still, Larissa opened one eye in expectation for the attack.

The clouds out the window beyond her sister were mountainous peaks now. She hadn't flown for years. And never to Europe. Wherever her crazy, wonderful old baba was, Ira would thank her for that.

"But with the help of the doll, she did everything the Baba Yaga asked, got the fire, killed her step-sisters and step-mother, was taken in by another old lady, and married the tsar."

Larissa took a slow sip from her tea, her lips upturned.

"I think you cheated the ending a bit."

"You looked like you'd recovered from the take-off."

The male flight attendant walked by again. Ira caught his cologne or maybe just his deodorant, that mix of male musk and maybe peppermint. Spearmint? Was there a difference? The scent made her relax into her seat, sweating drink in hand, tiny red straw to her cayenne pepper painted lips.

When she closed her eyes, she saw Baba Vira against the black of her eyelids. She walked away toward a definite destination. A forest path. A wooden, spired fairytale cottage. Ira couldn't quite place her, but she had no doubt that she wasn't lost at all.

11

Vira (May 1941)

The paint on Lesya's wooden nesting doll had dried nearly a week ago. The twins had talked through their plans for their own, guiding Lesya's and their mother's brushes to add their dark blond curls, flowered red and yellow scarves upon their heads to match the aprons tied around blue dresses. One nesting doll held a favorite baby doll, and the other a small plate of cookies.

Vira sat beside her mother feeling tied to the chair. The tiny paintbrush had been put into her hand. The paint had been placed before her on the table.

"We need to finish these matryoshka today." Her mother's voice contrasted starkly with the twins singing under the table at their feet, the same song, over and over again.

"*Cuckoo, cuckoo, ptychka mala...*" Cuckoo, cuckoo, small bird... Cuckoo, cuckoo, small bird....

Vira and her mother had the two biggest nesting dolls in the unpainted set Uncle Oleh had given them. Halya, the youngest by thirty minutes, would go inside Helena, the elder twin, Helena inside Lesya, Lesya inside Vira, and Vira inside their mother. The responsibility of the biggest was to take care of the others, but Vira wondered if an inner nesting doll had ever wanted so badly to break free.

"Your father said Uncle Oleh will be returning soon."

Her mother painted the biggest matryoshka's face. The eyes were stunning, the precise blue that could bear down on her oldest daughter, under eyelashes as fine and pointed as needles.

The mouth, though, wasn't right. A flattened streak. This doll pressed her lips shut—whether forcing her voice to be silent or combatting the draw of a well-known sweet tooth, Vira couldn't decide.

Vira pushed back her chair.

"You stay," her mother snapped. "You cannot move until your doll is done."

She nudged her chair back into place. After dipping her brush in the yellow paint that still smelled of the mustard seed, Vira swirled a few flowers onto her doll's dress. Upstairs, Ivan banged and thumped as he packed his bags, readying to return to the city, to rejoin his peers in the Lviv symphony.

"What are you putting in the hands?" Forcing pleasant conversation in less than pleasant moments was a specialty of her mother's.

"I still don't know."

"Why not a rooster?"

The doll's bare hands in front of her had the space for a colorful bird. The idea wasn't a terrible one—a rooster for fulfillment of wishes. She could almost see it there with its tail feathers in green and yellow and red. But she didn't want to admit that to her mother.

"Not a rooster."

"Some yarn and needles. You have a talent for design."

Her mother spoke without looking away from her work. Her brush added a touch of pink to her doll's cheeks then she wiped it off with a rag on the table.

"Uncle Oleh said these dolls had to tell our stories. I'm more than sewing."

"And I'm more than a mother, and your sister is more than a friendly girl with welcome bread."

Vira's eyebrows raised. She didn't think they really were. She started to scoot out her chair again but stopped herself.

"May I go get a book from my room for ideas?"

"Come right back."

She shook off the invisible ropes as she stood. From the hall, she could see that the truck of Soviet soldiers outside still hadn't moved down the hill. The soldier's uniforms were crisp if dusty, their expressions sharp.

Her Uncle Oleh called them murderers everywhere but to their faces. Ivan was convinced Galicia, their region of western Ukraine, would be free of their presence soon. Her father said they needed to be calm, to wait and see. Vira had always been terrible at waiting.

She crossed past her father's study with his thick leather ledger full of notes on his bees open on his desk. She traced her fingertips along the stair's wooden railing as she slipped upstairs. In Ivan's room, clothes and music sheets lay across his bed, covering every space but his empty, open suitcase. A suit and vest hung ready in his open wardrobe. A hat sat upon his dresser. His viola leaned against the wall near the door, more sheet music scattered on the floor beside it. A rich yellow ribbon stuck out of a thin book on his dresser.

The floorboards creaked underneath her as she stepped into the messy space. Pencils littered the floor. Folded clothing piled on a chair. A sketch of the insides of a beehive decorated the wall over his bed. Vira knew the smell of him would linger for days after he'd gone—that mix of honey and wax for his viola.

If boys painted nesting dolls, Ivan's would certainly hold his viola—but boys were always so much more than just one thing, Vira knew.

From the small window across the room, Ivan could be seen outside talking to their father. Such pride and camaraderie existed in their exchange, their father's hand resting on his back, not directing him one way or another.

A candle on Ivan's bedside table had dripped wax all over the hand-made cloth it sat upon. Vira had stitched the eight-pointed stars upon it and its border of triangular wolves' teeth. God, strength, and wisdom. These ideas didn't always fit her brother, but he tried to live them all the same.

"Vira?" Her mother called from the bottom of the stairs. She would only dare to raise her voice that loud when the men were all out of the house.

"Still looking," Vira called back even louder, knowing the tone would bother her mother.

A runner that matched the star and wolves' teeth design also ran across Ivan's dresser. A pair of stainless-steel scissors, a model of a car, and the thin book with the yellow ribbon bookmark sat upon it.

"Fighting the Bear, Refusing the Wolf," read the title. The author was Slavko Ukrayina, a pen-name no doubt. Glory to Ukraine.

Vira opened to the bookmarked page, careful not to bend the paper.

The Wilderness
Baba Yaga lives in the forest,
But Baba Yaga lives on her own,
No bears attack
No wolves come to prowl....

Her Uncle Oleh's work, she had little doubt. She could almost hear his voice reciting the words.

He thought that Ukraine had an independent future and that this independence could happen soon. She'd heard him say so only the day before. These words couldn't be as dangerous as her father insisted. They were just words, not battle plans.

The next page began a new poem titled "The Famine of '32" about foreign dignitaries touring Ukraine only to see rosy-cheeked Russian actors in traditional peasant costumes presenting loaves of bread, showing off Ukrainian dances while the real, emaciated people of the villages were locked behind the metal doors of a nearby town's factory, starving and dying in a great secret from the world.

"What are you doing?" Ivan walked through his doorway,

ripping the book from her hands.

"It's Uncle Oleh's, isn't it?"

"It's not for you. You don't understand these things."

"Bears and baba yagas?"

"This isn't some fairytale." He placed the book down on the dresser and shooed her out the door.

"You aren't so much smarter than me." She spit at him like she had when she was a younger child. It landed with accuracy on his cheek.

"This is why no one will marry you. Grow up, Vira."

She walked backward away from him toward his door, and her foot brushed against his viola, forcing it to clang disharmoniously against the floor and the disheveled sheet music. She bent to put it back in its place but stopped, crouching beside it on the floor. "Do you feel so wise because of this?"

Ivan crossed his arms in front of him.

"I know what the world looks like beyond these walls. You never will. Mama and Tato trust me, at least, to leave the house without shaming the family."

She swept the scissors from the dresser and picked up the viola's bow.

"Vira!"

The bow's horsehair string popped and curled with a delicious pang. Ivan tackled her and tore the scissors away.

And when he did and her hands were bare, she brushed him away, stood, and walked out the door.

Her mother waited for her at the table. Kalyna branches with their bright red berries now filled her matryoshka's hands—the bush representing the mother and the berries the children, though kalyna was also the national tree of Ukraine. Vira wondered about any deeper meaning. Her hands still trembled from the popping of the bow string.

"Cuckoo, cuckoo," the twins pleaded.

"*Cuckoo, cuckoo, ptychka mala...*" she sang absentmindedly. Little hands clapped, while Lesya picked up the song by the kitchen sink, where she readied the big pot for the night's borscht. Their voices blended together like bread and honey. They always had. Their mother didn't join in.

Vira picked up a brush and dipped it in black paint as she sang, forming the outline of a mask in her doll's hands. She gave it a long, crooked nose and teeth.

Who were the women in her family, after all? Her mother had her clear role. Lesya always had welcoming words and the best of manners. The twins loved their dolls and their cookies. And Vira was the liar, the sneak, the one not to be trusted, the one who prized bravery and following one's heart above all else, and the one who would fight for her place in life harder than any man she'd ever known. She held the Baba Yaga mask. No bears or wolves, Russians or Germans, frightened her either.

Her brush glided over the wooden doll, and girl and doll faced each other, both with the same smile of satisfaction.

"What are you doing?"

Vira thought her mother's expression didn't look so different from the Baba Yaga mask.

"Finishing my matryoshka," she answered. The paint glided on as if enchanted, like it knew exactly what shape it needed to take. Across the room, Lesya sighed at their basket of eggs. "And helping my sister." Vira jabbed her paint brush into the bowl of paint, turned her nesting doll a degree farther away from her mother so it could begin to dry before its next layer, and stood from the table, her sister giving her an easy excuse. "I'm going to get geese eggs."

"Cuckoo, cuckoo," Halya and Helena pleaded, and Lesya started the first verse again.

"*Ty nam spivala, pravdu kazala, shchezla, shchezla, schezla zyma ....*"

Vira walked down their long, poppy-bloom decorated hallway and closed the front door behind her, silencing her sister's voice, the giggles surrounding it, and the scowl that somehow almost reached an audible pitch. Nearby, the geese honked and walked toward her, sensing the bread she'd grabbed and now held up in her apron. Their long white necks reached out, and they encircled her.

"Get back, get back," she spit at them, throwing bread-crumbs over their heads. One approached and hissed, trying to nip at the loaf. She kicked dust at it, wanting to hiss back. Leading the birds toward the pond, toward their nests tucked away in the low branches, she threw handful after handful just out of their reach, clearing a path for herself.

The truck of soldiers still parked there, unmoving. Vira counted the days, touching her thumbs to each of her fingers. She had seen soldiers on the street near their house for five days in a row this time—not quite a week, but not quite a coincidence. A goose nipped at her apron, and she pushed it away with the toe of her boot.

The soldiers hadn't noticed her, their heads lowered to their papers, their long guns slung over their shoulders. Vira's skin prickled. The warm breeze of the morning didn't help.

She tore bigger chunks from the bread and tossed it at the honking birds. Their nests were just ahead, where the tall grasses met the water-reeds. The ones with eggs had mother geese sitting heavily upon their frames of twigs and grass. The shallow side of the pond held endless frogs and water bugs that scattered when she neared. Vira had caught frogs here plenty of times before. But never a goose egg.

The big birds followed her closely, honking, sticking out their thin tongues and sharp beaks. She crumbled the remains of the loaf in her apron. The soldiers looked up to see her, so she busied herself with her task, flinging the crumbs into the air before moving toward a nest set apart from the others. She'd seen Ivan do this before. It couldn't be so hard.

Vira grabbed the white mother goose at the top of the neck, trying to move it off the nest so she could get at the eggs. The bird was heavier than she guessed, and its soft white feathers were damp and slippery. The animal honked in surprise, possibly in pain, when Vira pulled it back and tried to shift it behind her. The other geese lifted their heads and their wings, but Vira reached into the downy nest and retrieved two brown spotted eggs. The mother goose nipped at her hand. She pulled back but didn't let go of the eggs. She ran as fast as she could in the direction of the hives. The geese flapped and rustled behind her, but they didn't chase her far. They circled their nests and remaining eggs, creating a honking barricade.

Chest heaving, Vira leaned against the closest hive box, feeling the bees buzzing inside, feeling the strength of a baba yaga, letting the sound vibrate her skin and still her heartbeat. Down the street, the soldiers all watched.

She held up the two eggs and curtsied in their direction. She didn't know how Ivan had made that look easy.

"What are you doing?"

When Vira flinched at the voice, she bumped the hive, stirring some bees from the wooden box. The insects buzzed about her, and she forced herself to be still as her heartbeat picked up again. Dmytro. She stopped leaning and straightened her shoulders. Countless rows of tall wooden boxes surrounded her, the sun casting long shadows behind each one. She sought out footprints in the morning dew that hadn't completely disappeared or bent blades of grass. No bees seemed agitated, a stranger in their midst.

Vira took a slow step forward, aware of the fragile eggs in her hands and one of the soldier's eyes still upon her.

"Good. If you can't find me, the men in that truck can't see me either."

Closing her eyes and following the sound of his voice, Vira tilted her head away from the hives, not as far as the big barn but somewhere closer. She blushed and opened her eyes to examine a nearby tree, ideal for climbing, near the footpath on the edge of their property which she always forgot ran so close to these hives. Dmytro perched low in its leafy green branches, the brown frayed vest he wore the perfect camouflage. His smokey smudges blended in with the shadows.

"*Proshu*, don't stare right at me."

Vira smirked at his manners and looked toward the barn.

"What are you doing there? My father and brother will kill you if they see you on our land."

"But my father and I are the best blacksmiths in town. They wouldn't force themselves to use someone else. Your father likes perfection."

"You're perfection?" She blinked as her skin flushed at her own words.

He raised an eyebrow, smile widening.

"Some say so."

"What are you really doing?"

He shifted his balance, leaning closer to the trunk, rearranging his grip to rest his arms on the limbs stretched out before him.

"Trying to figure out those soldiers." He propped one leg out beside him, his shape becoming one with the tree's form. "And hoping to see you."

"What do you know of them?"

"A few of them came into my father's shop this morning demanding engine parts. My father encouraged my sister and me to leave."

"Noncia's here?"

"She's at edge of the orchard."

The slamming of the truck door on the road silenced them both. The three soldiers walked toward Vira's house with tight lips and otherwise blank expressions. In the five days, they'd never done that before. The man in front had papers tucked under his arm, and all three had their guns off their backs and in their hands.

"Run away with me, Vira."

She warmed at his words before the reality of their meaning sunk in for her.

"They've already seen me," she said without looking in his

direction or the soldiers'. "I'm sure it's nothing." She looked down to the eggs in her hands. Fear didn't fill her mind, but it had permeated her vocal cords.

She stood too close to the house to ignore them. One of the soldiers nodded to her, lifting his hat.

"Careful."

She didn't answer Dmytro. Instead she moved toward them. She could show them the kindness of the Galician people and what a true Ukrainian woman could be. There would be no trouble here. She could handle this. But her hands grew cold as she came closer, then her whole body, as if she walked in the presence of ghosts.

"Good morning, gentlemen," she said, meeting them at the front door. She raised her voice louder than she had to. "May I help you with something?"

"Look at those fine goose eggs," the soldier in front said. She held them up proudly, imagining Lesya's surprise at their speckled shells delivered by her hand. "May I?" He took the large eggs from her fingers without waiting for her answer, slipping them into a pouch of his uniform.

She forced herself to close her mouth. The geese had resettled around the pond, missing the transfer. Vira coughed, fighting the urge to question him, fighting the urge to open the man's pouch and reclaim her prize. Or to smash the eggs hard with an open palm thrust against the pocket. The men looked down upon her unmoved, their mustaches waxed, their shoulders broad in their uniforms. Terror rose in bumps across the skin of her arms.

"Does Ivan Bilyk live here?" the lead soldier continued. He pulled a handkerchief from a pocket and wiped his brow.

The heavy wooden front door opened before she could think how to answer. Her father had his bee ledger in his hands.

"May I help you?"

Vira slipped inside between the door and her father's tall mass, shrinking herself as best she could and fleeing to the kitchen.

The warm room flushed her face, but it could have been her relief at what felt like an escape. Her mother was gone. Two cloth dolls lay forgotten on the floor, and Helena chewed on a hunk of beeswax. Vira took it from her grasp, replacing it with one of the discarded dolls—one that had once been her own.

"What happened to your idea of eggs?" Lesya asked.

"Where's Ivan?" she whispered. Upstairs, footsteps creaked the floorboards. Vira raced to the stairs and up them.

"Ivan..." she said, grabbing the fabric of his sleeve as they met at the landing. "There are soldiers asking for you. What have you done? Where is Uncle Oleh?"

"I heard father," he answered, as if she had just mentioned neighbors at the door. He moved down the stairs, nudging her against the wall as he passed.

"No, stay here with us. Tato is handling it. Uncle Oleh spoke of the youth in the Lontsky Prison, no actual reason for arrest, just suspicion of work with the Underground, please...."

But he shrugged her off.

"We just have to wait a little bit longer to be free of them. You'll see."

His footsteps thudded, heavy on the steps, anything but discrete. When they reached the bottom together, she could see the geese at the pond out the window. When they had been younger, Ivan had once made her so mad, she had caught a frog and stuck it down the back of his shirt. She still hadn't figured out any better solutions for getting his full attention. But her cold hands were so empty.

"Every disadvantage has its advantage," he said, moving toward the front door. But her feet wouldn't take her any farther. The thought of her goose eggs in the soldier's pouch made her body tighten.

When the door opened, she shrunk back, retreating to the shadows of her father's wide bookcases then past the kitchen door and down their poppy-painted hallway until her hand found itself on the brass doorknob at the back of the house.

She twisted it, her hand feeling one with the chilly metal. Then she ran, past the last of the hives, past the barn and the stables, past the fields of what would soon be tall wheat, swaying in the summer breeze. The movement brought warmth to her chest, spreading to her shoulders and arms, but her fingertips still felt like ice.

She ran to the line of the woods and then along their edge, avoiding their shadows, a child running from home—perhaps that's all she was. She ran for the orchard, not knowing where else to go.

Vira banged into something, knocking the air out of herself. She gasped and fell to her hands and knees, fingers lost under the dead leaves of last year's autumn. A girl stood above her; long, dark hair windblown and speckled with ash, yet no grease smudged Noncia's beautiful face.

Young cherry tree leaves just beyond them shifted in the breeze. Neither spoke, though Noncia extended a hand. Vira took it and came back to her feet. The forest birds rustled and called. A cuckoo sang.

Not so far away, a gunshot rang out.

Vira cried out involuntarily, not letting go of Noncia's hand. Her eyes filled with water. She couldn't turn around. Her legs refused.

"Can you see what that was?" she whispered.

Noncia shook her head.

"Is my brother okay?" the girl whispered back, squeezing her hand. Vira's fingers didn't respond. Against the girl's skin, they were frigid.

"I think so." Vira's voice quivered. "But I don't think mine is."

12

Larissa

Her children were probably getting ready for bed at home, standing pajama-clad and watching the rabbits that sneaked into their backyard in the evening hours to eat from their veggie garden. Anna and Alex loved those rabbits so much, Larissa didn't have the heart to put up netting or chase them away. The bunny garden, they called it. Almost everything they harvested had teeth marks—if they had anything to harvest at all. But after the little brown bunnies with the white fluffy tails had been named—Olga and Sasha, Baba Vira's suggestions—she cherished the bunny-watching as much as the kids did.

Larissa handed the cab driver the address of the Palace of Culture and Science. He nodded and didn't bother taking the paper from her. She couldn't open her mouth to speak. She didn't have the words. She didn't know what language to think in.

They entered a long stretch of road with a grassy median. Its lush green was not so different from home, but the billboards were indecipherable—beautiful women, toasting glasses, televisions, musicians, something involving a close-up of a man's eyes. The flamboyant script covered them in its strange letter combinations and accents tossed in like decorative flourishes, touches of whimsy, design ideas weaned from Pinterest.

Their taxi driver whispered into his cell phone. He steered the car with one hand—one wrist splashed with something Larissa couldn't figure out, the maroon mark an explosion of Crayola markers. When he scratched his forearm on the steering wheel at a stoplight, Larissa's body tightened, and she pulled her hands into her lap, away from the interior fabric of the car.

Beside her, Ira rested her chin on her propped-up fist, and Larissa fought the urge to move her sister's most likely germ-covered hand farther away from her face. Ira didn't notice, though. She leaned her ear closer toward the cabbie's phone conversation.

Larissa raised a hand to push her hair behind her ear but didn't finish the motion. She opened her purse, squeezed hand sanitizer into her palm.

Buildings were becoming more numerous. Buses with red trim surrounded them. Renaissance-inspired candelabra street-lights hung over the road. Larissa knew the city had been flattened during World War II but didn't have any idea that it had been rebuilt to mimic its century-old style. The columned facades and meticulous ironwork were stunning yet illogical among other sleek, modern structures.

"This way," her sister whispered as the cab pulled to a stop. The English felt luscious to her foreign-stuffed ears.

Huge movie billboards and a glass-fronted shopping district greeted them. Larissa had been expecting quaint stalls of pretzels and pierogis, bearded men and fur-coated women. She blinked at the city, letting it settle on her eyes. Masses of cars shifted and slowed at a stop light. Tracks rattled as trams moved in line with the vehicle traffic. Across the street, a mother and child exited a storefront with bags of purchases heavy in their arms. Even the little girl's arms. She was about Alex's age. She beamed up at her mother.

Ira tightened her hold on Larissa's elbow and slammed the cab door shut. "Did you catch the cabbie's conversation on the phone? Polish and Ukrainian are closer than I thought."

Larissa spun around, away from the mother and child, away from the cabbie. Then the Palace made her lose her balance. She imagined the biggest chunky block creation on her playroom floor, maybe using every wooden block of every little child on her street, with a final flourish of spikes and spires added onto every available edge and roofline, just in case anyone was curious about the intent of intimidation. The wild megalith took up nearly a whole city block.

Ira's hand still held her sister's elbow, pulling her toward the looming structure.

"Was he debating murdering his girlfriend?"

Larissa rolled her eyes. "The cabbie?"

"Maybe I lost something in translation, but I swear, he was plotting, Lyalya."

"You're the one plotting."

"Murder? Never."

"Your next seduction?"

Ira just shrugged at her sister before they walked the broad path toward the entryway. One of the entryways. So many options. Perfectly manicured beds of white flowers along the sidewalk led them forward. The columns on this side were bulbous, almost pregnant. Far above them, a dark clock tower loomed like it kept time for angry gods. More chunky masonry grew like it had been recently watered. Tiny spears sprouted upon ledges. Larissa looked for hiding gargoyles.

As they neared the doors, three teenage girls chatterd on a nearby bench. All dressed in folk costumes, peasant skirts, embroidered blouses, flowers in their hair, they glanced among each other and their mobile phones, each clutched like a mismatched accessory in their hands. The folkdance exhibition, Larissa reminded herself. People didn't actually dress like that here. Her grandmother's stories and her reality couldn't settle in her mind. Music floated from the Palace now, deep, heavy, sinking into her skin—perhaps the melody she had once found for Baba Vira on YouTube that had sent her grandmother to a chair with her face flushed. Her frail legs had to be propped on an ottoman. Her eyes had closed and were lost in a memory that she never shared.

"Do you know that song?" she said to Ira. Larissa swallowed, humbling herself to her sister's relationship with their grandmother.

Ira's steps forward had fallen in line with the music, each footfall led by a pointed toe.

"I think there was another boy before our grandfather. Maybe even when they were apart."

"It's always boys with you."

"I think it was for Baba too."

Larissa walked again, pulling Ira along with her this time. They were within the Palace's massive shadow now, following signs for the International Folkdance Exhibition. She waited to see their baba sitting on a bench tucked into an eve, surrounded by dancers in costume, laughing her head off at her trick to bring them all together.

"But Dgidgo was her one true love. She told me—".

Ira walked faster, away from Larissa's glare.

"Our *dgidgo* was a war husband. They barely knew each other then had four years apart. Things happen."

The heavy doors swung open easily. Inside, their shoes echoed on the marble floor under a three-tiered chandelier, its light dancing across the ceiling and walls. Stefa was in the Congress Theater with her girls, this she knew. They would be dancing six times today. Larissa wished she knew where they were on their schedule. Her copy had been left on Baba Vira's dresser back home. Maybe their baba would be sitting in the front row, tapping her wrinkled hands on her lap.

"She always told me about knowing he was the one, about the feeling of love overtaking you, leaving you breathless, leaving you without a doubt. She told me that on my wedding day, right before I walked down the aisle to meet Greg."

"Are you sure she was talking about our *dgidgo*?"

Larissa's palms sweated as she pulled on a door. Something about it seemed right, almost warmer than the others. It whined as it opened, revealing darkness, far-off lights overhead, curtains as tall as the columns outside.

"Are you planning on taking the stage?" Ira raised her eyebrows. It made her forehead wrinkle. Those wrinkles made Larissa feel better.

She started to ease the door shut when a voice from inside stopped her.

"Lyalya?"

A chill exploded down her spine. Only after she swallowed did she recognize Stefa in the dim light.

"How did you find us?" their mother's old friend said. Her voice was hushed, the stage just feet away. Its lights streaked across the floor, but not where Stefa stood. Her tired eyes and crows-feet were darkened but not erased in the shadows.

"Luck," Ira answered.

Larissa tried to make her eyes adjust. Stefa's bouncing but closed-lipped gaggle of twelve-year-old dancers surrounded her in the wings, but Larissa still rushed into the woman's arms, pressing her cheek into hers and allowing herself to linger, allowing the tears that fell to be squeezed between their skin.

"Where is she, Panya Stefa?"

The woman tightened her arms around Larissa.

"I'm so sorry you had to come all this way. I didn't know what else to do. With all these girls. With..." She threw her hands up in the air, releasing the embrace.

The dancers fluttered around them, flower wreaths in their hair. Fabric sunflowers and cornflowers, hollyhocks, poppies. Ribbons streamed down to their shoulders, flying through the air like electricity when they moved. Larissa reached out a hand to untangle the red, yellow, blue, and green ribbons that had become entwined within the sheaves of wheat.

Ira watched the dancers, combing her fingers through her hair. Larissa knew she wanted to braid it, grab an extra floral crown, and join them. X's marked places for dancers to line up before they entered the stage. Ira toed the blue tape on the ground.

"She left me a note." Larissa put a hand on the shoulder of one of the dancers as she passed. The girl paused, allowing her collar and vest to be straightened. Larissa's blue jeans clashed with her surroundings, a betrayal of her heritage. "She disappeared on purpose."

Stefa's face tightened. She shepherded her dancers into lines in the wings of the stage. She nodded at them, holding their eyes, squeezing their hands in silence. The curtains loomed high over their heads, disappearing into the darkness above. The girls fidgeted, but the toes of their red boots stayed on the tape marks on the floor. Larissa remembered being one of those girls, costumed, made-up, pretending to celebrate a heritage she didn't feel much connection to. The flowers always made her scalp itch.

One of the girls was paler than the others. She stood still as a wooden doll, expression as locked on her face as if it had been painted.

"That's Annabelle," Stefa said, following Larissa's stare. "Her parents are one of our other chaperones, but their train was delayed.

The girl's skin looked moist.

"Is she okay?" Larissa whispered. "Is it just stage fright?"

Ira lingered near the girls, a step away from being in line with them, ready to high-step onto stage.

"She'll be fine when her parents get here."

The notes of the *Kolomyjka* began. The girls walked onto the stage, pointed toes leading each footfall, stepping together in a line one after the other, arms spread out, welcoming the audience to their party. In their straight lines, Annabelle alone was crooked. She moved more slowly than the other girls.

"Your baba planned this." Stefa didn't turn from her dancers in the light of the stage.

"You don't look surprised," said Ira.

"Are you?" Stefa asked. She gripped an extra floral wreath in her hands, tracing its long ribbons in her thin fingers.

"But Baba's ninety-one years old." Larissa shifted her weight ever so slightly from side to side.

"Do you know how she reached that age?" Stefa still didn't turn to the sisters, but she tilted her chin in their direction. The dancers twirled and high-stepped, kicking their legs behind them as they traveled. Annabelle was still a step behind, the only girl without a wide smile. "She lost her whole family in the war. She lost everything. She adapted. She's always found a way to survive."

"She tells us the stories."

"But have you ever thought about what she had to do?"

"She seduced Nazis."

"Not that simple, Irena."

Annabelle's lips moved. They heard her faint voice on stage as she lost her position with the other girls, as her gibberish distracted the others.

Stefa took a step forward, just to the edge of the darkness, where the lights of the stage reached their limits, where a curtain veil blocked the audience. The girls stepped forward and back, arcing one arm over their heads. Annabelle teetered. The other girls didn't notice. They turned in unison, ribbons flowing behind their decorated hair.

"She's diabetic. I didn't even... Her parents were supposed to be here already. Your baba was supposed to be here already...."

Larissa broke into the stage light in the same moment that Annabelle collapsed onto the wooden floor. The music bounced, a lively celebration around them. The other girls dropped their arms and their practiced expressions. Larissa cradled the girl's head, bringing it into her lap. Her eyes fluttered but didn't focus. Not on the stage lights, not on Larissa's face. The heat was strong here. Beads of sweat trickled across the girl's brow.

"Annabelle. Annabelle!" Larissa lifted the girl to a seated position, hugging her, using a free hand to reach into her purse still strapped across her body. She fiddled through its contents—crayons, lip gloss, passport, wallet... If the girl was diabetic, she needed... Larissa's fingers found what she sought, the little brown packet of organic raw sugar. With her one arm supporting Annabelle's limp form, she ripped it open with her teeth before pouring the grains on the tip of Annabelle's exposed tongue.

The girl blinked. Someone thought to turn off the music. In the audience, someone coughed. Voices murmured.

"Annabelle, help me help you," Larissa whispered. The other girls had retreated to the edges of the stage where Stefa and Ira still stood. Annabelle swallowed and opened her mouth like an infant, a huge, lanky, fully-toothed infant. "That's it."

She pulled off the girl's floral headband that surely made her head itch. When she rested it on the stage beside them, its shadow spiked into a crown of thorns.

"Someone, please go get some water," she called off stage. She couldn't make out the faces there behind the lingering dancers. Somewhere Stefa watched. Somewhere Ira stood by. How did she ever agree to let Baba Vira join this ensemble?

The stage lights dimmed, adjusting over their heads to a soft blue light. The girl she held took a deep breath as another dancer ran back on stage with a water bottle. Larissa took it, twisting it hard to break the seal. When she raised it to Annabelle's lips, the girl's cheeks flushed. But embarrassment was good. Embarrassment was healthy.

"Thank you," she whispered.

"Ready to exit stage left?" The girl nodded, and Larissa helped her to a stand. She wobbled. The other dancers offered their shoulders and their encouragement. With their arms around each other and their red boots retreating, they were the oddest of armies.

"Your parents are in a taxi on their way." Stefa's phone still glowed in her hand.

Annabelle nodded slowly.

Ira hung back in the shadows.

Larissa stayed with the girl, watching her breathe, watching the color return to her skin, sensing the energy seep into her young, thin limbs.

"I'll meet her parents," Ira whispered before darting toward the exit, but Larissa knew it was just a means of escape.

A basket of sunflowers sat on a table by the door, stopping

Ira's momentum, freezing her with her hand on the knob. That hadn't been there a moment ago when they'd walked in. She pushed open the door a crack, just enough to cast light on the discovery. Larissa's shoulders tightened when she saw what Ira must have seen immediately. A crooked-nosed mask sat atop the flowers. Its teeth were jagged and yellow. Its chin pointed. And it grinned.

13

Ira

The stage door banged behind Ira when she took off running, passing dancers in fluffed out knee-length skirts of every color and women whispering and comparing notes on their clipboards. Ira tried to retrace their steps out into the sunshine, the way someone making a delivery would have come in.

A group of girls in yellow crowded the hallway around her next turn. Yellow ribbons fell from blond hair. Yellow fabric matched their yellow shoes. The gaggle of them chatted and laughed, spilling themselves across the narrow passage. Ira felt her shortness of breath, like the girl on the stage, lightheaded, pale, about to fall.

One of the yellow girls noticed her and shifted to the side, nudging another out of the way. The glimmer coming from the incandescent lightbulbs tucked into the crystal lighting over her head made her dizzy. But Ira blinked. She nodded. She darted through them, feeling their ribbons shift and move around her.

"Excuse me, excuse me," she repeated, weaving, dancing, hearing her sister's manners rubbing off on her. "I need to get through," she shouted louder. Bodies swarmed around her, yet she saw the end, the last girl, ignoring her while she played a clapping game with a friend, the sound of their palms touching again and again echoing off the hallway walls. Beyond them were the doors. The light of the sunshine, not as painfully yellow. Real. The promise of fresh air. The smell of flowers.

At the wide glass doors of the entrance, a man in a gray uniform stood still, looking down at his phone. A short sprig of baby's breath sat on his arm, clinging to him, refusing to be a part of any delivery. Ira rushed toward him.

"Did you just deliver that basket?" She grabbed his arm, nearly pulling her face into his. He pulled back, wincing, confusion clouding his expression. "The sunflowers. *Soniashnyky!*" she repeated in Ukrainian.

The deliveryman didn't answer. He cleared his throat and shifted away from her. But they were somehow alone at the end of the marble hall, the light bouncing off the stone floors. The sunshine peeked through the glass doors beside them.

The man said something she couldn't decipher—something that sounded like a curse. He pulled a note from his pocket and stuck it into her hands. Upon it, Vira's beautiful slanted script detailed the time of delivery and specific stage door.

He left the note in her hands and escaped her, out the doors, down the marble steps, and across the wide white sidewalk past the fountains and flowers toward empty benches where nothing familiar still lingered.

Larissa's hand on her shoulder made her jump. Her sister was out of breath. She'd been running too. Ira passed her the messenger's instructions and pushed open the grand doors. Her sister followed.

"How do we even begin to find her?" Larissa's arms crossed over her chest.

A bird swooped over their heads toward a nest tucked into the cornice. Larissa's body stiffened, curling in on itself. Ira raised her hand to the creature as if she were Snow White and the gray pigeon would alight upon her fingers. When it didn't, she moved her hand closer toward Larissa's face, beckoning the bird again. Her sister pushed Ira's hand away.

"I thought maybe it was a messenger pigeon."

"It's a miniature velociraptor."

Ira raised her hand again, but Larissa leaned away, pressing her back against the stone building. Ira dropped her hand and leaned back with her sister. How was it that old stone smelled different from the cement of her apartment building? There was something dusty about it. Ancient. Full of spice. What was a

Polish spice?

Beyond the wide sidewalks, horns honked. Two mopeds sped by, weaving between the bigger vehicles. A crowd poured out of the underground station across the street.

"How'd you know what to do with Annabelle? Neither Anna or Alex are..." The rest of the sentence hung in the air as if Ira's memory had lapsed on a major family conversation. Larissa didn't immediately interrupt the confused silence while other tourists walked past them, speaking German, French, and maybe Dutch.

"No one in the family's diabetic." Larissa brushed her hands on her jeans. "Just things you learn if you pay attention, I guess."

"Why do you have sugar packets in your purse?"

"How do you think I get Alex to eat cooked vegetables when we're out at restaurants?"

Traffic stopped on the street before them. People lined the sidewalks. Far off, music blared. Drums. Woodwinds. Cymbals.

"I always wondered what it was with that kid and veggies. Wait..." Her voice slowed.

"What?"

Across the Palace's city block of criss-crossed walkways and manicured gardens, a massive face stared back at her, a nonsensical giant set of eyes, a long and crooked nose, and a scowling mouth. Its features were unconnected to one another, a literal parade of facial parts, thin black legs sticking out below each costume. The street was visible between them. People nearby stopped and cleared a path while the face moved. Its ears became unaligned, as if one had stopped to listen more carefully. Its wild gray eyebrows were lines of scratchy straw.

"What?" Larissa pressed.

The face marched, the bent nose moving jarringly one way then the other. Only the mouth and eyes remained steady, brutal, locked in an ancient stare that Ira wanted to place somewhere back in her childhood and also in the mask that nestled with the sunflowers.

Her own finger felt crooked and gnarled as she pointed. Her sister shifted her weight beside her.

"What is that?" Larissa squinted.

"Baba always said witches were real."

The face's features distorted and reformed when it turned a corner. Scowl followed by long nose, out of line ears, followed by eyes that lost and found their symmetry, then went out of sight.

"She's there somewhere, frightening the crowd into submission."

Ira cut down the steps and across the wide sidewalk. Larissa, who she had never been able to beat in a footrace her whole life, was right at her side, past the red and white flowers shaped into designs of interlocked diamonds. Ira grimaced and pushed her legs harder. Bodies were blockades around the bus-stop shelter. Walls of slowly meandering tourists, maps in hand, obstructed Ira's path and view. The fast-moving street traffic didn't give her another option.

"Where are we going?" Larissa said through tight lips, keeping pace with her sister while Ira wove and scurried around everyone she could. A traffic light turned red, and Ira cut across the road.

"Baba's here somewhere, I know it," she said between huffing breaths.

"You're going to get us hit by a car."

"Only if you're slow."

"You're going to get us lost."

"No more lost than we are without her."

Ira pushed farther down a side street. There were fewer people here away from the main thoroughfare. An old man sat on a storefront's steps. A woman pushed a stroller. Ira saw her sister's eyes flick to the child inside, but she only sprinted faster, harder.

At the next block, she turned left and was forced to stop in the crowd. But this wasn't for any parade. Where had they lost the baba yaga parade? How could you lose a baba yaga parade?

Market stalls covered the sidewalks, selling pretzels, bread, honey, and woodwork. Fresh sausages hung from metal rods. Shoppers and tourists swarmed in the street.

A block away were the modern skyscrapers, but here, they'd stepped back in time.

Ira panted beside her sister who somehow wasn't nearly as out of breath.

Before them, women had white aprons tied over their long skirts. They offered sunflowers, hollyhocks, and dried herbs. A heavy-set man struck a hammer on his anvil, red-coaled furnace at his side. A pair of nuns dressed in brown habits passed them.

"If you think Baba's in this crowd, we'll never find her." Larissa put a hand on her sister's shoulder, but Ira shrugged her off.

"Or maybe we will." Ira darted again into the crowd. A troop of musicians tucked into an alcove played clarinets and flutes, stepping hard on the whitewashed bricks to create their own percussion. Ira slid behind them, passing a woman with clear plastic bags of pierogis.

"Ira!" Larissa called after her.

The market stalls ended after a few blocks of vendors, and the streets became less crowded. Art galleries, bookstores, and cafes gave way to university buildings and a stone archway.

"We should go back. We're getting lost. Baba's not here." Larissa trailed a few steps behind her sister.

"She is." Ira's heart beat almost painfully in her chest. Her lungs were about to explode, but she broke into another run. She ran for blocks, inhaling the smells of the city—dust and stone, onion and dough. There was something just beyond her sight here. She could feel it like a string wrapped around her ribcage, pulling her forward.

Only a tall red brick wall stopped her. Old Town Warsaw. Brick turrets and a crenelated barrier guarded the oldest part of the city. Beyond it, a huge castle showed off its red roof, three towers, and aura of a fairytale. Kings and queens must have lived there. Ira stared, hands on her knees, bent over in exhaustion. Horse-drawn carraiges must have brought guests to royal balls there. Galant noblemen with a flair for romance would have invited the beautiful girls to dance.

"If Baba was here," Larissa huffed, catching up, "I think you probably ran past her."

"There." Ira straightened herself.

"You see her?"

"No."

"Then what?" Larissa stayed by her side as Ira forced her legs forward, slower this time. That's as much as they could bear. The buildings surrounding them here looked like they were built in the Renaissance—all snug proximity and architectural flourishes, care taken over every decision in the keystones and cornices and balcony railings. Nothing quite compared to this stateside. But that wasn't what had caught her eye.

The statue Ira approached wasn't imposing, not like the figure atop a massive column farther into the square. This woman's wavy stone hair was tied back, revealing her bare breasts and curvaceous hips and belly. One arm held a sword high and ready for battle, while the other possessed a massive shield. Below her torso, waves thrashed around her mermaid tail.

Larissa combed her fingers through her hair, wrinkles creasing her forehead.

"Look at her. She's awesome." Ira circled the statue. The mermaid's face was so serene, so feminine and beautiful, so fierce.

"She's a mother," Larissa said in the same moment Ira said, "She's me."

The mermaid before them was out of place in land-locked Poland, in the midst of this ancient town square, surrounded by nostalgic horse-drawn carriages and tourist stands selling soccer scarves, miniature coats-of-arms, flags, and wooden matryoshka dolls. Somewhere a massive Baba Yaga hid.

Somewhere their baba played games.

Ira bent to retrieve the loose sunflowers that had first caught her eye, resting on the ground by the statue's base. She plucked one up and struck the mermaid's pose, and her sister rolled her eyes.

"Are these sunflowers from Baba too?"

"Maybe the basket of flowers had a note. Why didn't we look for a note?"

"There was a mask."

"That didn't mean to find a Baba Yaga face, chase it across the city, get lost, and look for sunflowers." Larissa dragged on her sister's arm like she had since they were kids. "Can we go back to Panya Stefa and the girls now?"

Ira nodded, but held her position, arm extended to the sky, imaginary shield before her.

14

Vira (June 1941)

Vira wanted to be done crying, but she wished Ivan could see this. The roofless vehicle had a single driver, but two more soldiers sat in the truck bed between boxes. A large gun perched on a small trailer dragged behind them. Vira could barely see the soldiers, such different soldiers, from this distance at her window-seat. Even with their strange red and black swastika armbands, she was drawn to them. Her breath staggered as she exhaled. The liberators of Galicia. Stalin's soldiers gone. Just one month too late.

Ivan's viola rested on its stand in the corner of the room, where it had been for years while he was a child learning how to play. Their mother had wrapped a black cloth around its long neck. He hadn't been home much in the past year, but the house still echoed in the absence of his music.

She walked across the room and sat down beside it, running a fingertip along the length of a string until stopped by the dark fabric. The silver-wrapped sheep gut released a high-pitched whine at the touch.

Vira's father came into the room and watched the truck as it went out of sight. He cleared his throat. They both knew now that Ivan had somehow been right. Independence was possible. Bandura and the Organization of Ukrainian Nationalists had declared an independent Ukrainian state. The Germans chased the Soviets out.

Vira plucked at the string that only answered in a whisper with the muffling fabric. She ripped the black cloth away.

"At least this is good news, Tato," she dared to say into the silence. Her father looked to the viola with red eyes. "The Germans, I mean," she pressed.

He shook his head, the motion in time with the pendulum of the clock on the wall. He cleared his throat again.

"It's not over," he said. "And we're not going to the dance this evening. It's not safe."

Vira's chin jerked up.

"But, Tato! Mama, Lesya, and I were going to give bread and salt to the German soldiers. And I just finished my new skirt!"

"No." He walked away. He did that when he knew she would protest. He walked out of the room a lot lately.

She flicked at one of the viola strings. Without the cloth to soften the sound, the sharp note echoed through the house. She plucked three more times like the machine-gun fire she'd heard so much about. Was that the big gun the truck pulled to keep the peace?

Why didn't her father see that it was over? They were finally free.

The echoes of the notes bounced against the room's walls, the poppy flower hallway, maybe even creeping up the stairs to Ivan's room. The twins were napping. Lesya probably had her nose deep into a book. Her mother was in the kitchen—she had probably overheard the new plan, but as always, she didn't speak out against her husband's wishes.

Vira wouldn't be like that when she got married. She imagined herself in hand-stitched wedding clothes, and all of her friends basking in her beauty. Across from her would stand a groom... She bit her lip. She didn't know who that would be. Dmytro came to mind, but if she married him, she'd leave this kind of life behind. Noncia had callouses on her ungloved hands. Her hair always fell free of its braid. Her face, the same age as Vira's, always looked so tired and dirty.

Vira ran her finger up the length of the silver string making the high-pitched whine fill the room again.

She wasn't supposed to go out without asking permission,

especially now, but that had never stopped her before. She stood up and walked toward the door. The normally squeaky hinges didn't give her away as she slipped outside.

The geese raised their heads but didn't harass her when they saw she didn't have any food. She walked toward the hives, letting the dew on the grass clean the dust off her leather shoes. She tilted her feet back and forth until they looked like she'd spent some time cleaning them the right way.

Beyond the beehives, the sunflowers bloomed, their wide faces as familiar as friends. As a child, she happily danced with them as they swayed in the breeze. She could weave circle dances around their stems so much taller than she, tapping her heel then toe into the rich black soil and pretending she was a girl crowded by admirers. But she wasn't a child anymore.

The buzzing amplified as she approached the bees. They had been the only thing to calm her since Ivan's death, pressing her body against the hive boxes, feeling the vibration of creatures so alive, so connected to each other, so indifferent to who the soldiers were or weren't on the roads.

Her father and one of her cousins had been painting the boxes a vivid turquoise and an eye-catching red. They stood in a pattern, ordered, vibrant, and serene. Vira didn't know why she felt the need to tiptoe between them. The insects buzzed out and around their homes, delighted with their beauty perhaps? Fulfilled because of everything they'd worked for inside? Ready to escape and discover something new?

Something jutted out from one of the still unpainted boxes in the third row. Vira crossed to it, trailing her finger across the worn side of the box, almost seeking a splinter, a sting. The paper had been curled by the wind.

I had to find a way to tell you. We're leaving tomorrow. I hope you get this. If you do, look for me in the usual spot.

Vira hadn't been near the hives in days. She knew the note could be for anyone—even for Ivan if someone in the Ukrainian

Underground didn't know he was gone—but the handwriting appeared to be the same as Dmytro's first note to her, the few words he dropped inside a rock right in front of her family, the one inviting her to meet him, which she'd refused and refused before that first night months ago.

The usual spot. The fallen birch tree. Her body flushed remembering the touch of his lips there, the feel of his hands on her waist. His dark eyes, even darker in the night's shadows.

Her fastest path to the woods was in line with the window of her father's study. She put a hand to the hive box, feeling its vibration, letting the sweet smell of honey fill her nose. Her father already said they couldn't go to the dance tonight. What else could he really do to her?

The bees hummed against the skin of her palm. She leaned forward and put the side of her face to the box.

Ivan was dead. He didn't always follow the rules, but at least he had lived while he could.

Vira peeled herself away and hid herself among the nearby sunflowers. They greeted her with nods of their massive faces. She wove into their tall stems, surrounding herself with tall green stalks and bold yellow petals, pressing far enough in that she wouldn't be detected by any windows from the house.

Wide green leaves caressed her shoulders as she passed, and she stepped carefully among them, not wanting to disturb their beauty. They weren't admirers of her dance today. They were accomplices.

The sunflower field nestled against the edge of their woods, the woods where Ivan had once told her Baba Yaga lived, and everyone knew Baba Yaga ate children who were not smart, courageous, and good-hearted. When Vira had protested that she was those things, Ivan had answered that he never doubted that she was smart or courageous.

She stepped into the shadows of the woods and whistled softly, a shrill warble a far fetch from any bird who lived there. She walked a bit deeper into the woods and sat down upon a fallen tree, the old birch. Its white bark was nearly peeled away to the bone. Vira whistled again then lowered her face into her hands.

Birds fluttered around the woods nearby, but none twittered back. A lark hopped in the leaves, the black stripe around its neck like a necklace it had donned for the occasion. A small rodent—a mouse or a hedgehog, Vira couldn't tell—rustled in the leaves nearby. Its black beady eyes rested on her for just a moment before hiding away.

"Vira," came a whisper.

Her head shot up. Noncia stood before her, as beautiful as ever. If she wasn't Dmytro's sister, she wasn't convinced she would like her.

"You got Dmytro's note."

Noncia moved to sit down beside her. The wooden beads of the necklaces she wore clacked together as she moved. She didn't normally wear necklaces. For a moment, Vira wondered if she'd gotten the idea from the lark.

"He couldn't be here any longer, so he sent me. Our family is leaving tonight."

"Leaving? What does that even mean?" The air left her lungs. She blinked. Her elbows dropped to her knees, but in her shift a beam of light that fell through the leaves overhead seemed to pierce her. Was it possible for light to pierce a soul? To find any last fragment of wholeness within and rip it apart? "Leaving?" she repeated, grasping for more but not finding another word to say.

"My father's nervous. A lot of the townspeople are. We've received news from friends in Poland. These German soldiers are dangerous."

"But they've freed us from the Soviets."

"And what they have in mind is worse." The hedgehog, definitely a hedgehog she now saw, had returned to its scurrying underneath the nearby leaves. Vira squeezed her hands in her lap, scrunching up her nose. She tried to lean back, out of the sun, back into the shadows. Her breathing thinned. Why wasn't Dmytro the one telling this to her? Why hadn't he said that this was possible?

"You can't just suddenly... how can you even...."

"My family has been talking about it for a long time," Noncia interrupted. "I want to go to a good school. To have a better chance. Dmytro does too."

"You two go to school now."

"Not one that takes us seriously." She shifted her weight and her necklaces clicked against each other. "I'm smart, Vira. I want to be a doctor. I want to work hard and study. To be acknowledged. To stop being a smoke-stained blacksmith's daughter."

"But that's who you are!" The words left Vira's mouth before she thought to stop them.

Noncia's lips thinned when she pressed them together. The lark took flight, taking its fancy ideas with it. Noncia's eyes followed the bird.

"People are moving everywhere," she continued. "It's our family's moment to do something new with ourselves, in a new place, a new life. Our father's been saving. He has friends abroad who can help settle us."

Noncia's braids sat neat upon her head, and she held up her chin like Vira had never seen before.

"Where are you going?" she whispered.

"Czechoslovakia."

Vira nodded, and Noncia turned back toward her. Hers were the eyes that held Vira together when her brother had died, when screaming filled her house and her mind, when the music stopped. She took Noncia's slim hand in her own, squeezing it, not wanting to let it go.

"I'm sorry, I—"

But her words were cut off when a yell broke through the air. "Vira!"

Nearby birds scattered at the interruption. Her father. She didn't know how his voice carried across the hills as far as it did. She shook her head, looked for the lark, but it was gone. The hedgehog seemed to be too.

"There's a forest in Czechoslovakia that's good for hiding. Slovak Paradise, they call it. We will be in a nearby city, but if the war comes... It could be safer for us. It could be safer for you too."

"But you just said you were leaving for a better life, not hiding in a forest."

"I hope so." She patted the neat braid arching up and over the crown of her head. "But it's good to know every possibility of how to survive. This war—"

"But we're at the end of the war!"

"I don't think—"

Vira's father called her name again. The sound of his deep voice sliced through the wind, silencing the end of Noncia's sentence. Vira stiffened and closed her eyes, wishing she could burrow into the leaves with the hedgehog or tuck herself into the folds of Noncia's skirt, to let herself be taken away too.

"Your brother?" she said, standing up.

Noncia shoved a hand into a pocket of her skirt, producing a small familiar rock with a hole through its center, and pushed it into Vira's hands. "He said to give you this."

Yet the hole bored through it was empty. No words. No goodbyes.

"Take it for luck, for remembering." Noncia closed Vira's fingers around the cool stone.

"Vira!" Her father's voice had become angrier—not concerned—angrier.

Through the trees, she could see the fields that separated the woods from their house. She needed to go now, to follow her father, to lower her chin and be silent as he fumed.

Vira turned back to say goodbye, but Noncia was already gone.

She ran back to the house, legs pumping under her long skirt, hair loosening from her neat braid. Face glistening from the exertion. Or her nerves. Or the summer heat. Her mother stood at the back door. She pretended to spit on the ground when she saw her daughter, superstitious as always at the first sign of anything wonderful or terrible in their lives. She'd come to think of Vira as the latter, she knew, but the woman stepped out of the way for her daughter to go inside.

Creeping down the long hallway, she could hear her father and Uncle Oleh discussing something in the front room. The rise and fall of their voices lacked harmony without Ivan's third inflection blended in. Whatever they debated, they were on opposite sides.

On the mantle over the fireplace stood the family nesting dolls all complete, just as Uncle Oleh had suggested. The second doll in line had a hideous Baba Yaga mask in her painted hands, allowing her to hide her beauty with something fiercer if she wanted to. Vira was proud of how it turned out, and the glimmer of respect in her uncle's eyes made her stand taller.

"I don't know where you should go, but not here!" her father boomed, throwing one of his books down onto his wooden desk. The room shook with the impact. Vira swallowed.

"Why can't Uncle Oleh stay, *Tato*?"

"Your father thinks I'm making it dangerous for your family if I'm here."

"There's no question about that. Go to your friends at the university or your friends outside of Galicia. You're being reckless." He crossed the room and put a hand on Vira's shoulder. The massive iron keys that had been passed down for generations jangled on his belt as he moved. "You're teaching my daughter to be reckless. Where have you been?"

"I'm being a revolutionary," her uncle answered, before Vira could think of how to respond. "The Organization of Ukrainian Nationalists—"

"If you won't be more cautious for yourself, all I ask is that you leave my family out of it."

Vira's father motioned him toward the door, and her uncle

nodded at the nesting dolls on the mantle.

"Vira understands."

"My oldest daughter is the last person who understands."

A knock on the door silenced them. Vira leaned toward the front window. Soldiers stood outside. They weren't Soviets. They were German.

"German soldiers," she whispered, stressing the first word.

Her father's grip on her shoulder tightened. Vira's mother came down the hall with her hostess's face in place.

"Take the children upstairs," Vira's father snapped at her. "Stay upstairs."

Her welcoming demeanor fell to one of fear. She nodded and returned to the kitchen, swooping up the twins in her arms and carrying them out of the way and up the stairs. Lesya was already up in her room.

"Back door, go!" Her father's voice cracked. Vira had never heard his voice crack. "I'm not lying for you, but get a head start."

Vira and her uncle both left the room at the same time, brushing shoulders, meeting eyes, then moving in different directions. She moved toward the stairs. The knock came again. Vira spotted Halya's doll on a table in the hallway. Her little sister loved that doll. It would comfort her if she was scared. She spun around to fetch it before anyone answered the door, but her body wouldn't immediately let her move back down. She forced herself step by step. Creaking stair by creaking stair. These weren't the men who killed her brother, she reminded herself. These were the men who were helping to liberate Ukraine. They were enabling true Ukrainian independence. Her stomach twisted. She crossed to the table with the doll and forced herself to breathe as quietly as possible, to manage to exist without the slightest rise or fall of her breast or the blinking of an eye.

"Yes, he was here," her father said. He'd opened the door. When had she missed him opening the door? "But he has already gone," he continued. No cracks in his voice. Only strength. Only the voice she'd always known. She never realized there was any other inside of him.

Language spit out in a German reply before being massaged by a second voice into a Ukrainian tongue.

Her father spoke exact German, but he wasn't going to make this conversation any faster by skipping the translator. Vira tucked herself deeper into the room off the hall where she wouldn't be able to be seen. She spoke exact German too. She could understand every word.

Had Uncle Oleh snuck out the back door? Gone to the woods? The stables to borrow one of her father's fastest horses? She moved toward her window seat. Her needlework lay there where she'd left it, but when she picked it up—at least a reason for her to be there—the needle and thread slipped and poked her in the palm, piercing her pale skin. A drop of blood fell onto the white fabric of her new blouse. She pulled a handkerchief out of her pocket to press against the tiny wound.

The men clomped down the hall. Her heart clomped inside her.

"*Wo versteckst du ihn?*" Where are you hiding him? The sounds of their voices echoed worse than Ivan's viola strings. The ring of it bounced off her skin, against the walls, against the ceiling.

A blond boy stuck his head into the room where she sat, but she didn't look up from her wrapped hand. He said something to her in German, but she didn't move or respond. He gazed about the room, allowing his eyes to rest on her for a long time. Her entire body went numb until he turned and walked away.

Behind him, her father stepped in only for a moment and looked in alarm first at her and then her Baba Yaga mask nesting doll. She understood the command. If these men were coming for her uncle, they knew of his work. They knew of his definition of a Baba Yaga. As soon as the soldiers had moved farther down the hall, she moved straight to the mantle and packed them up, one by one. Halya inside Helena, Helena inside Lesya, Lesya inside of Vira, Vira inside their mama, Marichka. She didn't put the collection back onto the shelf but kept it in her hands—her hands that were cold, shaking, and smeared with droplets of blood. She gripped the dolls tighter so they didn't slip from her grasp.

The footsteps clomped. Their trail of caked mud dirtied the hall rug outside the sitting room door. It probably trailed all the way down their beautiful flower-trimmed hall. They moved deeper into the house toward the stairs.

Vira wanted to do something, but what could she do? She couldn't save her uncle or fight these men or protect her family. She held the nesting dolls close to her chest.

The barking of German came from deep in the house. The heavy backdoor creaked open. Boots stomped faster. The yelling was cacophonous, an insult to Ivan's viola surrounded by torn black cloth now on the floor. Its new bow string stared at Vira, catching the light of the sun that cut in the window. An automobile engine started outside.

Hours, minutes, seconds later—she couldn't tell—a military vehicle came into her sight, pulling off down the road. She could see her uncle inside.

Vira ran out the front door after the soldiers' truck on the road, past the goose pond and all the way past the fields of her family's land to the place where the road forked. One way led to Lviv, where Uncle Oleh worked as a professor and Ivan used to play with the symphony. The other led to their own small town. Vira didn't know which way the car had carried her uncle, but she knew she couldn't run all the way to Lviv.

Her boots kicked dust up over the hem of her skirt, but she didn't slow to a more dignified pace. She ran past her neighbor's cow fields and the church on the outskirts of town—only stopping at the large elm tree she'd always wanted to climb as a child, the tree her mother never let her scale, the tree that now held the body of the dressmaker's daughter, strung up by the neck like a fanciful decoration, a yellow star of David sewn onto her cream-colored sweater.

Vira collapsed to the groud then. She hugged the nesting dolls to her body, almost not realizing that she'd carried them with her, but she always carried her family with her, their lives, their stories, their fates, whether she wanted to or not.

15

Larissa

Larissa blinked the sun and street dust out of her eyes. She walked away from the mermaid statue, fairly certain that her sister would follow, but refusing to look back, refusing to give in to the mommying instinct. She wasn't a mom right now. She was just a granddaughter.

People swarmed around her, bees too close to her skin. They spoke to each other, and she didn't try to translate. She tucked in her shoulders and tucked down her chin, interrupting the flow of the crowd, pushing through to return the way they'd come.

Her shoulders jostled strangers'. Her hair flew into her eyes. She gripped her purse, double-checking that both pockets were zipped shut. When she neared the stall of the blacksmith, sparks flew from his anvil. The fire behind him was stoked and crackling, and the long knife he hammered glowed a ferocious red.

Women crowded the next stall buying and selling sunflowers. Bouquets with long green stems stabbed out of the arms of every customer walking away. But there was no wild hair of Baba Vira, no bony neck or borscht-stained hands.

She escaped into a nearly empty side-street but for a man pulling a wooden dog on a string, mumbling to the carved animal and clicking his tongue.

He barked at her when he sensed her approaching then scolded the wooden creature so harshly she almost wanted to protect it. Larissa pressed herself against the wall of the building opposite the man to sidle around him. Ira's hand on her back pushed her forward. She knew it was Ira's hand without turning.

Music swirled in the air as she pulled herself around the corner, an accordion, clarinet, and cymbals—rapid-fire, melodic, yet not at all.

The mouth came at her first, slanted and jagged toothed, marching to the rhythm tugging at her in the breeze. The crooked nose turned the corner, followed by one eye. The other lagged behind a beat, giving the Baba Yaga parade a cyclopsian illusion. She was in the middle of the street, and she didn't know how she'd gotten there. Ira's hand wasn't on her back anymore. Where was Ira's hand? Why was she looking in the costumes for Ira? The face came closer, straight at her, the face she sometimes saw in her own mirror in the darkness.

"Baba?" Ira called out, as if the giant face would answer her. She was there with Larissa. Of course she was. Standing just as frozen in the middle of the parade's path as the black stockinged legs under each body part, each marching to their own complementary rhythm.

Larissa jumped out of the way, talking Ira's hand and pulling her back to the sidewalk.

The mouth passed her first, then the nose, ears, and eyes. Scraggly eyebrows. A serious-faced accordion player. Then it was gone.

Larissa jostled other people in the crowd and continued to push forward. Heel. Toe. Heel. Toe. The familiar steps turning from dance to skip to run. There had to be a note in that basket.

"I'm with you," Ira called out behind her. Larissa kicked up loose pebbles, part of her insides wanting to extend a single arched arm into the air to twirl around every cut corner.

In only a few minutes, they returned to the gold-framed posters announcing upcoming performances and the crystal chandeliers and medieval glass goblet lighting over their heads. The Palace of Culture of Science sounded so grandiose, so enlightened, but Larissa suddenly looked around the marbled halls, stripping away every aspect of flourish, and imaged Stalin's government workers once roaming here, crafting propaganda to deceive people, taking lives of nonconformists as simply as they erased pencil scratches from paper. Or maybe that was just Baba Vira's stories suddenly filling her head.

She was a character in one of Anna's *Magic Treehouse* books, transporting from a spot in the serene woods behind her house to an old palace, where her blue jeans clashed with the lavish architecture.

"This way." Ira turned left then right. They passed more columns, these squared and crisp as military regalia. Larissa wondered if she only pretended to know where she was going, when Ira put her hand on a knob and twisted.

Inside, the basket of sunflowers sat on a side table. The mask was nestled amid them, the jagged-toothed smile a challenge in the brighter light. The girls played sing-song hand games, clapping, snapping, and patting their legs. Annabelle's parents hovered over their daughter, and Larissa's heart hurt. Somewhere deep in its fibers, her blood pumped out toward her every extremity, but it stopped acutely at the ends of her fingertips. She didn't know how to stretch it across an ocean and across time zones. Her fingertips were so far away from the end of her normal reach.

"We were wondering where you two went," Stefa said, coming quickly to their sides, hugging them both tightly. Mirrors surrounded by lights covered two walls. Below them, long counters lined with stools acted as dressing tables for dance troops, ballerinas, or government mouthpieces of long ago.

Larissa prodded Ira to go to the basket, to dig through the stems, to search behind the mask. They tried to describe the Baba Yaga face marching down the street. She allowed herself to melt into Stefa's tight grasp and to wait for her grandmother to burst into the room.

With all the lights, the bright room didn't have any shadows.

Larissa took a deep breath. She closed her eyes, and envisioned Alex's rug-burned knees from sliding into an imaginary home-plate on the carpet. She thought of Anna flopped on her belly with her colored pencils, where she could stay happily for hours.

Ira's fingers moved through the stems. She lifted the mask then brought it to her face and, turning toward her sister, shook her head.

"Your baba has always had her own agenda." Stefa finally released Larissa. Across the room, Annabelle's mother had a medical kit open by her side. "I don't know why I believed she was coming to help with the girls. She would never set foot in this place."

"I didn't think Baba had ever been to Warsaw."

Stefa frowned.

"I mean, this building built by the Soviets. Your baba knew too much of what Stalin and his army did."

"The war was a long time ago." Larissa's voice was unsteady.

"You know Stalin's soldiers killed her brother."

"We know, and her father and uncle."

"No, her father and uncle were killed by Germans."

Larissa's heartbeat reverberated inside the limitations of her own skin. Ira, still holding the mask to her face, plucked a stem from the basket. Behind them, the girls chattered and sang. The lights were overpowering.

She swayed on her feet, finding her balance, feet rooted to the ground, breathing in through her nose and out through her mouth.

"Go to my apartment." Stefa leaned forward to trace the sharp lines of the mask's nose with her finger. "Maybe the flowers were to tell us she is safe here. Maybe she waits for us. The girls have one more dance, but yes, I'm sure she will end up there."

Larissa's feet didn't feel rooted to anything. Her breaths turned shallow, and her heart beat like it tried to create waves across oceans. Ira's nod caught in the mirrors of the room, cast-ing endless reflections of hope, bouncing off one another into the infinite abyss on the other side of the looking glass.

"Did she paint this?" Stefa took the mask from Ira's hands.

Only then did Larissa notice the string she'd used on Anna's birthday wreaths. She took a step back, knocking over the basket of flowers. The stems scattered by the sisters' feet. Their brown faces were speckled with seeds, reminding her of the freckles her children wore in the summertime.

Ira scrambled to pick up the flowers, returning all but one to the basket. Larissa pulled out her notebook to take down directions. The pen shook in her grip. The Baba Yaga mask stared at them from Stefa's hands, like another mirror.

16

Ira

The crowded subway car bounced under their feet, and Ira twirled a sunflower through her fingers. Stefa had given them the keys to her apartment three metro stops away. The idea of a couch to collapse on sounded beyond superb.

When the subway entered a tunnel, the windows blackened. Ira imagined they shot through a cave and tried to make out the rough, imperfect texture of the underground walls. She sought out stalagmites, wolves, or bats.

The twirling sunflower brushed her cheek. She had forgotten she still held it. Their subway car broke into the light once again.

"At least we know Baba's okay," she whispered to her sister, offering out the long-stemmed flower. The tracks shifted her toward her sister then away. Larissa held onto the metal pole between them with white knuckles. She didn't take the stem.

Ira wished she had someone to pluck the golden flower's petals over. Next to her, Larissa's lips pursed, and her nose crinkled. But Ira supposed she'd look the same way in Montreal or New York or any other crowded city buzzing with non-mommy life. Ira hooked her elbow around the pole.

"My sister loves me." She plucked a petal, letting it flutter to the ground between them. "She loves me not. She loves me, she loves me not."

She stopped after four when Larissa wasn't amused, the petals festive litter at her feet. A few others in the car were watching her—a teenage girl with thick plastic glasses and bright red lipstick and a gray-haired man around Stefa's age.

She shrugged to the nearby girl and handed her the flower. The girl's eyes were suspicious of the gift, but she took it, bringing it to her nose, not looking away from Ira and Larissa.

Something seemed so real to Ira about the strangers crowded so close. Body odor. Heat. Musk. Something so vital. She eyed the bodies nearby, her skin warming. There were a lot of beards here. Scruff. Body hair. She wasn't opposed. But she blinked away the thought. They were on a mission to find her baba, with not that much help from Stefa, whom she barely even knew.

Baba Vira had met Stefa's mother in a displaced persons camp in Austria after the war. Ira knew they'd remained close through their emigration across the ocean and through the years of braving Winnipeg winters. Both women eventually relocated with their husbands and young families—Baba Vira to Rochester, New York and Stefa's family back to Europe—but they had kept in touch. Some visits had lasted for years if she knew the stories right. Ira remembered Panya Stefa coming to stay when she was a child and the way she would chatter on and on with her mother. There had always been tins of shortbread cookies and a familial bond that only made her miss her absent mother more.

When the metro doors slid open, the sisters escaped up the underground station's escalator. The long tunnel of studded-together sheets of metal twinkled with dots of light—nothing fluorescent, nothing greatly luminary, just tiny spots of illumination, Tinkerbell's forgotten entourage. Larissa climbed up the last flight of stairs, and Ira followed behind her, out into the sunlight beyond the tall metro entrance in the angular shape of the letter "M."

The Vistula River greeted them, slow and greenish gray. A broad suspension bridge crossed over it, and there she was again—the mermaid, sword in hand, breasts bared, tail raised out of the waves, shield clutched tight in preparation for the attack. This statue dwarfed the first one they had seen in Warsaw's Old Town. This was a mermaid giantess.

Both sisters took in a deep breath, imperfect mirrors of each other. Ira stretched out an arm toward the statue, wishing she still had the long-stemmed sunflower to act as her own sword, wishing she had the mask she'd left in the dressing room as her shield.

"She is so badass."

Larissa rolled her eyes.

Ira didn't lower her fist. She raised it higher, her other hand moving to the bottom of her shirt, lifting it upward just an inch. She could bare her own breasts right here. Her sister couldn't understand the blood in her veins. Even if it was almost the same as hers.

"We need to get to Panya Stefa's." Larissa plucked the fabric of her shirt out of Ira's hand. She smoothed it down over Ira's thin belly. But Ira didn't immediately lower her imaginary weapon. She wondered what it would be like to create waves with such an immense tail. To swim away and disappear into the depths whenever she wanted.

She let herself be pulled along. They followed the directions given to them across busy streets dusted with time. Panya Stefa lived only blocks from the river station next to the Copernicus Science Center, next to their mermaid.

Ira stepped over every crack in the sidewalk. She spoke to everyone they passed with a Ukrainian greeting, the words falling heavy and sweet on her tongue, something decadent and made from scratch by her baba.

"*Dobrehden ... Dobrehden ... Dobrehden....*"

Most people didn't respond to her. Some frowned. One spit. Yes, she knew it wasn't the right language for this country, but she was closer to Ukraine than she'd ever been before. Larissa put a hand on her arm to silence her, only looking up when the door at her side matched the number in her notebook. She dug into her purse for the key, retrieving it faster than Ira expected from the bottomless depths of her mommy-bag.

The key turned in the lock effortlessly. Ira didn't know why she'd expected a fight.

Inside, the smell of beets and sauerkraut seemed to settle on her skin. A collection of plastic dolls swarmed the front room, on shelves, on tables, on windowsills, and pedestals on the floor. Each wore her own hand-stitched blouse and skirt, needlepoint-accented scarves, silk flowers clutched in tiny hands. Ira thought of Baba Vira's childhood friends killed in the war. Stefa's aunts and uncles too. Ghosts stared out at her through the eyes of the dolls. There were the murdered storytellers and poets, the captured priests and professors, the imprisoned lawyers, artists, and musicians—anyone in a position of power poised to make other people think. Then they came for the landowners and doctors, anyone who had property they could seize and reclaim for Russia, then for Germany. And all the women could do was hide like wooden nesting dolls—hide or run.

Ira knew her grandmother had run. She thought she herself would have run.

Ira sat on a couch almost as thread-bare as the hair of the grandfather she barely remembered. When the war started, her *dgidgo* had been studying to be a priest, the Ukrainian Catholic kind that could marry. He was a charismatic force in his community and mathematical genius on the side. And after he survived it all, for the rest of his life, he'd told anyone who asked that he was just a man who worked with tools. Those were the words that always made Baba Vira cry—whether because of all they'd lost or how humbled they'd become in their factory work across the ocean, Ira never knew. But there was something there left to discover.

The dolls all faced Ira, ready to chat. Maybe, to Panya Stefa, they did.

Larissa took a seat beside her. The coffee table before them had a glass already upon it and a bottle of an amber-colored drink, hand-labelled in a rushed black script.

Lipstick was on the glass's rim. Drops of *medivka*, the honey liqueur, remained at its bottom. Ira debated getting two more glasses. The dolls continued to stare with their rosy skin and synthetic eyelashes. Against the opposite wall, a hutch nearly overflowed with wooden nesting dolls. Some of the matryoshka were open, showing off the next tucked inside; others stood in long lines descending in size. These were not cheap, tourist shop dolls. Each was different, from the scarves in their painted hair to the items clutched before them—flowers, sheaths of grain, a honeycomb, a military-style rifle, a tiny kitten, a pitcher of milk.

Ira stood and took a step closer before retreating to the small kitchen, fumbling through cabinets, and returning to the living room with two small glasses in her hand. They were rose-tinted, etched with tiny flowers.

"What are you doing?"

"Panya Stefa said to make ourselves at home."

"So that means we drink?"

"When in Poland."

The bottle's sticky cork released without much of a fight.

"No, *ni dyakuyu*." Larissa slipped into her Ukrainian manners unconsciously, waving away the offering.

"So polite." Ira didn't stop pouring the second glass. Instead, she filled it higher than the first. "Just two fingers." She extended her pointer and pinkie fingers next to the glass, their grandmother's old joke. "We drink to Baba."

"I don't think so."

Ira reached forward, swapping her own smaller drink for Larissa's.

"But we haven't actually found her yet."

"She needed this adventure."

"I didn't."

"You absolutely did."

The plastic dolls across from her on the floor smiled. The closest one had its little arms raised seeking asylum. Thin colorful ribbons fell from its hair across the white fabric of its shirt, the wide sleeves, and the floral apron. No, not seeking asylum. It danced.

"If I was Baba, you wouldn't say no," Ira added when her sister didn't move. "Your kids aren't here."

Larissa wrinkled her nose.

"I'd say no."

"Sure, sure, no thank you, *ni dyakuyu,* once or twice until you gave in." Ira picked up her two-finger shot. *"Dai Bozhe,"* she added, before tipping it into her mouth, her accent flawless in her toast to God, though her religious zeal was admittedly questionable.

Ira picked up the other glass, putting it in Larissa's hands before leaning back beside her.

"It might help you relax a bit, Lyalya," she whispered.

Larissa frowned again at the nickname. Ira knew she hated it.

The dolls surrounding them stared Larissa down, some perverted form of Ukrainian peer-pressure from their stands on the floor, from their poses on pedestals, shelves, and a long thin table that stretched across the opposite wall.

"Dai Bozhe," Larissa said, her voice low, her cheeks reddening before her lips even touched the glass.

She took the shot fast, shuddering when the sticky amber touched her lips and burned down her throat. She covered her mouth, trying not to cough, but she couldn't hold back.

"You okay, there?"

"Ukrainian women can hold their liquor."

Ira smirked at their grandmother's words coming out of Larissa's mouth. Every birthday, holiday, or funeral, their baba would insist upon a proper toast. Usually vodka. Occasionally something homemade. Nothing, she could remember, that was quite as strong as this.

Revving engines made both of their heads turn. Outside, one white-haired woman hugged another on the back of a yellow moped. Helmets couldn't tame their fly-away hair. Ira couldn't see their faces. She didn't recognize the coat the one on the back wore. But her knobby knees, those wide familiar hips, and that hair....

The woman's head bobbed as she spoke, as she laughed, as if the pair considered stopping here at this apartment but decided against it. The engine roared to life again, and they flew down the street, around a corner, and were gone.

"Baba!" Ira called after them. She almost didn't know when she had stood and pressed her face so close to the window glass her breath fogged it up.

"Was that really—?" Larissa was right beside her.

"Yes!"

Ira set the glass still in her hand on the windowsill before running out the door.

"Baba!"

Larissa followed her down the few cement-block steps to the sidewalk, looking like she wanted to tackle her sister like Ira had seen her tackle Anna and Alex to dress them before school. A man stood next to another moped on the opposite side of the road, staring at them as a cigarette burned between his lips.

"A ride?" Ira called out to him, cursing the fact that English was the first language to jump to her lips, but she refocused herself.

There was a way she could change her stance and her voice to enchant someone that Ira had learned a long time ago. She held the eyes of the stranger, not letting herself blink, letting her eyes smile without the rest of her expression following. Baba Vira had taught her the art of allure when she was still a teenager. Just another piece of her Baba Yaga magic, magic as real as she was, as real as Vira, as real as the short life-line on her hand.

Ira gestured to herself, to the man to the bike, and then in direction the two women had just disappeared down the street.

The man raised his eyebrows, but he flicked his cigarette to the sidewalk. Beside her, Larissa leaned toward the still flaming litter but seemed to restrain herself.

"*Chodźmy.*" His deep voice rumbled as he stretched to straddle his bike. He nodded his head, and Ira ran toward him, draping her long, lean leg over the bike behind the stranger, before wrapping her arms around him.

The motor vibrated underneath her as she pressed herself against him. He hadn't offered her a helmet, so she held onto him as tightly as she could as they took off. Ira laughed. Then they swerved and flew.

"Ira!" Larissa's call after them faded away quickly, lost in the sound of the engine and the beat of her heart.

This was how you found a missing grandmother.

Her hair whipped out behind her. The cotton of the man's shirt felt soft in her embrace.

They cut around the corner the first bike had taken. She closed her eyes and trusted in her intuition. Sometimes, she felt she had powers to make the unimaginable happen. She had ever since she was a child and decided that they would ride elephants at the circus. Larissa had rolled her eyes. Ira had approached the clowns. An hour later, they'd been riding high in the center ring.

When they flew around another corner, Ira opened her eyes. The yellow motorbike was there. It was actually there! Just taking off at a stoplight that had slowed them.

"That bike!" she shouted in the stranger's ear, pointing. The buildings leaned in around them as they shot through the streets, covered in ancient dust and almost forgotten history. The man smelled good, like salt and sausage and engine oil.

The yellow scooter took a left, and they gained ground on them, cutting off cars, horns blaring. The man she hugged yelled, snorted, and said something over his shoulder at her.

She didn't answer. Instead she whooped like she was on a rollercoaster ride as they gained speed. Their path led them to a road along the river. The giant statue loomed ahead, growing bigger and bigger as they approached. She was fierce. She was brutal. Ira's hair flew into her eyes. She blinked it away, and the statue was gone.

Pedestrians crossed on the block ahead of them, and they had to slow. School children barely looked at the traffic. Ira found herself panting, tapping her fingers against the stranger's side as one child paused to tie a shoe. Tap. Tap. Tap. The man squirmed, ticklish, smiling, but she pointed ahead. The road had finally cleared.

When they took the path the yellow scooter had followed away from the river, they returned to the newer part of the city. Tightly compressed apartment buildings surrounded a white palace-like structure, raised on red bricks as if on the shoulders of its cheering fans. Long winding steps with voluptuous balustrades led to its entrance. At its cornice, nude figures stood out in bas relief surrounding a silhouette cameo. Fryderyk Chopin. The classical composer? But then it was gone, replaced by a massive mural of musicians in colors that seemed to challenge the steady palette of the city, whites, tans, and grays replaced with reds, greens, and blues. Ira almost forgot to look for the yellow scooter. She squeezed the man in front of her, breathing in his warmth, his sweat, and the cigarette smoke that clung to him tighter than she did.

He cut down smaller city streets, zigzagging between blocks. Was he following them still? He had to be following them still. Ira's hair blew back behind her. She blinked when it flew into her face but didn't dare release a hand from her driver's broad body so she could see better.

They swerved in and out of a traffic circle with a massive sculptural palm tree at its center. Unless it was a real palm tree? Ira released a hand and pushed her hair back. Her driver said something over his shoulder and laughed. Horseradish lingered on his breath. She nodded and made a noise that could have been acknowledgement or agreement. She had no idea what was needed, but he laughed again as they jolted forward.

Soon glass-walled buildings, sleek storefronts, and massive billboards drowned out the city blocks that ached for years past.

An empty yellow scooter nestled between two parallel parked cars. Ira's heart sped up. Her lungs filled with air—musky cigarette-infused air, but still.

When their bike slowed and pulled to the side of the road, she was momentarily distracted by the reflection of her clasp on this scruffy Polish stranger in a mirrored window. Damn, they looked good together. But she just thanked her driver with a kiss on the cheek and jumped off her seat.

Ira ignored the eyes of her driver tracing over every inch of her skin. She adjusted her neckline, pushing her hair back behind her shoulders. Where were the old women in the crowd?

A tram rumbled down the street-side tracks. The man before her said something, but she didn't understand it. Throngs of people crowded the sidewalks. An arched opening led to an underground metro stop. Graffiti or maybe more murals blanketed the cement walls nearby.

And she couldn't find the women who had left their yellow scooter behind. The man said something more she couldn't decipher before driving off, leaving Ira behind, scanning the crowd, the mix of youth and age in this city, soccer flags hanging out of apartment windows and flowerpots with cascading vines.

She turned, but the yellow bike's passengers were lost. And apparently, so was she.

17
Vira (June 1941)

Vira sang the words she had known by heart for as long as she could remember. Her sister's soft voice sounded beside her as they walked with all of the other guests at the wedding. The musicians waited a few blocks away where the ribbons had been strung and flowers added festivity to the perfect early-summer day. The group's voices lifted into the air, a blessing for the couple carried by the wind.

The decorated wedding bread, the *korovai,* led the procession—its intricately shaped dough flower buds, leaves, deer, curls, doves, and fish, held high by one of the bridesmaids Vira didn't know. The couple, Eugenia and Teodore, followed hand in hand.

Everyone around Vira smiled. Joyously, senselessly smiled. She tried, but the expression refused to stick on her face. They proceeded along the street where the traveling Roma's stalls had been only a few days before. Dmytro's father had sharpened knives and tools right there on the corner next to the butcher. She had often seen Dmytro there or even once or twice on the thatched roofs along this street, making repairs with his father. Flowers bloomed in a tiny greenspace Noncia had tended to when she thought no one noticed. Hollyhocks and poppies had been her weakness.

Shops owned by Jewish families had been shuddered. Posters outlining new regulations in bold black print were plastered on their windows and on the brick masonry of the synagogue.

The singing voices surrounded her like a swaddling blanket,

holding her tight, inhibiting any understanding of the world around her. She wanted to stretch out her limbs, to cry out, to wail. No one else seemed to pay attention to the gun shots rumored to ring through the nights at the overcrowded Lontsky Prison, or the Roma's sudden absence, or the Jewish policies that seemed to clear the town of almost everyone but those leaving the church gathered in folk dress for the special occasion.

German officers, their mouths in thin straight lines, their eyes never meeting Vira's own, watched the wedding procession.

Lesya's voice became stronger as they walked, joining the older trills and warbles. She stared at the couple, at the bride's embroidered sleeves and colorful vest, at her dangling red cherry drop earrings.

"You will have your chance, Lyalya," Vira whispered to her, trying to focus on the celebration.

"Mama said I have her blessing if I want a husband."

"She did not!"

"She did this morning. With all the men going to war, she said I should find a husband now before they're all gone."

An accordion player joined their proud intonations as they rounded a corner. The priest had said that their blessings joined those of the heavens for the happy couple, that one couldn't be happy alone, that marriage is what made a soul complete. Vira's voice sang along but she wasn't sure if she agreed. A musician on a kobza joined in, and another blew into a short wooden sopilka.

A German soldier, who stood nearby, tightened his jaw. The muscles of his entire body seemed tensed, twisted, ready spring to life upon command.

Lesya leaned in toward her sister. Yellow, blue, and red flower petals from her braided crown brushed Vira's cheek.

"Mama said you needed to find a husband too."

Vira tried to push away thoughts of Dmytro's skin, the color of golden baked bread when he wiped away the ash. His eyes were almost the shade of the black earth under the tilled sunflower fields.

Toasts were shouted, and a drink was put into her hands. She raised her arm with the guests around her, but she didn't put the honey liquor to her lips. Eugenia was a friend, a girl she had played dolls with when they were small and a girl she had whispered secrets with when they noticed the attentions of boys. She looked exultant as her new husband murmured into her ear. Her cherry earrings tickled his nose. Dmytro had whispered to Vira like that, his breath warming the skin of her neck as he told her how beautiful she was, how his aunt guessed that her life would be fused together with his, a link welded into a chain.

"Vira." Her mother's arm wove into her own, squeezing it more tenderly than she expected. Her mother's eyes weren't smiling either. "You've heard what your father and the other men have been saying."

She nodded. Lesya had begun to dance with some of the other girls. Her father spoke with a group of men she didn't recognize. He looked restrained, his big eyebrows furrowed and the lines of his forehead as creased as the old map of Galicia he kept in his study. He stepped toward the men as if he would take their hands in his, like he would toast them instead of the married couple, but then took a step away, crossing his arms as if displeased, though his face didn't agree with his posture.

"I'm not sure how much time you have." Her mother took her by the shoulders and turned her so that they were face to face. She arranged her face into a carefree, joyous expression, letting the stress in her forehead's wrinkles momentarily fall away, but Vira knew it was only for the benefit of anyone watching on this happy occasion.

"Time for what?"

"Time for finding a husband. You're sixteen."

"I'm not an old maid," Vira hissed in a whisper.

"This war might make you one." Her mother's voice lowered to match. "Keep an open mind."

"But Ukraine is ours now. The Soviets are gone."

"And the Germans are now here."

"They're helping us gain our freedom."

Her mother took Vira's hands in her own and pressed into them, kneading them like the dough of the *korovai* bread that she had helped fashion.

"Ivan was too naïve. You need to be smarter than that. We all do."

Vira's heart beat as if it tried to make up for her brother's absent one. A chill grew inside her that climbed up her throat. She swallowed it down and blinked her eyes repeatedly. People were clapping and tapping their feet. Voices joined the musicians for the familiar refrains.

"Just look around. There are many nice young men here."

Vira nodded again and walked toward her sister to join in the dance. He father left the group of men to intercept her. Her shoulders straightened, and her posture lifted to perfection with his eyes on her.

"We need to leave here soon. Tell your sister. We will leave as soon as the *korovai* is cut. You go dance now."

"*Tak*, Tato."

The musicians hollered and played faster as the circle dance began. One by one, the guests linked themselves together. Vira's sister grabbed her by the hand, and she was pulled into the dance, an unfamiliar man's hand gripping hers at her other side.

The accordionist danced as he played, and others around them clapped their hands as Vira fell into the pattern of steps to match the others. Step to the side, cross step, step to the side, cross step. The guests cheered, as the two bridesmaids entered the circle, linking arms around each other's backs and dancing shoulder to shoulder, stepping and kicking in unison with fast steps. The circle rotating around them paused its movement only for a moment to let them back in.

The man at Vira's side let go of her hand as he took his turn in the center of the dance. He threw his arms out to the side as he squatted low and kicked high, first one leg then the other. The groom laughed and shouted at him, and the man jumped high into a split, touching both of his toes, his eyes meeting Vira's.

When he moved to take his place in the circle beside her, Vira felt the tug of Lesya's hand. The music swirled in the air like the smell of medivka on everyone's breath. Vira forced herself to blink away any other thoughts but the eyes on her sister, the eyes on her.

Lesya squeezed her hands and grinned madly, beautifully. She counted off in a whisper to the beat of the music.

"*Odyn, dva, treh.*"

The sisters twirled together in the middle of all the wedding guests, every spin ending with a kick out and a bent knee, as if adding momentum to their next twirl. Their arms moved in unison over their heads then outstretched to their sides. Years of practice had their motions down to perfection.

Spinning as fast as they could, refusing to let their bodies get dizzy, they both laughed as they clapped their hands in unison at the end of twirl number six.

Light-headed, Vira stepped back to the circle as it moved again in the other direction. The bride and her bridesmaids stepped into the center, shimmying in their small circle. Then two older men, neighbors Vira recognized, performed high kicks and leaps of their own. Vira's hand was squeezed, and she turned to find the eyes of the young man upon her.

"You and your sister?"

She was swept up as she agreed, letting herself be pulled back to the center by his hand, letting herself pull her sister along too. Another young man joined them at the middle of the circle, and they wove themselves together, arms around each other's backs. They spun so fast, and the girls bent their knees, letting their feet leave the ground. Their red boots flew through the air. Their skirts fanned.

The group around them yelled and clapped louder.

Vira put a hand to the flowers woven into her hair when she returned to the ground. The man at her side didn't immediately loosen his arm around her back as they returned to the outer circle.

"You are from this town?" he asked.

"*Tak*," she answered, clapping along, "and you're not. How do you know the happy couple?"

"The groom is my cousin."

Vira's mother and two other women moved to the center of the circle, hands on their matronly hips, turning two steps to one side, two steps to the other.

"I am Mykhail."

"Vira."

"So I've heard."

She looked away from her mother. He clapped along with the music, but his gaze was only on her. Her face reddened. Her sister beamed at her side.

"May I see you again?" he said, letting his voice drop as low as it could to still be heard over the music and the guests.

"How long are you in town?"

"I fear not long." He nodded as discretely as he could toward the German soldiers watching over their celebration. Vira didn't know how she'd forgotten about them, their straight lips, their cold blue eyes, their freshly shaven faces.

"But they're here to protect us, to help us keep our independence from the Soviets." Her voice wavered. She felt herself blushing. Her skin was hot. She didn't know where they'd taken her Uncle Oleh.

"I don't think so."

Lesya broke from the circle to do a solo dance. The ribbons tied to the flower crown in her hair twirled about her as she moved to one side then the other, lifting her knees up high, stepping so gracefully and so intricately, Vira knew she had been practicing all her life for this one moment. Lesya's face was one of pure joy, and the poppies woven through her hair matched the red in her cheeks.

"They call our land the *Lebensraum*," Mykhail whispered.

Vira's nose crinkled at the unfamiliar accent of the German word. She clapped as her sister did one final twirl, the eyes of the wedding party upon her.

"Our soil is the richest in Europe. Our land is the most beautiful. They say the Führer wants it for his people."

Lesya's eyes sparkled as she rushed back toward Vira's side. Across the circle, Vira's mother looked at her daughters with her chin up, an expression as pleased as any she'd ever worn.

Across the street, a high-pitched whistle blew, and four German soldiers rushed toward them. They shouted one name then another. The circle had stopped moving, but they broke through the remaining linked hands. The musicians silenced their instruments, and a wooden flute fell from someone's hand. Its hollow rattle echoed amid the shifting footsteps and murmurs of the wedding guests. The groom put an arm around the bride and whispered something into her ear. Her earrings brushed against his nose, but he didn't laugh this time.

The officers grabbed the two men her father had been speaking with, bending their arms behind their backs. Mykhail took in a deep breath by her side.

"I wanted to delay, but—" he whispered, not finishing his sentence. Beads of moisture had come to his brow that hadn't been there even after his dancing. He clasped her hand tighter. "Marry me before I die for my country?" he whispered.

The accordionist shifted out of the German soldiers' way. His instrument exhaled as they passed.

"You need to talk with my father."

"I already have."

18

Larissa

Following the instructions on the calling card ate up more of her minutes than the meandering voicemail Larissa left for Greg and the kids. Maybe they went out to an early lunch. Brunch. Alex would enjoy that word.

Her husband didn't cook much more than toast—except for his mother's potato soup that took him an entire day every winter. One full day per year. He said it was his quota. The soup was good, though. He had potential. Maybe he'd cook for them. Maybe Anna and Alex would even help, wearing their curlicue monogrammed aprons and chef's hats that Santa had brought them last Christmas.

Stefa coughed in the next room, a hack that combined with a gurgle and maybe a belch. Larissa let go of the phone resting in its cradle on the knife-scarred kitchen counter.

"Thanks for letting me use your phone." She returned to the woman's side, handing her a glass of water.

Stefa nodded and coughed again into her hand, and Larissa took a seat. The cuckoo clock ticked. The dolls stared through their plastic eyelashes. Outside, a car horn honked twice and someone shouted something. Was it friendly? Was it vulgar? She had no idea. Where was Ira?

Larissa folded her hands in her lap, wondering if they would someday look as grotesque as Vira's. Her skin was freckled but mostly smooth. Tidy cuticles. Nails short and unpainted but shaped to perfection. But her hands had deeper creases than they used to. And were the tiny hairs on her first knuckle becoming more pronounced?

Four nesting dolls on a nearby table looked nothing like the ones she and Ira had played with as girls. Those matryoshka had been more traditional. Larissa's set of four had worn pink dresses with a floral trim and a white apron. She'd called the biggest one "Baba," the next in line "Mommy," the third "Lyalya," and the fourth "Baby Ira." Ira said she had both sets of dolls now. She'd have to get her dolls back to give to Anna. She'd like the pink too.

"Ira will be back, and don't worry about your baba, Lyalya." Stefa leaned forward and put the biggest matryoshka in her hands. "If she wants to be found, she'll let you find her."

The doll in her hands was so light. Baba. Why wasn't she thinking about Baba?

"And if she doesn't?"

"Then she'll become a baba yaga of the woods that the children will talk about for years to come."

The disconnected face came to her mind. Ira had a point: its long nose, wild eyebrows, and crooked mouth did kind of resemble her grandmother.

"Baba told my kids we had a baba yaga in the woods near our house. They get jittery when we drive by in the dark." Alex curled himself into a ball in his booster seat, hugging his knees. He always stuck his lips out and scrunched his nose when he was nervous, trying to be brave.

"Maybe they're all the better for it." Stefa shrugged, and Larissa stiffened.

She tried to relax her shoulders and neck. She breathed in through her nose, thinking about the voice of her favorite yoga instructor. *In good, out shit.* Stefa didn't know her kids. She tried to let down her defensive mommy posturing. It came on quickly sometimes. This wasn't actually about her kids. She had good kids, baba yaga or not. She was damn proud of those kids. What she wouldn't give for a bedtime cuddle with Anna right now, feeling the warmth of her as their foreheads pressed together and stuffed animals were piled into the hug between them—or one of her questions about ballet dancing, the dangle at the back of your throat, or what people did all day in heaven.

Larissa ran a fingertip across the painted braid that crossed the crown of the doll's head. Yes, Anna would like her old nesting dolls. This one's floral crown had small yellow sunflowers and blue hollyhocks—colors of the Ukrainian flag.

"You can find your baba soon. First, we bake." Stefa heaved herself to a stand and pulled Larissa to her feet. She turned Larissa's shoulders, pointing her toward the kitchen, and gave a push between her shoulder blades.

Dolls lining the shelves of the short hallway were turned toward her, an awkward receiving line. Their blank eyes looked through Larissa as if toward something beyond this world. In the kitchen, painted spoons hung from the walls. Splatter from cooking projects speckled the surroundings. Her fingers itched to clean.

"Was your family a part of the independence movement too?"

Stefa pulled out a wooden cutting board stained red. Larissa winced before reminding herself it was probably just beet stains. "My father was. He was sent to a labor camp." Stefa opened cupboards that stuck with age and some sort of jelly. She discretely wiped her hands on her pants while Stefa pulled out container after container. Flour. Sugar. Molasses. Something cloudy and gelatinous. Something that might be fennel seeds. "So many died, caught between Stalin and Hitler. They just wanted their own country, their Ukraine. Still do."

The cabinet slammed shut. Larissa jumped.

"I didn't know there was a time between the Soviets and the Germans in Galicia." The sound of the Ukrainian region tripped between her tongue and her lips. "How far is that from here?"

"That part of Ukraine borders Poland—it was a region of Poland too for a time before the Soviets took it back in the late 1930s—not far. That's why my father knew all the Polish nursery rhymes. He was a child during that period. But short train ride, short drive." Metal mixing bowls clanged as they touched down on the countertop. Stefa scooped out flour, dumping it into the bowl.

Larissa took the chipped wooden spoon Stefa handed to her. Its missing section gave it a snaggletooth.

"Baba always told me that after a time, the soldiers of my grandfather's Ukrainian regiment were either sent to the labor camps or to the front lines of the Germans as human shields."

"That's simple version, *tak.*" Stefa pulled out packets of yeast and shook them absentmindedly. She ripped them open with her perfectly aligned dentures. The tiny grains fell into the metal bowl like dirtied snowflakes.

Stefa coughed, not turning away from her ingredients. The fennel seeds were tapped into the mix, and Stefa touched the snaggletoothed spoon in Larissa's hands. "Stir."

Larissa hadn't realized how awkwardly she'd been hovering over the old woman. She took a step toward the counter.

"What are we making?"

"Bread."

"What was..." She pointed to the last ingredient disappearing into the mix as her spoon circled around and around.

"*Kmin.*" Stefa combined water, molasses, the coagulated cloudy substance, sugar, and salt into a saucepan and turned on a burner. Some of the salt had missed the pan and tumbled across the stovetop. "Keep stirring," the old woman repeated.

Larissa's face felt flushed. She dropped her head. No fires were starting from the salt. She could clean the kitchen for Stefa later, clean it better than it had been in years, probably. The mixture in front of her blended like it knew its task. Her wooden spoon made easy progress. Progress was good. She stirred more.

She imagined Baba Vira making a crazy attempt at preserving the independence of present-day Ukraine—a knife in her teeth, a cloud of white hair. It was absurd. Completely absurd. But Baba Vira's logic had never made sense to her. She caught rainwater in bowls and yelled at thunderstorms. She valued a well-told lie.

Stefa turned off the burner and moved her pan toward Larissa's bowl.

"Keep stirring."

But Larissa didn't know how without letting the boiling liquid touch her hands. She rearranged her hold on the spoon, holding it higher, only with her fingertips. Her strokes became weaker, stabs in the powder, the way Alex stirred when he wasn't paying attention.

"I won't burn you, Lyalya." Stefa laughed.

The hot pan tipped toward her bowl with a shaky hand. The molasses mix didn't want to let go, lingering on the edge of the saucepan, ready to glob down anywhere but where Stefa's haphazard pour directed it. Larissa let go of her spoon. The mixture collected on the saucepan's rim, forming a giant blob preparing to fall. Larissa's eyes sought out paper towels, but she didn't see any. She nudged the bowl just an inch to catch it. The light brown drop slid down the edge of the inside, and she picked up her spoon again, sweeping it deeper with a practiced hand. Her usual cooking partners missed a lot too.

"Your baba and her mother, her sisters went to Czechoslovakia first, to wait out the war," the old woman added after the ingredients were combined. "Stir harder."

Larissa had to lean into the sticky, unyielding mix now. She pushed the spoon around the bowl wishing she had her apron-clad children by her side. They would enjoy this struggle against the ingredients. They'd be clapping, cheering her on. Stefa sprinkled in another type of flour, thickening the dough more.

"Keep mixing, Lyalya. Harder."

Her spoon dragged like she paddled through wet clay. The dough became more consistent, though, smoother to the eye if not the spoon. Baba Vira had called herself an actress who never touched the stage. *Lying can keep you alive, Lyalya.* Larissa stopped stirring.

Stefa plucked the spoon from her still hand.

"Use your hands now," she prodded.

Larissa reached for the sink to wash, but Stefa grabbed her by the wrists and plunged her hands into the dough. She tried not to wince but could feel the dough squishing under her nails, in the spaces between her fingers, in the prongs of her diamond ring.

"Any filth you have on you came from God."

Larissa tried to focus on the familiar motion and kneaded the dough, pressing hard against it, feeling its resistance.

The dough felt good in her fingers. She could build something of this. Castles or kitty cats. Dragons. Snakes. Stefa plunged her oily hands into the bowl beside Larissa's, and together they divided the dough into two balls, plopping them onto a floured section of the counter.

"The Slovakia part is the part I don't know well. Do you?"

Stefa covered the balls of dough with a dishtowel and looked to the microwave clock. Larissa's hands were white. She brushed them off over the counter. Stefa wiped hers on her skirt.

"You need to ask your baba your questions."

"If we can find her."

"When you do."

19

Ira

Ira's purse had her phone, passport, wallet, and lucky acorn, but her purse was back in Stefa's apartment. Where was Stefa's apartment? Past a palm tree, past Fryderyk Chopin, near a mermaid. Good lord, it was like a six-year-old made up these directions. She blinked and blew air out her lips. Was it the *medivka*?

A traffic light changed on the street behind her, and the city sped by—cars full of people who didn't know her, bikes with riders who couldn't care less, buses with hulls shellacked with advertisements, splattered with words she didn't understand and smiling faces that didn't seem to actually be smiling at her.

Could you smile with an accent? She tried, but the woman passing by only twisted her neutral expression into a frown in response. Ira was pretty sure her smile with an accent was doing something funky to her eyebrows, plus it kind of hurt, so she dropped the expression. If befriending the locals didn't work, she'd figure this out another way.

Parked and all by itself, the yellow moped down the block nearly blinded her with its cheerful disposition. If she stayed by the moped, she'd be there when her baba came back to it with her friend. Simple. Easy. Obvious. Well, obvious beyond the fact that Baba Vira had a moped-riding friend in Warsaw.

The scrawny shape of her body in that coat, the wild hair that escaped any attempts at taming, hair that embraced the wind blowing through these old city streets full of dust from her not-so-far-away childhood. It had been her, Ira was sure of it. Right age, right posture, right rebellious nature.

Ira threw herself into the flow of foot traffic down the sidewalk, carried by a gaggle of teenagers pushing her forward, nudged by a straight-faced executive type, straight-out colliding with a woman talking to herself near tears—whether she wore ear buds or was just losing her mind, Ira wasn't quite sure. The woman threw her arms up and moved on before Ira even had a chance to apologize. The crowd progressed. She rolled in the waves of it, nothing more than a mermaid absorbed in Poland's foam and froth and bubbles.

The yellow moped's front wheel leaned against the curb. Her heart sped as she neared it. Her body heat intensified. When she dove out of the foot traffic, Ira caught herself against a nearby magazine kiosk. The bike seemed to be waiting for its owner to return, its front headlight like an unblinking eye, mirrors tilted upward like antennae, double-seat like a shell that hadn't finished growing. She'd wait too.

She looked at her nails like there was a chip in the paint that wasn't there, posturing like she knew this place, like she knew someone, like she had full control of the situation.

Conversations she almost but didn't quite understand flowed over and around her. Storefronts gleamed, beckoning shoppers. The tram beeped as it rode on its tracks parallel to the road beside her. A deep base rhythm escaped from the nearest shop every time someone opened the door.

Ira pushed herself on top of the short and squat metal magazine box, graffiti tagged and rusted at the corners. When Baba Vira and her friend returned, they'd laugh. They'd probably dance. The *Kolomyjka* would make so much more sense here than in an American airport, or in an American child's bedroom, or on a scratchy video of her parents' wedding, her beautiful mom twirling and glowing, her young father embracing the absolute confusion and joy of it all.

Horns blared behind her. Someone yelled down the street. The deep base thumped like the deep pulse in her skin then silenced itself behind the surprisingly soundproof glass.

A man came out of the nearest shop, pointing at her and shouting. His cheeks reddened as his words flew, but she'd been too distracted by her memories to catch a single one. Had Baba Vira been making trouble and he needed her to get the old woman out of it?

"*Schodzić!*" he said. Again. Pointing to the metal magazine box she perched on then the sidewalk.

"Oh," she said, hopping down. "*Vybachte.*" Sorry. But she was more sorry she couldn't save the day. Run into the shop to discover Baba Vira tangled in a messy web of yarns, save her from a rogue robber by throwing grasshoppers gathered in her purse and pockets. Wow, she wished she had a purse or even just better pockets.

The man smirked at her Ukrainian apology, shook his head, and went back inside.

She nodded back to him before taking a small cross-step then a side-step, before freezing on her small little square of sidewalk. A small circle by her shoe glinted in the afternoon sun. Ira squatted down to see better. A two zloty coin. She'd assumed Poland had used Euros, but, of course, Larissa knew all about zloty, the conversion rate, and the history of the coin. She'd been taking about it for a while on the plane. Ira hadn't really been listening, but she didn't remember Larissa saying anything about how beautiful they were.

The coin on the sidewalk was bi-metallic, was that the word? A silver circle on the inside, surrounded by gold. Bronze? Brass? Whatever it was, American coins seemed so dull in comparison.

She traced her finger along its ridges, the leaves, the curves. But when Ira tried to pick it up, but the coin didn't budge. She tried to wedge a fingernail underneath it, to unstick it from whatever it was caught in—there's a thought that would gross out her sister—but even as she traced her nail around the full circumference of the cool metal, the coin wouldn't budge. The gleaming number two stared back at her with such promise, the silver and gold together assuring so much assistance. A metro ride back. A taxi. A phone call if phone booths were still a thing here.

The zloty coin seemed cemented into place, or at least attached by glue stronger than her nails could fight. Her squat fell into a cross-legged plop onto the sidewalk, next to the coin, next to the magazine box, and next to the moped, which two women were now climbing onto.

Ira's head jerked up.

"Baba!"

The woman in front with her hands on the handlebars blocked the second woman. Her portly bearing shifted, though, as she turned to her companion at Ira's voice. She leaned to the side so Ira could see.

The second woman pressed her lips together, her eyes narrowed with wrinkles when she smiled at Ira. Sweet-looking lady. Wild hair. Freckles turned age-spots spattering the bridge of her nose. This was probably someone's baba, but not hers.

"*Tak*?" the woman said, her expression wide and helpful.

The word was right—Ukrainian or Polish, maybe the languages shared the word—but the speaker was wrong.

Ira just shook her head, returning her attention to the coin in front of her, to its tiny ridges that suddenly seemed like mountains to climb, not looking up until the yellow moped was gone.

If she found money on the sidewalk once, maybe she could find it again. Maybe this time, it wouldn't even be super-glued to the pavement. Ira pushed herself up from her seat by the metal magazine box. Storefronts with sleek glass windows stretched the length of this block. She could have almost been in any city in the world but for the zloty coin staring up from its place by her feet.

Across the street, people rushed up and down the stairs of a metro stop. There could be a loose metro card or token, lost change or cash. Or if not a way to ride, she could probably find a map. Metro stops always had maps. She'd recognize the name of the stop where she and Larissa had gotten off maybe. Surely. And if she found any money, she'd get on. Problem solved.

Ira wove through the crowded sidewalks toward the crosswalk.

Their stop had been on the river. She'd totally recognize that stop on a map.

Ira breathed in the city as she joined its masses. She could do this. It'd be fine.

Though the ground approaching the station didn't offer much charity. A gum wrapper, a balled-up flyer, a crack in the cement where a determined weed grew through.

Ira wanted to applaud that little weed.

She blew her breath out between pursed lips. The honey sweet taste of the *medivka* was gone now. She wondered if Larissa was freaking out, if she'd had another shot. Ira would have probably had another shot if the situation was reversed, but she guessed the situation never would be reversed. The feel of that man's warmth in her arms had been one of the highlights of her day, though. Baba Vira or no Baba Vira, the attempt had been worth it. She'd find her way back.

She slipped her thin fingers into the change return slots in the ticket kiosks. Again and again, cold, smooth metal emptiness was all she found. But the city map was just where she thought it would be, metro routes in red and blue and gray slashed across the city.

There was the river, and the blue metro line ran parallel to it. There wasn't just one stop. There were so many. Or maybe the red went closer. It did seem too, but then so did the gray. The gray seemed a more minor route. But how did she know the difference? And had they been on a minor route?

The brakes of the metro echoed deeper in the station. A recorded message played about the closing doors or minding the gap or something else essential yet mundane.

Palm tree. Chopin. Mermaid.

None of these landmarks were on this map.

Disembarking passengers flooded the station, swirling around her, a mighty tide controlled by train schedules if not the moon. Ira grabbed the arm of someone passing by.

"Mermaid?" Her voice broke. She didn't know the Ukrainian word—or the Polish.

The man shifted his weight away from her but didn't yank his shirtsleeve free.

"*Zhinka*," she said. "*Zhinka z ryb'yachym khvostom.*" Woman with fish tail. Her lack of fluency in this moment flushed her cheeks, but she raised her chin higher.

The man pointed to the map, tapping in a rapid succession of beats in multiple places before walking away.

What was that supposed to mean? Were there lots of mermaids? Was he trying to confuse her?

She looked to the mark that identified where she was. That was easy enough to find. And she saw the river. A long sidewalk followed along it, she remembered. If she could just get to the river, surely wherever she reached it, she'd be able to see the mermaid. That mermaid was massive. And the bridge! There had been a long suspension bridge.

She tried to memorize the way, to choose the most direct path. She tried to see the route she'd ridden on that bike.

Palm tree. Chopin. Mermaid.

She nodded her head, bouncing on her feet. She could do this. Ira turned and traced her steps out of the metro stop, back to the crosswalk, down the street past the parking spot of the yellow moped and the metal magazine box. She didn't even look for the zloty coin. Her legs took long strides, every footfall in rhythm. At the end of the block, she had stepped off the stranger's bike. They'd come from the right, she knew, so she cut down that street, "al. Jerozolimskie," a street sign told her. She would never be able to remember that name, but this wouldn't be so hard.

20

Vira (June 1941)

Vira's mother fretted over her oldest daughter's hair, tucking in loose strands, lacing a flower or two or three or seven into the tightly woven braid that folded around her head in a crown.

Her father paced from his favorite button-tufted armchair to the window, around the border of the rug to the corner of the room where Ivan's viola lay in its stand. Its silent strings vibrated in Vira's mind. They sang. They crescendoed. Ivan had known Mykhail. They met at the university in Lviv and attended OUN meetings together, dreaming of an independent Ukraine. They were probably both equally delusional.

When Vira looked to catch her reflection in the window pane, she saw him walking down the long dirt road toward their house. He neared the pond full of geese. He was probably nowhere near as agile at stealing eggs as her brother.

Lesya sang songs with the younger children upstairs. One of them yelped and cried out, and Vira's mother glared at the stairs with her lips tightened as if she could shush the voices above by mere motherly concentration.

Mykhail knocked on the door harder than Vira expected. She painted a smile on her face. This wasn't how she was supposed to be courted. The decision shouldn't already be made. She couldn't imagine how this mustached young man could ever press her against a tall birch tree, running his hands through her hair, making her gasp with the wanting of him. In her pocket, the weight of Dmytro's stone anchored her body. She couldn't shift her footing, her posture, or her gaze from the long road before their house.

Her father pulled open the door, and her mother put a hand to her shoulder. She wasn't sure if the juddering creak was from the movement of the old door hinges or her body's first step forward. Mykhail entered in his soldier's uniform. He removed his deep green cap from his head. The brass buttons on his coat needed shining. She supposed he needed a wife for such things.

Vira forced herself to straighten, pushing any thoughts of Dmytro from her mind, knowing the blush that had come to her face could be understood as a sign of purity and inexperience.

The young man shook her father's hand and greeted him before turning to her. His hazel green eyes were full of expectation.

"You look *harna*, Vira."

He took a timid step toward her and reached for her hand. Only when her mother's hand pressed against the small of her back did she give it to him. She tried to find his heartbeat in his grasp. She tried to imagine their love lines pressed together, but they only drowned in his sweat.

"May we go for a walk, Pan Bilyk?"

Vira knew her father would say no. A walk alone with a man would be unseemly, inappropriate, vulgar in her parents' eyes. Beside her, her mother remained mute. Ivan's viola strings were silent too. Her brother would have made a joke right about now in his overconfident way. Instead, her hands were cold with a slight tremble against Mykhail's.

Her father cleared his throat once, then again, as if the first time was insufficient. He opened the door for them.

"Of course."

The rock in Vira's pocket tried to hold her back. Mykhail squeezed her hand and pulled her gently forward, and with her parents' eyes upon her, she allowed herself to be pulled.

The sunshine that had been so soft and sweet only hours before had become brutal. Mykhail took her gently by the arm but didn't continue walking after the first few steps out the door. He didn't seem to know which direction to choose.

"This way," she directed him, tugging on his arm. The muscles under his uniform were surprisingly solid.

They turned away from the honking geese that waddled in their direction. She felt the heat of his body, the blood under his skin.

He allowed himself to be guided, and they walked silently toward the far side of the hives, where the soft buzzing met the trickling water of the stream.

Vira's father and his men had finished painting the boxes only the week before. They were turquoise, green, yellow, and red—colors chosen as if to capture everything still spirited and alive. The bees buzzed inside. Her skin vibrated when she left Mykhail's side and leaned against one. The smell of flowers and honey surrounded her. She wondered if the tiny yellow and black insects would fly into the blooms tucked into her hair. She wondered if the swarm of bees would make him take a step away.

A single bee escaped the hive and buzzed in the air between them.

"You don't want to marry me, do you?"

"I don't know you," she whispered.

A second bee joined the first, looping and dancing in the air.

"I've been hearing about you for years."

A whistle blew out on the street in the distance but neither turned to look. Vira tried to hold her gaze on his hazel green eyes. They were nice eyes. And his face was strong and handsome, straight nose, strong jaw.

The two bees didn't deter him. Instead, he took a step closer toward her.

"Ivan told me all about his stubborn sister who put frogs down his shirt or beet dye in his wash basin when he crossed her." His eyebrows lifted as if waiting for her to refute the actions. She bit back the emotion that wanted to escape her mouth. "And his friends told me about a beautiful girl that all the boys fought over, who none of them could win."

Mykhail reached for her hands again. His touch was warm, not so terrible, really.

"When I met you at the wedding, I wanted to be the one to win."

"What makes you think you could?" she whispered. The two bees danced by the flowers in her hair, diving between their faces.

"Besides your father's permission... nothing at all."

A whistle blew again from the street. Voices carried in their direction. The sound of a motor interrupted the hum of the bees.

"I've volunteered. I report in a week."

"Volunteered for what?"

"To do what I can. I've joined the *Okhoronni Promyslovi Viddily* to protect Ukrainian factories."

"Who are you fighting for? For Ukrainian independence?"

"For whoever keeps me alive."

"My brother would never say such a thing."

"Your brother is who convinced me."

"He would never." Her eyes were becoming wet, but she didn't turn away.

"No." Mykhail looked toward the road. A small group of German soldiers marched behind a collection of well-dressed men. He put his hand on her shoulder and steered her toward the cover of the nearby sunflowers. Their wide black faces and yellow petals soon stood over them like guards.

"But I don't want your brother's death," Mykhail whispered. "I want to survive this to come back to you."

The assembly on the road came closer. German shouts and mumbled replies. Was that the priests from the church? And the lawyer with the bottomless stomach when her mother served her famous borscht? She shifted behind the stalks to see better, but Mykhail tightened his hold on her.

"We have to be still," he whispered, his arms quickly wrapping around her, his mustache brushing against her ear.

Mykhail bumped into a tall stalk, stepping against the base of its stem. It leaned awkwardly, not broken but no longer as beautiful. Vira wanted room to see, to move, to dance among these familiar stems, but she remained still in his arms. She rooted her feet to the ground as if she'd find strength in this soil. Her soil. Her once favorite place.

The whistle blew again, and German was shouted on the road only meters away from them. The first footsteps plodded along. Commanding footfalls followed.

"Where are they going?"

Mykhail pressed his lips to hers. They lingered warm and soft. His heartbeat pulsed in his hands now. They had moved to clutch hers. They squeezed her fingers with fear and ferocity and fervor. His heartbeat thumped. Hers thumped against it.

"Marry me before I die? It probably won't be for long."

She didn't push away his lips. She let them implore and revere her, and she kissed him back. Tears ran down her cheeks.

"*Tak*," she whispered, the word spoken against his lips. "Okay."

21

Larissa

"I use electric mixer," said Stefa. "But you needed to sweat. Good for body. For heart."

The old woman dropped one of the balls of dough, now risen, into a bread pan. The knife she used to slice an X onto its surface was bigger than was necessary, a tool for butchering not baking. When Stefa turned to point Larissa toward the plastic wrap, Larissa tried not to jump away from the shifting blade.

Not able to set the plastic on the sticky counter, Larissa performed her rituals mid-air. She stretched the thin translucent sheet out and ripped away a section so quickly that none of the corners had time to crook or stick. She swaddled the second loaf and held it in her arms, while Stefa bent to put the first in the oven.

"This, we trade." Stefa stood upright and took the plastic bundle from Larissa's hands. "My neighbor is butcher. He gives me meat when I bake for him."

"We didn't actually bake for him."

Stefa picked up the big knife and used the dull side of the blade to press an X into the top of the plastic. She handed Larissa the knife and walked toward the front door. "When I come back, we make ribs."

The front door closed before Larissa thought of an answer. She had followed Stefa out of the kitchen, the fingers of one hand held up so its flour wouldn't dirty anything, the other still gripping the knife. But maybe the flour wouldn't make much difference. Dust covered the shelves, the tables, the window-sills, the blinds. It blanketed the sofas minus all they'd already stirred up with their presence.

Larissa was good at being useful. If she just had a few minutes, she could make a difference. Rags and cleaning supplies shouldn't be hard to find.

Flicking on another light switch, her finger smeared the wall. She'd fix that too, but now she could see the place better. Rings covered the coffee table. The pillows on the sofa were lumped. She could start with the accumulation of dust on the windows. Weeks of dust. Months of dust. Maybe years. Clear daylight would make a dramatic difference, and that was attainable. The energy of accomplishment would ease Larissa's nerves. In five minutes, she could tranform this dim apartment.

Larissa turned toward the kitchen, and the knife in her hand thwacked as she twisted. Beside her on a wall shelf, a doll's head tilted, its too-thin neck hacked like a tree-trunk in a cartoon.

"Oh God." The brunette's eyes closed in its new position, tiny eyelashes lowering making it appear drunk and dazed. Larissa raised her flour-covered hand to her mouth.

Some of the flowers in its hair floated down to the floor like tossed petals on a grave.

She held the knife at arm's length as she navigated down the hall past sepia-toned pictures and Ukrainian dance team awards. She dropped her weapon in the sink and scrubbed her hands clean, settling for drying them on her own shirt rather than any of Stefa's dirty towels before returning to the mangled doll. Its body stood rigid in its stand on the wall shelf. She tilted the head upright again, and its eyes blinked at her. Voices chatted on the street, and her hands wanted to move faster. They flailed through the air, trying to find their dance, remember the right movements, hear the right beat. A groan escaped her lips. The head couldn't just be tilted like a disjointed Barbie. She needed her hot glue gun. That would save the floral crown too. She'd make it look even better actually. Pinworthy. Instagrammable.

The voices on the street passed. Her hands settled.

Larissa tilted the head farther, trying to see if she could find a pose that didn't look as if the doll had barely survived a guillotine. Her shift produced a pop as the old plastic cracked. The head detached completely, falling into the basket that the doll's body held.

Her hands went cold. She brushed her hair behind her ear and took a deep breath. Broken toys were her wheelhouse, she reminded herself. There was always a way, or if there wasn't, there was always a deception.

Tilting the doll-stand back, she forced the body to lean backward. She propped the head up, balancing it between the neck and the wall. Its little eyelids dropped to an ill half-open. Time could have done that damage. It could have just tilted. With the cleanliness of the place, Stefa wouldn't even notice. That's what she repeated to herself over and over, as she tiptoed to the kitchen to find the rags and as she cleaned her flour smudges off the wall. That's what she mentally recited as she picked up the phone, praying she had just a few more minutes alone. The windows could wait just a few minutes longer.

She had to talk to her kids. She had to talk to Greg. Her hands trembled as she listened to the high-pitched chirping ring. Even the sound of the ringing phone needed to be translated here. She tried to take a deep breath, but she couldn't fill her lungs with anything but apprehension.

"Hello?"

The house around her had begun to smell of baking bread, doughy and sweet. She closed her eyes and soaked in the familiar voices. Her children were playing in the room somewhere near her husband. Laughing. Alex sang. Greg said something else, but her heartbeat was a metronome to the rhythm of her son's little song. The Itsy-Bitsy Spider maybe.

"Sorry, what?"

"I said it's great to hear from you. We've been thinking about you."

"God, I've been thinking about you." She opened her eyes to look at the cuckoo clock with its long pendulum swaying on the wall, trying to do the backward calculation. "Have you eaten lunch?"

"Yes, I remembered to feed the children. We went out for sushi."

"What?"

"We had peanut butter and jelly sandwiches."

Larissa traced her finger through the remaining flour on the kitchen counter. She made a tiny heart then added an arrow through its middle, but the arrow looked more like a crack than she'd intended. She wiped away the design with her whole palm.

"Did you cut them with cookie cutters? Anna likes hers in the shape of a kitty, and Alex likes a rocket ship."

"We had squares, and the kids ate every bite."

The kids chattered about something in the background. She thought she heard her name. She tried to see them—still in their pajamas, knowing Greg. Anna's hair unbrushed and hands covered in stray marker. Alex's face covered in an ear-to-ear milk mustache, one sock on, the other lost to the world.

"Have you found Baba?"

Larissa traced a star in the fine white powder.

"Not quite. She's okay, I think. But she's..." A crash sounded through the static-filled line. "Are you okay?"

"Lincoln log demolition."

Larissa nodded, flicking flour from her fingertips. She stepped toward the sink but didn't want the water to drown out one second of this call. The knife stared back at her. She took a deep breath.

"Greg, Baba's gone somewhere. We're trying to track her. This whole thing is crazy...."

"Track her?"

Larissa grimaced when Greg laughed, but the kids' voices had come nearer again. She heard her name. Her real name. It wasn't Lyalya. It wasn't Larissa. It was Mommy. That name had always fit her best.

"Wait one second. One second," he whispered away from the receiver. "So what does this mean for you?" Greg pressed on, voice stronger in her ear.

"I don't know yet." The chattering turned to song again, definitely the tune of the Itsy-Bitsy Spider, but with something different about it. "Can you put the kids on?"

"Sure. But you're doing okay? You haven't killed Ira?"

One of the flowers from the broken doll's crown had stuck to her shoe. She peeled it off and placed it on a section of counter not covered in flour.

"We're doing okay. She's... I'll let you know as soon as we have a plan."

"You'll find her. Enjoy the chase, okay? We've got everything covered on the home-front."

The voices of her kids became crisper and louder. She was on speaker-phone now.

"They have a song for you," Greg said again, and she pressed her ear harder into the plastic phone. She didn't care that it was sticky. Her children twittered, and Anna counted them off, one-two-three.

"Great-baba and my mom-my got on an air-uh-plane," they sang together to the familiar itsy-bitsy tune. She closed her eyes and imagined their little fingers following along with the song, crawling upward through the air. But what were they doing for this version? She imagined their arms outspread, tilting to one side then another, cutting through imaginary clouds in their playroom.

"I love it," she said when they finished. "I love you so much. Do you know that?"

"Love you too, Mommy," said Anna.

"Uh-huh," Alex said still in his sing-songy voice. "Did you get to fly the plane?"

"Not this time," she answered. "Maybe on my way home."

22

Ira

"Palm tree, palm tree, palm tree," she thought again and again, with every exhalation. Her breath heaved. She slowed her pace just a bit. She didn't realize she was saying it aloud. An older man walking in the same direction, grinned at her.

"Palma," he said, pointing down the street.

Her heartbeat quickened. She pushed herself on faster.

This section of the city wasn't full of skyscrapers. Flat-fronted buildings lined the street in whites, tans, beiges, and grays. Apartments over storefronts. Office buildings. No flourishes or fuss here. The wide avenue spoke of simplicity, utility, clarity, and understated charm.

The street seemed to just go on and on, with the same buildings, in the same neutral style. Multiple times, she thought she was going in circles, yet she hadn't turned. The city played tricks on her. Baba Yaga magic.

But after another block, something ahead caught her eye. A palm tree? She needed to get closer. A monument? A pedestal? A sculptural traffic light? She hadn't realized how much she had slowed. Ira started to jog, not trusting her eyes.

A red and mustard yellow tram rumbled by. After it passed, she could see ahead more clearly. It was definitely the palm tree, standing there as illogically as a mermaid in landlocked, temperate-weathered Poland. The palm tree grew larger and larger as she came closer, but it was no mirage. It didn't disappear.

Ira closed her eyes and tried to remember her bike ride. She was fairly sure she needed to take a left, and she didn't allow herself time to hesitate. What had Larissa learned by now? Was she with Stefa? How much was her sister panicking?

Trees in large metal pots lined the street she now walked. Gray awnings stretched out to the sidewalk. The sun sank lower in the sky, but it didn't yet blind her.

She remembered the red store signage with the scribbled cursive script. She remembered the balcony with the white and red Polish flag.

Ira nearly skipped across the street to the next block. Yes, she remembered that coffee shop, its familiar green umbrellas over outdoor tables just outside its doors.

Two women and a child stood on the next street corner, and Ira slowed her pace. Their expressions were worn, eyes tired, faces drawn. The child traced a green leaf up and down one of the women's legs. Two instrument cases rested by their feet. They looked like they were about to play.

Ira leaned against a nearby street sign. She wished she had that two-zloty coin for a tip.

She looked for hoops in their ears or bangles on their arms, but none were there. She inhaled deeply, searching for the incense she expected to permeate the air around these women. Frankincense and myrrh. Maybe bay leaf. Ira had once played with gypsy incense combinations she'd found online. Her nose tried to dissect the absent smells.

Larissa's voice was in her head, "Roma" not "gypsy." "Gypsy" was a slur people didn't realize was a slur. Gypsy. Gyp. Gypped.

But Ira wasn't stereotyping. She'd done her research. She was full of respect, admiration really. She'd always wondered if she'd had the gypsy Sight too. The Roma sight, she mentally corrected herself.

The girl leaned down to one of the instrument cases and traced her leaf across the curves of its body, a violin or viola maybe. Ira wished she could take a seat, but there was nowhere nearby. The green umbrellas with their patio furniture were too far back. There wasn't even a metal magazine box nearby.

A bit closer to the women, a bench rested under the shade of another potted tree. It would be awkwardly close to sit to strangers, but if she was waiting for them to play, she supposed it would be all right. She inched closer. She smiled at the girl with the leaf when she looked over, but the girl only tugged on one of the women's dresses in response.

The woman looked down to the child, who whispered something, then over to Ira.

Ira smiled back. She lifted her chin, filling her lungs with the air of this old city, even if it wasn't incensed in this moment like she'd imagined. The sun beat down on her, warming her tired body. She was exhausted. She hadn't felt it until she'd sat down. Her legs quivered. Her feet ached.

The women said something to each other and turned back to Ira.

"I'm in no hurry," Ira said to them. She didn't want them to quicken their preparations on her behalf. She was here to enjoy every second of this experience. Though, she should have at least used Ukrainian. "*Vybachte—*"

"May we help you with something?" one of the women said to her. She held Ira's eyes with a gaze Ira couldn't escape.

"You speak English!"

"Yes." She blinked and gripped the younger girl's hand. "And you look like you're waiting on something."

Ira shifted her weight on the bench.

"Aren't you going to play?"

"Play what?"

"Your instruments?"

A car passed by and then another. A leaf fell from the nearby potted tree, and the girl's eyes followed its slow, twirling descent. Ira wondered whether the woman had heard her answer. She parted her lips to speak but didn't get out any words.

"You see us standing on the corner so you think we will play for you?" The woman's dark eyes narrowed, her mouth tight.

"Weren't you...."

Ira's heart pounded. She had gotten something terribly wrong. These three women. They just looked like they would perform on the street corner, collect the tips to take care of their daughter.

"No." The woman bent forward and scooped up the leaf that had landed near her feet. She handed it to the girl without letting her gaze leave Ira's. "I am speaking to my daughter's music teacher. She just finished her lesson. Classical violin."

"I'm so sorry. I—"

Ira pushed herself to her feet, fumbling her way off the bench. She had just been sitting there staring at these women, assuming lives for them which weren't close to their truth. What did she know of their truth? She tripped on something but didn't see what. A crack, a twig, the embarrassment in the air.

Classical violin. Wait, classical violin....

"Chopin!" she spit out, the only thing she could think to say.

The woman crossed her arms over her chest, her narrowed eyes unmoving.

"I mean, I'm lost. I'm trying to find Chopin. Then the mermaid."

The woman let out a deep breath. Her daughter trailed the leaf again up and down her side. She pointed down a side street.

"Two blocks," the woman said. "Take a left, then your first right."

She turned back to the other woman and squeezed the child's hand before plucking another leaf and tapping it on the girl's nose. She giggled.

Ira nodded. She walked backward and nodded. She didn't know why she kept nodding. No one looked at her anymore.

Taking the turn the woman suggested, a restaurant's sign caught her eye, a moon caught in fisherman's netting. The sign over the door read "Nocny." The word meant nothing to her, at least she didn't think it did.

She felt the heat on her face. She hadn't meant any harm. She just thought....

Nocny. Another sign perched out on the sidewalk.

Ira bit her lip and pressed onward. She had directions to follow now, though she definitely hadn't made a friend. Baba Vira was the one who could make any friend when she wanted to. She just didn't want to much anymore. She'd rather cackle at the parents Larissa always tried to impress or scare the neighborhood kids who were rude to each other. Scare them into being better people, the way of the best fairy tales.

Ira's hand went to her mouth, and she stopped walking.

Nocny. The angular letters clung to her mind but shifted, transformed. Noncia. Her baba often spoke of her wartime friend, though she never mentioned her name when planning this trip. Why hadn't she mentioned her? Of course she should have mentioned her. They still traded letters.

Noncia must have been the one at the airport. She'd stolen away with her baba, just like they had escaped decades, a lifetime, ago. Ira didn't know why it seemed so suddenly obvious, but it absolutely was.

The late-afternoon sun cut down the streets in narrow slices, shining in Ira's eyes. The shadows moved illogically around her, sunlight blocked by canopies, street lights, and thick black bars on windows.

"Noncia lives in Slovakia, in Spišská Nová Ves," Ira whispered like she was practicing. Larissa wasn't going to like this, but maybe she'd be impressed that Ira remembered exactly the town. "Baba Vira always said she wanted to see her again."

The shadows danced across her once more, and she stopped and shaded her eyes, sure their movement wasn't at random. She swore she saw a profile out of the corner of her eye. But then it was gone.

Noncia had been with her baba through the war years, through what young Vira had assumed was widowhood for the longest time.

Darkness moved over Ira's face, more than the shadows of cornices and balconies. She peered down the street toward the afternoon sun. She walked west apparently. Somewhere far beyond the limits of human sight, the States were that way—the States with so many of their folktales and legends stolen from other lands. Maybe Ira was meant for this old world.

Ira spun around when the shadow returned. It crept across the building beside her before darting down the street.

The long shadow of a witch loomed on the gray pavement. Mouth agape and teeth bared, its long pointy nose bent across a manhole, the sidewalk, and up the wall of a building. Ira pivoted quickly to discover its source. But there were no flowerpots with long-petaled plants that could have been that nose. There was no source of that mouth, those teeth.

A stray cat, all black, emerged from behind a cement stoop.

"Did you see that shadow?"

The cat didn't answer.

"It was a Baba Yaga," she continued as the animal held her eyes.

Yet now the shadow was gone.

"Aren't black cats magical? Do I need Baba Yaga's help, or am I trying to escape her?" she asked.

The black cat meowed then slinked on. Ira crossed her arms before her, momentarily concerned that she'd somehow stereotyped and offended it too. She tried so hard to be a good person. To be respectful. Mature. She didn't know why it sometimes seemed so far out of reach.

Another shadow danced across her. A clothesline or far-off flag? Her imagination was playing tricks on her. Yet the dark figure rose again on the building beside her now, two stories tall—wide-mouthed, eyes glowing in slits, nose reaching for the third floor.

Ira took a step back, staring first at the shadow then toward the sun.

When Ira spotted its source pop out again from a balcony two blocks away, she ran. Little hands held black silhouettes attached to sticks that were stretched out to catch the lowering sun, casting the massive shadows that fell down the street. The thin arms pulled the shadow puppets back again, hiding them behind a stone balcony.

Ira waited for a motorbike to whir by then darted across the road. One little face appeared as a child stood from her crouch on the balcony. A second head popped up, laughing before ducking again, sticking out the Baba Yaga silhouette, making it tremble across the buildings, making it shudder, shiver, and again disappear.

She needed to see those puppets up close.

A red and yellow tram rumbled down the next road. Ira saw it, judged its speed, and figured she could beat it. She sprinted fast across the four-lane road, stepping around a puddle and grinning at a mustached man who watched her in fascination.

Her foot slipped in the divot of the tram's tracks. Pain burst through her ankle as a surprisingly high-pitched beep sounded. Two cars-lengths away. Closer. Her short lifeline throbbed on her palm. The yellow and red tram didn't slow. Her shoe slipped off as she stood and pushed herself forward, but her ankle collapsed under the pressure, heel throbbing. Body pressed against the pavement again, she rolled.

The grime of the street stuck to her. Her hair brushed against the pavement and fell across her face. The tram beeped again, high-pitched, loud, aggressive, a child spitting newly discovered curse words.

The tracks jarred her body, banging her elbows and knees, but she kept her sight on the curb.

The tram rumbled by her, crushing her lost shoe and her dignity, but nothing else. The shadow of a Baba Yaga fell across her but darted away when she looked up toward the balcony. Ira sat up and dropped her head, allowing her messy hair to fall over her eyes.

After a moment, she used a street sign to pull herself up to a stand, wishing someone was there to offer her a hand—Larissa or even the women with their instruments. Even through their aggravation, they'd remained kind. One of them would have offered a hand. Ira wondered if there would have been any magic in it, then she chastised herself for the thought. What was wrong with her?

The gray of the road had rubbed off on her clothes. Ira leaned hard against the metal sign.

Her sandal was shredded, its faux-leather cut into unrecognizable strands. She wondered if real leather would have held up better.

The children's laughter echoed down the block.

Ira straightened her back, lifting her chin. She put more pressure on her weak ankle and winced. Her heartbeat pulsed in the injury, rushing blood through her body, telling her she was alive.

Those kids had met Baba Vira, she was sure of it.

Their balcony was only a half-block away. She hobbled every step of the way with as much dignity as she could muster.

"Where did you get those puppets?" she called out as soon as she could. "*Lyal'ky.*" She pointed to the shadow puppets. "*Zvidky?*" She shrugged her shoulders and held up her arms in what she hoped was a universal question posture, hoping the Ukrainian and Polish continued to be close.

The girls looked down from their sculpted cement balcony. The corners were crumbling, but the detail captured by its architect was preserved under the layers of city dust and pollution.

"Baba Yaga," the bigger one whispered.

The younger one continued the story, but her words were indecipherable. Then she spun on the older girl, growled, wagged her finger at her, and then made her scream before they both burst into more giggles.

Ira leaned against the side of the building, letting her forehead rest against the cool stone. Her grandmother had given her Baba Yaga shadow puppets when she was a girl. Her baba had told Ira that she needed help terrifying other children.

Ira moved slowly, stepping tenderly. All she could do was

nod at the mad brilliance of her baba in action. She might have been wrong about the yellow moped, but this was unquestionably her grandmother's work.

23

Vira (July 1941)

The priest she had known since she was a little girl had been jailed—so had many of the others from neighboring towns. The traveling priest who visited their village didn't wear a collar or robes. He wore a plain brown suit and shoes that were shinier than any of her father's.

Vira shared her wedding with four other couples. Without time for more preparations, she wore her new blue dress, the one made by the dressmaker's daughter and her mother, the one she hadn't been able to step into since the day her friend's body dangled like a loose thread. Her mother insisted, so she put it on, trying not to feel the smooth fabric against her skin, trying not to notice the perfect symmetry of each bow that went down the front or the tiny buttons hand-stitched onto the sleeves. The daughter's eyes were better than her mother's. Vira knew exactly where her hands had been.

She wished she had a real Baba Yaga mask to slip over her face so she could run into the woods and rage and scream and roast the bones of offending children. A house with legs that could turn around or run away whenever anything she didn't want to see came near.

There wasn't time for her to travel with Mykhail to his home two villages away, so her new husband had been handed a key to a house in her town. He didn't know the owners, nor did she.

There were so many empty houses now—houses of OUN members, houses of scholars and musicians, writers and artists, Jewish houses. Houses of those that offended someone Russian months ago or someone German in the past two weeks. Vira didn't know which had been vacated and which had been emptied by force.

On their wedding night, standing inside their single-night home, Mykhail pressed her hand to his lips. His mustache tickled her skin. The dust in the room tickled her nose. There were so many books here, volumes in Ukrainian, in German, in French, and in English. A pencil lay on a table next to a newspaper, like it was just put down for a moment, like the reader had just stood to get a cup of honeyed tea.

Mykhail traced the edge of her sleeve and moved bow by bow toward her shoulders, as they moved deeper into the house. Vira shuddered, needing to get out of her blue dress, to get away from the memories of death in its stiches. His hands moved toward her neckline, and she guided his fingers to remove it from her cold body. One of the tiny buttons on the sleeve flew through the air toward the bed with a layer of dust upon it.

There was a night with Dmytro not so long ago that she thought her virginity would be lost long before marriage. In that, at least, she'd been respectable, after all.

In the morning, she ironed Mykhail's green uniform and shined the tarnished buttons. His cap rested on a table by the door. She stared at it as she waited for him to reappear in this borrowed house, in this borrowed life where she was the good doting wife and he was her loving husband.

"Where are you going?"

"Kyiv." He put a hand to his mustache, clearing the last of their breakfast's crumbs from its rough hairs. "But I don't know for how long or where we'll go next. Not out of Ukraine—at least, I don't think so."

She allowed him to squeeze her hands, to move toward her to nuzzle her neck, to move his hands over her body, but she didn't promise to write him every day as she knew she should.

"How can you fight with the Germans?"

"I'm protecting our factories."

"They're German factories now, aren't they?"

"They're fighting off the Soviets at least."

"They took away our Ukrainian independence."

"I'm not sure we ever really had it." His voice muffled in her hair and then in the fabric of her shirt. "I told you, I'm not fighting for my country anymore. I'm fighting to survive." His eagerness flattered her. She didn't push him away.

"I'll be here when you get back."

"I have no clue when that will be." Mykhail pressed against her as they stood, pushing her against the wall of the small sitting room. A cross-stitched garland of roses, red petals and green leaves fell from the wall, clattering to the floor. The wooden frame broke. Mykhail didn't notice.

Vira's mother had spoken to her of the physical demands of being a good wife, of the wants of men's bodies, of the required submissiveness to one's husband—that sex was the bee sting that went along with collecting honey. But she hadn't been right. It was becoming one with the hive that held the swarm inside.

When she waved goodbye to her new husband at the train station, her hair was once again loose and messy. She hid it under a scarf tied under her chin. Mykhail was packed closely between young men she knew and absolute strangers. They all wore the same green cap, the same collared shirt, the same brass buttons. But Mykhail's buttons reflected the sunshine. She blew him a kiss goodbye, and the train wheezed into motion.

Lesya, at her side, had joined her to walk her back home—her home that wasn't where she was supposed to be now that she was a married woman.

They passed the elm tree, thick with leaves hiding its secrets. Vira didn't know who had cut down the dressmaker's daughter's body or what had become of her family. All the Jews she had known had disappeared soon after the travelling Roma. The yellow stars of David had been sewn on their clothes. She'd heard the Roma were given upside down triangles. The dressmaker's daughter had worn her star on her favorite cream-colored sweater, the one with the ruffles she had knit with her own hand. She had such talented hands with her thin fingers, short tiny nails, the scar that ran across one thumb from a long-ago mistake with the scissors.

"Is it different now?" Lesya brushed her blond curls behind her ear.

"Is what different?"

They passed the churchyard and the graves beyond. The short headstones had grown in number since the last time Vira had glanced their way. A few crumbled at their corners, grayed and sun-worn.

"Being married." Lesya blushed. She clasped her hands together in front of her, unclasped them, and smoothed her skirt.

The church cast a long shadow over the graves, stretching out into the empty field beyond, taking ownership.

"Oh." Her sister's red cheeks became redder. Vira linked arms with her as they walked along the dirt road. "It is different."

"Good different?"

"You'll have your own husband one day and see for yourself, Lyalya." Vira wanted to pinch her sister's rosy cheeks but didn't. They were a true match for Lesya's wooden doll.

Vira untied the scarf around her chin and let her wild hair blow in the breeze. It tangled and strayed, and she absolutely didn't care. Her little sister pressed her lips together and put a hand to her curls.

Far down the road, a figure ran toward them, a skinny body who moved in spurts, the way their mother had once advanced the time the sisters had seen her chased by the geese. Vira pushed her wild hair out of her eyes.

The sun was in their faces. They squinted to make out the woman. Her arms flailed in their direction. A voice carried in the wind.

As the figure came closer, both girls broke into a run.

"Mama?" Lesya called first "Mama! What's wrong?"

Their mother stopped running and bent over her knees, resting her elbows there huffing, puffing, reminding Vira of the delivery of the twins. She'd been in the room every painful hour of that labor.

"Mama?" she added tentatively, wrapping her arms around her mother once they reached her, supporting her so she wouldn't fall.

Lesya put a hand to their mother's forehead and looked down the road toward their house, still a half mile away. Their mother put her hands to her belly then her still heaving chest.

"What's happened?"

"They're taking your tato. To jail, with Oleh." Her words made her tremble. "They think he's a member of the Underground with Oleh and Ivan. With Mykhail..." A wet drop fell into the dirt of the road. Vira didn't know if she'd spit or if it was a tear. She hugged her mother tighter.

"Mykhail stopped fighting for independence."

Her mother shook her head and waved her hand into the air.

"Your father never was a part of it." The sisters wove their arms around their mother and turned her toward home. "They tied your father's hands. They raised sticks and..." She finished the sentence with her hands instead of her words. She covered her face. "They put him in the back of their truck," she added. Her voice escaped in a final burst, running away when she couldn't.

They came to the fence made of woven branches that contained their sunflowers. The giant blooms all looked away from them, preferring the glow of the harsh sun.

"They're talking about sending Oleh away, some sort of camp," their mother continued. "His brother might deserve it, but your father has never...."

A military truck rumbled down the road toward them, and

the women stepped out of the dirt road to the grass along its side. A stray stick from the fence caught Vira's skirt and poked at her leg.

Her mother's hand sprung out and talon-gripped Vira's arm. In the shadows of the truck-bed, Vira's father sat silent, face swollen. He met their eyes and held them. Turning his body as the truck drove away, he put a hand out to them. His restraints forced his other hand to rise as well.

"He's done nothing. They'll question him and release him." Vira whispered. The stick pulled at the fabric of her skirt as she tried to move.

Her mother stood on her own now, but the sisters didn't let go of her.

"If Oleh's mistakes were so large, your father will pay for it. *Klopit*. Trouble. He's always been *klopit*." She turned her head, matching the posture of the sunflowers. "We're going today."

"Where are they taking Tato?" Lesya walked again, and the three women stepped back onto the dirt road. The fabric of Vira's skirt pulled then ripped. She knew she should care but only wanted to be free. The scratch on her leg burned. A drip of blood slipped down her calf.

"I don't know. But we need to leave here, leave Galicia."

No clouds blocked the sun, but a gray haze hovered over their land. Vira blinked at it twice, expecting it to be in her head.

"We need to leave Ukraine," their mother said more forcefully, gaining her footing, easing her weight on her daughter's shoulders.

Lesya kicked a pebble down the road. The road bent, and they fell into the sunflowers' shadow.

"The Germans allow travel among allied regions."

Vira's body tightened at the word "allow." All her uncle had wanted was to make his own rules, for Ukrainians to make their own rules.

"Where are we going?" Lesya's brow furrowed as they walked.

Their house came into view, its tin roof gleaming in the sunlight, its glass windows showing off everything their family had worked for. A thin trail of smoke wisped up from the kitchen.

"Halya! Helena!" Vira wasn't sure who screamed the names or if they all had.

The sisters ran as fast as they could while their mother crumpled to the ground like she had been beaten instead of her husband.

Vira reached the big brass doorknob first. The metal wasn't hot. There weren't any screams coming from inside, but she was terrified there weren't screams coming from inside.

She pushed it open with Lesya at her side. Their white-washed hallway with the hand-painted trim of red poppies wasn't filled with smoke. The air didn't smell dangerous.

"Halya?" Lesya called out. "Helena?" Her voice cracked on the second name. The twins were two. The officers wouldn't have touched them. They couldn't have touched them. The gunshot that killed her brother echoed through her veins.

Vira reached out to squeeze her sister's hand before directing her in the opposite direction. Lesya ran to the kitchen while Vira darted upstairs, past Ivan's room, past the room she shared with Lesya, to the nursery. A big bang sounded from that room, followed by a small voice, followed by laughter.

Vira broke into the room to see her littlest sisters with handfuls of ribbons they twined around their dolls' bodies, around their wrists, around their hair.

"They're here!" she called down the stairs.

"The fire's in the back of the house! We need to get out of here!" Lesya's voice returned.

The heavy hinge of the front door groaned.

"Pack a trunk," called their mother's voice from downstairs. It had stopped trembling. "We have time to pack a trunk, *tak*?"

When Lesya ran into the nursery, Vira scrambled to their room, tossing open the trunk that had been reserved for her move to Mykhail's house. She tossed out armfuls of her best clothes, removing the new dishes and wedding linens. She tossed in brushes and blankets, pillows, soap and cream. The nesting dolls sat together on the sisters' dresser. Vira inside their mother, Lesya inside Vira, Halya inside Lesya, Helena inside Halya.

Vira grasped them in a tight fingered embrace and wrapped them in her favorite red fringed shawl.

Lesya walked into the room behind her, carrying an armful of the twins' clothes and an old backpack of Ivan's.

"At least they're out of diapers." Her mouth was a flat line— the flat, defeated line Vira had always detested in their mother. "Mama's with the twins. We won't be able to manage more than the one trunk and maybe this old backpack. Save room for clothes for mama."

She threw her own clothes in, skirts, shirts, boots, and sweaters.

Outside the window, the hives burned, their red and yellow and turquoise paint disappearing into flame, into smoke. Clouds of bees swarmed the air.

"Where are we going?"

"Mama says Czechoslovakia."

"No Russians or Germans there?"

"I don't know. No fighting there at least."

Vira nodded. She tucked her shawl into the trunk. Without even thinking, she grabbed the string that held Dmytro's stone and tied it around her neck.

24
Larissa

While Stefa sat by her side, Larissa's hands grappled at her purse by her feet, digging through crayons and hand-wipes, her wallet, her passport, dental floss, a stain stick, a toy car, a doll's brush, and a mini notebook, pen clipped to its spiral rings. She wished she had a swiss army knife to defend herself against the impossibility of the situation. But that would have been confiscated at the airport.

"How long until we eat?"

"An hour, maybe two."

Larissa flipped open her notebook, turning to the sticky tab marked Warsaw. She had the numbers for airport security, the airline contact, the official at customs, the Warsaw police officer who she'd talked to when she'd tried to file the missing person case, the other officer they redirected her to, who had told her it was too soon for anything official.

The carved wooden cuckoo clock ticked on Stefa's wall, its pendulum lethargic compared to Larissa's pulse. Her grandmother had been missing almost twenty-four hours now.

"How do I get to the police station?" She stood, sliding her purse onto her shoulder, looking around the room to see if she needed to bring anything else. Creepy plastic dolls. Wooden nesting dolls. Half-full bottle of medivka. No.

Larissa traced the line of her lips. The medivka must have washed the color away. She fumbled in her purse again, finding her beeswax-based gloss.

"Call them."

"I already have."

"There is nothing else to do."

"They can't hang up on me if I'm there."

Larissa stepped outside to wait for the taxi after Stefa called one for her. Maybe she should have waited inside. That would have been more polite. She was actually kind of rude—kind of Ira-like—to rush out barely saying goodbye. And now she just stood on the sidewalk outside Stefa's apartment door.

The cement there was cracked. A weed struggled to grow through, fighting against footfalls and the lack of fresh air. A car rushed by, creating a wind. She brushed a stray lock of hair back behind her ear and pulled out her notebook again.

Baba Vira had been seen getting off the plane.

A witness saw her meet an older dark-haired woman at the baggage claim.

She'd sent flowers and a mask to Stefa, no note attached.

Where on earth was she? It was like a game from their childhood, the frantic searching behind curtains and under beds, around closet doors and in the crevices underneath the stairs.

Her taxi pulled up in front of her, and she stepped inside, whispering the Polish word for police station that Stefa had just practiced with her. She flipped a page of her notebook and showed him the address.

After the driver with long fuzzy sideburns nodded and turned back to the road, she returned to her notes. The faux leather seat she leaned into smelled of garlic. Her nose crinkled, and she leaned toward the cracked open window, closing her eyes, saying a prayer, slowing her breath.

When the taxi swerved to the side of the road, Larissa grimaced at the driver before noticing the blue letters of "POLICJA" hanging across the arched entryway of the building next to them. They weren't perfectly centered on the canopy—as if the printer wanted to end with a single "e" rather than add the two additional letters. She tilted her head to the side.

The driver tapped on the screen that marked how much

she owed him. Larissa sat up straighter, apologizing in English, then Ukrainian, before pulling out the proper amount. She tipped him before leaving the cab, but she wasn't sure whether the amount was generous or stingy.

Within the shadows next to the door of the police station was the Polish seal, the white eagle with its wings outspread against a red background. It looked fierce and ancient. Larissa tried to adopt the same demeanor as she opened the glass door. She was a doer. She did things. She took control of PTA meetings, organized meal drop-offs for friends and neighbors with new babies, and conquered her kids' oddly complicated show-and-tell schedules. Surely, she could track down her grandmother in a foreign city when the police refused to help. She'd make them help. She'd demand it.

Larissa steeled her determination and her smile. The cool air conditioning inside met her skin. The man at the front desk barely lifted his eyes to her. He typed quickly on a computer, pausing only to hold up a finger for her to wait.

Larissa rooted her feet to the ground. She was a tree, an oak. Her roots extended past the old tiles into the dirt of this old place, deep past the rubble of World War II when this city had been nearly flattened to the ground, deep past whatever lies or omissions her grandmother had produced. She cleared her throat.

"*Vybachte...*"

The man's eyebrows rose, but his eyes didn't elevate from the screen. Larissa walked forward, laying a hand on the desk.

"*Czy mogę ci pomóc*" Her brain worked slowly translating the Polish to Ukrainian to English. Could he help her?

"Yes, *tak*," Larissa stumbled. "I do need your help," she continued in Ukrainian, hoping the close languages would continue to serve her well as she explained her grandmother's disappearance and the updates she'd already received from the airline, airport security, the witness at baggage claim, and the Polish police officer who refused to make a case of the lost old woman.

The man focused back on his computer screen.

"Your grandmother's name?"

"Vira Bilyk."

The officer grunted, something almost canine. At least, Larissa thought it was the officer. She didn't think a dog sat by his feet. She leaned forward just a bit, peering over the desk. The man shifted his monitor away from her before picking up the phone.

When he hung it up, he stood, and Larissa prepared herself for an argument. She wasn't ready to leave yet.

The man tucked a white police hat that had been sitting on his desk under his arm. The blue stripe around it was a brighter blue than the dark navy of his uniform.

"*Proszę*, follow me."

Larissa obediently followed. The tile floor in the long hallway he led her down reflected the bright ceiling lights. It looked recently waxed, definitely freshly mopped. She couldn't see a speck of dust or a smudge of a footprint anywhere. The walls were white, stark white, bleached white.

When the officer paused in front of a door, she nearly bumped into him.

"*Pani* Oliver," said the officer inside the small room, when she met his eyes. Larissa nodded. She'd almost forgotten her married name.

The man across from her was younger than she was. His face barely hid the puffed pride of a little boy on the playground, playing soccer with his friends. She was right to have come. The first officer grunted again and urged her into the room before leaving her side. "How many hours has it been now?"

Larissa tried to be an oak, to stretch her roots into the ground where she stood.

"It's been twenty-two hours."

"Not yet twenty-four," the officer replied. His chin had a scar upon it like he'd once fallen from a see-saw.

Larissa's roots dissolved underneath her. She took a step

forward before dropping into one of the chairs across from the officer's desk.

"You have contacted who she was supposed to meet? Any other family or friends?" His boyish face had already been distracted by something flashing on his computer screen. "There is nothing we can do...."

Pulling her purse into her lap, she reached for her notebook. Her list of contacts. Her lists of what they knew. Her list of Baba Vira's lies. Her list of Polish words and their translations. She didn't plan on moving. She could scribble lists right here for as long as it took. She was really good at scribbling lists. Preparations. Back-up plans. Possibilities. The officer pushed breath out of his mouth in an exaggerated gesture.

"Do you have access to her banking information? If she continued to travel, there might be a record." The officer paused, checking his computer screen. Larissa closed her notebook and pushed it back into her purse past the aspirin and pocket-sized sewing kit. "Let me lead you to an area where you can wait."

"Where will my phone get reception?" Larissa forced herself to stand. "And can I fill out any paperwork you have now so everything will be set the second we hit twenty-four hours? If she doesn't have her medication...."

She let the line trail off to let him think of what it might mean. She needed to track down her sister who was probably off having her tarot cards read or learning how to gaze into a crystal ball.

"I'll see what I can do about the papers," he said, walking away from the wooden bench in the waiting area where he'd deposited her like a toy put away. *Lyalya*. Doll baby.

The white blank walls surrounded her here. She held up her cell phone. It had a signal.

Her cell service allowed her to call her credit card company, but there was no activity on the card she'd given her grandmother. She set up an alert to be notified the moment it was used. The officer returned with papers to fill out, promising to file them when the time had passed. She'd still call him to remind him, though. She wasn't sure he was old enough to remember.

Larissa walked out of the station toward the taxi the officer had called for her. There was no way to reach Ira except to find her too now. God, where was Ira? She imagined her sister's voice calling her name and turned around to scan the streets around her. But no one was there. Larissa was all alone. *Lyalya.* Her whole life she'd been trying so hard to lose that nickname, to become something more than a doll, empty of brains, empty of power.

She tried to look forward to the stories her grandmother would tell on the flight back about her adventures. There'd be a magical element to it all somehow, she knew. Becoming a Baba Yaga. Something heroic about saving the lives of the next generation.

Saving lives. Larissa thought of Annabelle. The girls were singing tonight. Annabelle would have another chance on stage.

"The Palace of Culture and Science, *proshu,*" she said to the taxi driver.

She had time to see Annabelle before she returned to Stefa's, before she started her second frantic search for her sister, before they all were found and they could all go home to Alex's tackle hugs.

Her heartbeat pulsed in her chest, and she needed to make sure Annabelle was all right.

The driver nodded, taking off as soon as her door closed.

In minutes, the giant palace appeared before them, even more angular and intimidating than she remembered it. Its miniature spires made it resemble a fortress while its countless columns made it a Greek revival sketched by a drunken hand. Too much vodka. Too much medivka. Between the columns and spikes reaching high up into the sky, dull rectangular office building windows stretched for stories. Stalin's gift to the Polish people had a bit of an identity crisis.

After she paid and jumped out of the cab, Larissa ran. The

faster she moved, the sooner she could get home. Anna and Alex would love this story, how she had to travel across the ocean to catch their great-baba in her attempted great escape. How Ira had tried to hide too. She ran like a character in one of their adventure books. If she had her trench coat, she would have whooshed. She had picked up clues in her notebook, met two giant mermaids, stormed a palace... It was bedtime fodder for years to come.

Once inside, she slowed her pace to a brisk walk under the ornate crystal chandeliers, walls of blocked glass, and posters showcasing upcoming performances.

When the girls and chaperones were not in their dressing room, someone pointed her backstage.

She crept into the appropriate badly marked door, entering the cavernous darkness with velvet curtains hanging from a ceiling so high she couldn't even make it out in the shadows. Stefa only handled the dances, not the songs. The girls were already on stage.

In the brightness leaking from the stage through the massive curtain panels, young voices called her attention. Larissa's feet carried her forward, her ballet flats designed for such silent places.

Their white puffy sleeved blouses, needlepoint-designed aprons, thick bead necklaces, and fabric headdresses accented with a golden thread caught every stage light and the attention of the huge, silent auditorium.

The girls stood in a semi-circle on stage, hands clasped in front of their chests while they swayed to the music that was just beginning. A single girl stepped forward. Annabelle. She walked up to the microphone placed center stage. A woodwind of some sort, a flute or a piccolo, sounded slowly, hauntingly. The girls added their voices as another instrument, their harmonizing notes filling the space around them. Annabelle opened her mouth, and Larissa took a step back.

The girl's young vibrato was practiced and refined. Her

Ukrainian accent was better than Larissa's.

Plyve Kacha Po Tysyni. Their singing teacher was making a statement. The old folksong had taken a new life mourning the dead of Kyiv's Maidan Square in 2014. A bold, kind of dangerous move. Larissa was glad Anna wasn't up there, having her name maybe put on list as a Ukrainian freedom fighter against pressures from present-day Russia. Sure, a recital in Poland was different from a recital in Ukraine, but they weren't that far apart.

The girls' voices joined together making the old folksong almost into a hymn, spreading itself into the air like incense in a church. Their small voices synchronized in an ethereal three-part harmony. Larissa shivered and clutched the edge of the huge velvet curtain at her side. Wordless vocalization, the pain of a mother, the pain of a nation.

> *Mother of mine, don't cry for me.*
> *You will cry for me in an evil hour;*
> *I don't know myself where I will die.*
> *I will perish in a strange land,*
> *And who will bear me to the grave?*
> *Foreign people will carry me out.*
> *Won't this be a grief to you, mother?*

She squeezed the curtain in her hand harder. Annabelle. Of all kids to sing these words, it had to be Annabelle. The footsteps that sounded behind her barely registered in her mind.

Annabelle's mother put her hand on Larissa's shoulder.

"Any word on your grandmother?" she whispered.

Larissa forced herself to swallow before shaking her head.

The girls took in a breath as one between lines of the song. Larissa took a deep breath with them, in through her nose, out through her mouth.

Then her phone vibrated against the insides of her purse.

25

Ira

Ira's ankle was slightly swollen, but her bright red toenails weren't even chipped. The sidewalk looked free of broken glass, so she slipped off her remaining shoe as well. A better look—more Bohemian, less clumsy tourist.

She walked on as gracefully as she could, trying not to wince, trying not to favor her good leg. She'd passed Chopin's museum and the mermaid. The familiar street of apartments greeted her. Panya Stefa's was somewhere just ahead.

"Lyalya?"

Ira's head jerked up. Panya Stefa stood alone on the cement block stoop of her apartment.

"Where's my sister?" Ira asked, hobbling toward the woman, then past her, into the apartment once more. The plastic dolls stared at her unblinking under their long lashes. Even the blond ones had the same dark eyelashes.

She realized Panya Stefa had been speaking rapidly, about Ira's limp, if she was okay, her missing shoe, but she was so tired. Ira collapsed onto the living room couch before turning to the woman.

"Your sister went to the police," Panya Stefa continued.

"They're arresting her already?" Ira smirked.

"What happened to shoes?" Stefa pressed as she came closer. "Oy, your foot!"

Ira's ankle was red but not noticeably puffy.

Stefa shifted the pillows that crowded the couch into a leaning tower of cushions for Ira to prop up her foot upon. The older woman moved herself to a different chair with an aged groan.

"It'll be fine by the morning. I've done worse drinking too much in stilettos."

Stefa hunched forward on her knees, trying to get a better look at the injury.

"I thought your sister would be back by now," she whispered, extending one finger and retracting it before contacting the skin.

Ira exhaled. A nearly empty plate sat on the coffee table beside her, a single slice of bread remained with a few sticks of *kabanos* sausage.

"Eat, Irena."

Ira complied without argument. The salty spiced sausage tasted like her childhood. She wanted to ask for more, but the phone rang and Stefa stood to answer it. The woman's shadow fell across the wall. Her silhouette was rotund but feminine, but her thin legs were like bones sticking out of her knee-length dressing gown. Ira closed her eyes and exhaled her *kabanos* breath through rounded lips.

"Irena."

Ira opened her eyes. Stefa held out the phone to her, and the shadow held out an object too—something to drop in a cauldron or to enchant with eternal life. Ira squeezed together her fist, hiding her short life-line.

"It's Lyalya ..." Stefa pressed, and the wheels in Ira's brain begin to move. Her sister. Their search. Where the hell was Larissa?

She pressed her ear to the plastic phone, noticing something sticky on the receiver. She nudged it with her fingers as Larissa talked, trying to determine what it was.

"We're going where in Slovakia?" she found herself saying.

Ira pressed the phone against her ear, not believing her sister's words—they were her words, her argument she'd been refining and rearranging the entire walk back to Stefa's apartment.

"Baba bought a train ticket this morning." Larissa rushed through the details that Ira didn't begin to absorb. She'd catch up later. The dolls around her stared at her with wide-open eyes. They wanted to befriend her. They definitely weren't her friends. One in the shadows of the hall had a chunk of plastic hacked out of its neck. That one, apparently, had once gone too far.

"Wait...what?"

"I bought both our tickets. Our train is the last one going to Slovakia tonight. We leave in two hours. Can you get to the station?"

After Ira hung up the phone, Stefa's eyes joined those of the dolls upon her.

"Apparently, we're going to Slovakia. Can I have a ride to the train station?" She explained what she could of her sister's discovery plus her own thoughts about Noncia.

"I have Noncia's address!" Stefa exclaimed, pushing herself up once again and disappearing into her bedroom. A closet door opened, and boxes seemed to slide around on shelves. "*Tak*," she continued upon reentering the room. "Spisska Nova Ves, Slovakia. Here is street number."

Ira took the envelope Stefa held out to her, with Noncia's handwriting clearly recording her return address on the corner. Wouldn't Larissa be impressed?

"And shoes? What happened to your shoes?"

As Ira told a simpler version of her story, minus the rushing tram and baba yaga shadow puppets, Stefa shook her head, sized up Ira's feet, then began getting the girls ready the best she could.

The bread that Stefa wrapped in foil was still warm. A shaped dove perched at the top of the loaf. Baba Vira used to make bread like that. Her grandmother's doves were always a bit less graceful, though. A bit bloated and crisped on the thin parts. Until this moment, Ira had thought that was the best that anyone could shape a bird from baked dough.

Stefa gathered more *kabanos* and a chunk of hard cheese, which she packaged with the bread in a bag on Ira's lap. Still reclined with her foot propped, Ira had given in to being still for as long as she was allowed. Stefa scolded her every time she attempted to move.

Finally, with, slightly oversized sandals on her feet, wedged into Stefa's little car with warm bread and cold meat, Ira watched Warsaw go by. The Vistula River cut a gray line along the city's edge. Its massive mermaid grew before her eyes as they sped closer—her shield and sword ready for a fight, her hair wind-blown, her exposed skin exuding the power of a siren. They cut past the curved wrought iron balconies, where no Baba Yaga shadows lingered on the building facades.

Old neighborhoods gave way to green spaces, thick trees, parks, and a sign for a zoo. Modern angles and glass-fronted storefronts were interrupted by the Palace of Culture and Science, its Gothic angularity mingling with vaulted arches and dull rectangular windows. Girls in folk costumes walked down its sidewalks with spurts of water from the fountains dancing in the air behind them.

The car jerked as it came to a stop. The train station stood before them.

"Go to your sister." Stefa squeezed Ira's arm and kissed her on her cheeks, left, right, left—always three times.

Ira nodded, thanked their old family friend, picked up the food and, grabbing both of their suitcases, stepped out onto the sidewalk.

The main terminal was a giant bubble—the ceiling so high, the room so long and wide, sunlight pouring in from every direction. Larissa sat on a bench waving with both arms, crossing them back and forth over her head as if she tried to land an airplane. Larissa's bulbous purse sat next to her.

"Why are you limping?" she called out as Ira came nearer. Larissa moved toward her, but hesitated, dropping a hand to her purse on the only available bench within sight. She peered around her cautiously, eyes narrowing, before jogging in Ira's direction while constantly looking back. The massive bag remained in her sight like a child too young to be unsupervised.

"I had a run in with a Baba Yaga."

"What?" Larissa moved to take the big package of food from her arms, and Ira let her. The thick and heavy smell of sourdough bread and meat sunk into her clothes. Stefa's poor car probably wouldn't be rid of it for days, though it might always smell like that. "I have a bench for us over here," Larissa continued when Ira didn't offer any more explanation. Heavy bag of food in hand, she took long strides back to her bag.

Ira followed behind, feet slipping slightly in Stefa's beaded sandals. They were actually beautiful, tiny colorful beads strung onto thin straps of braided leather. She would have felt guilty about taking them, but they were too perfect for regrets.

At the center of the massive terminal, potted trees and flowers nestled amid benches. Larissa's bench was at the precise middle. People hurried and rushed with bags over their shoulders. They stared down at phones. They stopped to examine screens of departures and arrivals. But in the middle, Larissa's face was calm and organized, her plans moving forward. This was the Larissa her sister knew. The people of the train station were nothing more than her marionettes, spinning, dancing, and darting in directions all around her.

Ira's ankle twinged as she stepped on it too heavily. She winced, and Larissa caught it, throwing her arms out as if preparing to catch her.

"I'm fine," she said through gritted teeth, finding her place on the bench beside her sister.

Blue digital kiosks stood around them, modernist sculptures in this unlikely garden space. Larissa nestled the package of food between them.

Across the hall, a massive billboard showcased a teenager with a partially-shaved head. He was leaping, singing, or playing some sort of sport—Ira couldn't tell. *Wolność Kultury, Kultura Wolności*, it said.

With their bags piled into a makeshift ottoman, Larissa

guided Ira's injured foot into an elevated position.

"You went shoe shopping?"

Ira thought about clarifying but didn't have the energy.

"Cute, huh?"

Larissa shook her head, shifting the bag of food onto her lap. She opened it slowly, like a present. Hunks of cheese, slices of thin *kabanos*, horseradish. She traced her fingers over the decorative dove at its top.

"Who knew a bird could be made out of bread dough so well?"

Ira could see the wheels turning in her sister's head. Her kitchen back home would be full of flocks of dough birds soon. Anna would be trained in their art like an apprentice. Poor girl.

Across the room, images of greasy food and frothy beverages argued for their attention, but Stefa's picnic won out over the "Golden Bites" from KFC and McDonalds' McCafe. Ira pursed her lips, trying to read the Polish words around the familiar signage.

"We still have about twenty minutes until our train. I already spoke to Greg, and he's booked us a hotel in a town called Spišská Nová Ves."

A hunk of sausage almost fell out of Ira's mouth. She blocked it with the back of her hand.

"What?"

"Spišská Nová Ves, Slovakia," Larissa repeated. She put down her piece of bread to fumble through her purse, pulling out a trifold pamphlet with a tiny train schedule and map of routes.

Ira chewed with a smile on her face.

Larissa took a dainty bite, not even spilling breadcrumbs. She chewed silently and swallowed, before pressing her perfectly filed fingernail to one of the lines on the map.

"The police gave me the idea to check my credit card purchases. Baba bought a ticket to Spišská Nová Ves with the card I gave her." She dabbed her mouth with a paper napkin, carefully, so as not to smudge her lipstick.

Ira nodded, taking another bite of the cheese.

"It's *Obman*."

"It might be."

When the sisters had been young children, in the days when their grandmother occasionally babysat for their parents to go out on dates in the city, Baba Vira had introduced a twisted form of hide-and-go-seek she called *Obman*. Deception. Someone would count to sixty, and the others would create a trail of misleading clues. Shifted blankets and pillows to make it look like someone hid under the bed. Opened doors to make it look like someone had left or entered a different room. Shadows of baba yagas always watching.

Their grandmother had been a master of clomping heavily up the stairs then silently tip-toeing down, sending the girls running the wrong direction once they reached sixty and opened their eyes.

"I thought the police weren't calling you back."

"I went there and told them she needed to be on her medications or she'd be delusional."

"You lied?"

Larissa dabbed again at the crumbs near her mouth then handed Ira another tiny folded napkin she had pulled from her purse. Folded. It had been folded inside her purse. Ira took it from her hands, wiping the crumbs on her lap onto the tiled floor.

"It wasn't a lie," Larissa answered, her voice soft. "Sane people don't play *Obman* across oceans."

Ira leaned over until her shoulder bumped her sister's. Then she bumped it again.

"Oh my god." She smirked. "Lyalya told a lie."

Larissa straightened her back, pulling away from Ira's shoulder. She folded her paper napkin, bending each of the corners inward collecting all of its crumbs within, not letting a single speck fall to the floor, before reaching into the bag for a piece of the sausage and a chunk of cheese. A static-filled voice interrupted over the station loudspeaker.

Larissa recrossed her legs at the ankle.

"You still have your passport, right?"

"I'm not one of your kids, Lyalya." But Ira patted her small purse all the same, feeling the angles of the thin rectangle inside. "Baba was always really good at *Obman*."

"We'll find her. She'll jump out from the shadows, cackling her head off, like she used to, saying she was watching us all along. Then we'll bring her home."

Ira raised her eyebrows, but she didn't answer. She wasn't convinced Baba Vira wanted to come home.

26

Vira (July 1941)

Vira's train dashed through the forest filled with darkness, past the wolves and bears and baba yagas. She put a hand to her heart. Lesya whispered of soldiers and gunfire, of the Ukrainian volunteers wearing old Czech uniforms dyed green, but Vira barely heard. Her fingertips reached for the stone necklace and lingered there on the bump of cloth it produced as it hid under her shirt. She traced her thin wedding ring with her other hand. No diamonds or sparkling gems, just yellow gold, almost as yellow as the sunflower fields that had hidden her first kiss with Dmytro ... her first kiss with Mykhail.

She wondered if the flowers had gone up in flames too.

The train station had been crowded, so many people leaving or fleeing or hiding away. There were no soldiers on this train, only women and children, the occasional old man—only the family members left behind.

Vira sat next to Lesya while her mother and the twins had the seats across the aisle. The twins had missed their nap. Their eyes were almost wild as they refused the dinner being offered to them, the rye bread and thinly sliced meat and cheese, pickles.

Two women in the row in front of them tightened their hands into fists and examined the wrinkled skin their clenched grip produced.

"Two children, see?" one said to the other. "That's what the Tsyhanka told me."

Vira shifted in her seat. The heel of her boot caught the

ripped seam of her dress. She hadn't thought to change. She hadn't thought to pack needles and thread.

"I've heard about that," Lesya whispered. "The gypsies say you can count the wrinkles around your pinkie's knuckle when you make a fist to see how many children you'll have."

"I don't think..." The words refused to escape Vira's lips. They choked her as if the ashes of their house and their fields filled her throat.

"I have three wrinkles." Lesya reached for her sister's limp hand in her lap. "Think I'll have three babies someday?"

Vira felt queasy at the thought of babies, of giving up her body for something else to grow inside of it. Everything was moving to fast. She hadn't even thought of the possibility of babies.

"Maybe they'll be Slovakian babies, Lyalya," she offered, swallowing.

Lesya's face fell back into the flat line she'd never worn before that day.

"Do you think all the Ukrainian boys will be gone?"

Vira looked down to her own hand and made a fist. Just one strong wrinkle stood out at her pinkie's largest knuckle, though a thin second wisp of a line might count as two.

The train whistle shrieked, and the brakes wailed. The entire car jerked, and Vira catapulted into the aisle, her elbow cracking into another passenger's shoulder. Her sister fell on top of her. The twins were flattened between their mother and the opposite window and yowled.

The train lights flickered and went out.

Lesya's warm breath panted in quick bursts. She didn't climb off her older sister, nor remove her knee from her side.

Outside, no electric lights shone. Tree branches moved in a choreographed dance with the glow of the moon, arms waving over their heads, swaying from side to side. Beams of flashlights cut into the darkness, passing by their train car.

"What happened?" Lesya whispered. Vira shifted herself,

removing her sister's knee from her ribcage.

Murmurs began at the end of the car as people pulled themselves up. A horse and wagon in the way of the tracks? Soldiers in these woods? A bombing in Košice. A baby wailed. The twins whined. The lights flickered back on, and a chunk of moist bread left Helena's hand and landed in Vira's lap.

"I'll find out."

Vira pushed herself off the aisle floor after coaxing Lesya back toward her seat.

"Where are you going?"

"The bathroom."

Lesya raised her eyebrows and pressed together her flatly lined lips. Vira almost stepped over the other fallen passengers but helped them up instead. Her torn dress would only be caught on their bags and flailing hands. She moved toward the front of the train car, toward the restroom, slowing her motion to eavesdrop.

"There were soldiers outside," someone whispered.

"German soldiers," someone else said.

"Where are our papers?"

"Where are our tickets?"

"Was there gunfire just before we were jarred?"

"Should we answer in German?"

Vira reached the bathroom compartment and pulled on the handle. It was unoccupied, but she paused in the aisle like it wasn't.

Outside the train, beams of light flashed through the woods over clean-shaven faces, over guns slung over backs. She leaned against the wall like she was impatient, but the angle allowed for a better view. Men's choppy voices barked orders at one another.

The traincar's door rattled and banged as it slid open a few feet from where she stood. Vira jerked herself back and nearly fell onto an elderly lady who sat next to the nearest window.

She whispered an apology but nestled herself into the empty

seat next to the woman just as three German soldiers entered their car. Their arm bands gave them away just like they had at home. Vira sat up taller and raised her chin. She didn't have a Baba Yaga mask face to scare them away like the old lady beside her.

A woman across the narrow aisle held the hand of a little boy who slept with his head on her lap. She hunched over and looked at the little boy's dark hair. Her body became rigid as the men took their steps closer and froze in the aisle at her side.

"Name?" one of the men shouted at her. "*Im'ya?*" he repeated in Ukrainian.

"Anne Fishbeyn."

"Where do you live?"

"We're going to Prešov."

"Where do you live?"

"We're meeting family who lives there."

"Where do you live?" The question came out as a growl now.

"Ternopyl."

The man looked over his shoulder to another soldier holding a stack of papers. The pages rustled in his hand in the otherwise silent train car. Someone nearby sneezed. Farther back, Halya begged for another pickle. The old lady beside Vira must have passed gas. A foul stink filled the air.

"Your husband was named Ilya?"

"*Tak*," the woman whispered. She still hadn't looked away from the sleeping boy in her lap.

The soldier nodded to those behind him and stepped out of the way as they grabbed the woman and the sleeping boy, who lurched awake with terrified rabbit eyes. She didn't struggle, but she didn't let go of the boy. She pulled him into her arms and hugged him ferociously even as she was prodded and pulled out of the car.

"And you, fräulein?" the officer said in German to Vira. She had known he was still there but hadn't been able to look away from the woman and the rabbit-eyed boy. The stench of human gas made her want to hold her nose.

"Schönen Tag, Offizier," she responded in crisp German. Her cheeks were pink. Her eyes were a greenish-blue. Her dark blond hair was neatly pinned back, Lesya's work after they had already boarded the train. She let the pungent air fill her lungs as she raised her chin higher.

"Ah, schönen tag, schöne Mädchen." His stiff countenance relaxed as he continued in German. She forced herself to smile as she nodded. Her skin warmed. Her heartbeat's every pulse tried to force a tremor in her calmly collected hands in her lap. When he finished, he laughed, and she joined him. She pulled her ticket from her dress pocket.

"Ich fahre nach... Spišská Nová Ves," she said, trying to spit out the words as smoothly as the soldier had. The eyes of the other passengers were on her, and she knew it. She put her left hand to the invisible bump of the stone under the fabric of her blouse. She didn't know whether it was the stone or the protection of her wedding ring that gave her strength.

"Ah, gnädige frau, entschuldigen sie mir bitte." He bowed his head to her and moved on to the next row of passengers.

The old lady beside her patted her leg approvingly as Vira closed her eyes and tightened her hold on the stone. The officer had assumed they were together. She didn't even know why she'd done it. Her breaths escaped her lips more rapidly as the soldier moved farther back toward her family.

She didn't open her eyes until the soldier exited the back of the train car. Helena whined for another pickle.

The old lady beside her patted her leg again. She took up Vira's young hand in her veined and spotted grasp and kissed it. Far behind them, Lesya coughed and whistled a secret bird call they'd made up when they'd been younger.

Vira whistled back, but she didn't dare to move.

27

Larissa

Their compartment held six red fabric seats—three across from three—and the sisters had chosen their sides and drawn an unspoken, imaginary line not to cross out of habit. Their bags perched on their respective borders. Larissa's crossed legs angled out but not too far. Ira repositioned her sister's phone cord that had strayed too much in the wrong direction.

Larissa had pulled out her bobby pins, as if she really would sleep, but now her hair kept falling in her eyes. She pushed it back behind her ears again, as if this would help her see the darkened scenes their train rushed by.

The rails hummed underneath her, a whisper that she was getting farther and farther away from home. The faint lights of small villages blinked as they passed them by. Stone houses immersed in trees. Shadows of wild forests. Car lights at railroad crossings.

Back home, her kids were probably having their afternoon snacks. Bunny crackers and squares of cheddar cheese. Greg probably wouldn't have the bunnies hop onto their plates. She hoped he wasn't coming up with exciting plans for every moment of their free time. Kids needed unscheduled time, after all. Time for nothing was what shaped them into thinkers, into problem solvers, into observant members of society. Boredom was essential for....

"Get some sleep, Lyalya."

Larissa pushed back her hair again.

"I don't want to miss our stop," she answered.

169

In the darkness, she swore she could see her sister rolling her eyes.

"Set an alarm on your phone. This is the longest train of the trip."

Larissa blew air from her lips then inhaled through her nose. The air was stagnant and dusty. She wanted to fling open the glass doors of their compartment but didn't know if that would be an invitation for others to come inside. She didn't know train etiquette. Or European travel etiquette. She lay down and nuzzled deep into her coat that she had folded into a pillow. The best tickets she could find gave them two stops on the way to Spišská Nová Ves. She wondered if she should have picked the other route. It would have taken longer, but it only had one train change. No, faster was better. She knew it was better. She'd sleep on their flight home. Tomorrow afternoon maybe.

Would they fly out of Bratislava? Wasn't that the capitol of Slovakia? Were they going anywhere close to Bratislava? Larissa crossed her arms in front of her but didn't close her eyes.

Outside, branches reached toward the train, extending their bony fingers. Across the compartment from her, sprawled across the three seats into her own make-shift bed, Ira sighed.

"Once upon a time," her younger sister started, "a king had three sons."

"I don't need a bedtime story, Ira."

"Apparently, you do."

A pair of passengers walked down the aisle outside their compartment, pausing to peer inside the glass sliding doors.

"Should we make room for them?"

"You reserved this for us."

"I reserved two seats."

Ira only answered by stretching her arms out over her head, making sure her thin body took up the entirety of her side. Larissa resettled, reluctantly laying down her head.

"The king decided that it was time that his sons should marry," Ira continued, extending one arm into the space between them like a breach of neutral territory. Larissa wasn't sure if the action was hostile. "So he told them each to shoot an arrow into the air, and wherever it landed, each would find his bride."

Larissa decided to ignore Ira's arm and pulled her coat over herself as a blanket.

"The first son shot his arrow high into the air, and it landed at the door to a merchant's shop. The merchant had a beautiful daughter who was giddy once she figured out no one was trying to kill her family and that she would get to marry a prince.

"The second prince shot his arrow, and it landed somewhere else with a beautiful maiden—a palace or a convent or something—and he too took an enchanting bride."

"A convent?"

Ira nodded in the darkness. She retracted her trespassing arm.

"It's how the story goes, Lyalya."

"Today's version," Larissa mumbled, but she let her sister continue.

"The youngest prince, Prince Ivan, took his turn and shot his arrow into the air, but this arrow got caught by the wind and fell into the middle of a swamp, sticking into a lily pad or something next to a slimy green frog. His brothers laughed at him, and he tried to pull out another arrow, but they all agreed that his destiny had brought him to marry the frog."

Larissa caught herself smiling at the familiar story. Alex had once said he'd be okay marrying a frog. He always thought youngest prince was the luckiest one.

She shifted the coat up higher across her shoulders against the chill of the train.

"They had a beautiful triple ceremony with the three princes marrying their newly found brides—the merchant's daughter blushing, the girl from the convent crossing herself repeatedly, and the frog croaking on some swanky velvet pillow that it was carried in on," Ira continued. Her own eyes closed as she spoke. "After the marriages, the king wanted to see the skills of his three new daughters-in-law, so he asked each of the three to bake a loaf of bread and weave a rug. Prince Ivan panicked, because he knew his frog couldn't bake any bread or weave a rug, but his little wife just croaked at him and asked him why he was so sad.

"Why the fact that the frog was now talking to him didn't freak him out, I have no idea, but when he explained what the king had asked of her, the little frog just croaked again, told him not to worry, and told him to go to sleep. Weirdly obedient to the weird-talking frog, he did, and the frog stepped out of the frog-skin to become a beautiful maiden. She called out the window, 'Nurses and cooks, come to me and bake a loaf just like those I used to eat in my father's palace, and make me a rug with threads of gold like I used to walk upon.' And these magical spirits came to her and helped her make the most delicious loaf of bread and fanciest rug."

Ira's voice was so much softer and kinder when she was telling stories. Larissa liked this Ira perhaps the best of all of her sister's faces. She allowed her eyes to close and for her body to relax into the vibration of the train.

"The king was so happy with the three wives that he requested that each of them be presented to the kingdom at a ball," Ira continued. "But Prince Ivan didn't want to be presented with his frog bride. He knew the whole kingdom would laugh at him. But the talking frog bride told him to wait for her, that she would get ready and meet him before the ball.

"Once she was alone, she stepped out of her frog-skin and dressed herself in the most beautiful gown, and when Prince Ivan came to retrieve her, he gasped at the beauty who confirmed that she was indeed his frog wife. At the ball, everyone gaped of Prince Ivan's beautiful bride."

When Ira paused, Larissa cracked open her eyes. The couple who had walked by their compartment before was back again, standing just outside. They were young travelers, college-aged maybe.

"We have room," Larissa whispered. "We should shift to share this compartment."

"They'll find some other place."

Both sisters watched the aisle outside of their compartment's sliding door, barely lit by tiny lights in the base of the walls. The girl pointed in one direction before walking that way. The boy followed behind.

Larissa took a deep breath and brushed her hair behind her ear.

"So this is my favorite part," said Ira. "During dinner, the frog who wasn't a frog anymore put chicken bones into one sleeve of her dress and she poured red wine into the other, and then later, as she danced with Ivan, she poured out the red wine which became a smooth lake with a soft wind blowing over it to cool the guests. She poured out the chicken bones which became beautiful swans that settled on the water.

"The other wives wanted to amaze the guests too, so they filled their own sleeves with chicken bones and wine, but when they danced, the bones flew out to poke people's eyes and the red wine spilled all over them and made a mess of the dance floor.

"During all of this, Prince Ivan was so enchanted by his beautiful bride that he snuck back to his quarters, found the frog-skin, and burned it. But at the end of the party, when his frog bride discovered what he'd done, she cried, explaining that it was a curse put upon her by Koschei the Deathless, and that she had only to wear it a short time more before they could have lived happily ever after together. But now, she was forced to return to Kostshei's Palace, where she would become his prisoner."

A bang in the hallway interrupted the story. A heavy shoe against the glass. The couple sat in the hallway outside their compartment.

"Prince Ivan sought her out, searching deep into the woods, but he couldn't find her."

Larissa didn't know how her sister could be so good at ignoring people outside her own skin. She shifted her weight as Ira continued.

"When he found Baba Yaga, she already knew what had happened and told him how to find his bride and how to rescue her by...."

The shoe kicked the glass door again. Larissa sat up to free up the two seats by her side.

Her sister groaned just before their compartment door slid open.

Larissa smiled tiredly but gestured to the two seats. The boy and girl nodded in return, falling into the two other seats on Larissa's side. The boy extended his long legs across the compartment, resting his feet next to Ira's on the opposite side. Larissa willed her sister not to growl.

"I never got why the old witch helped him," Larissa whispered, trying to distract her.

"Because she's so much more than just a witch. She keeps kids in line, making sure they grow up right, and she helps those who deserve it. If they are truly good. If they are brave. If they are smart. She's fierce but not always bad."

The couple leaned against each other and whispered.

"Eating people is kind of bad." Larissa pulled her purse into her lap and moved over another inch so her hips didn't have to touch her new neighbor's.

"People are more complex than you think, Lyalya."

The couple talked in Polish, whispers growing absentmindedly louder, the oblivious chatter of early-twenty-somethings. Apparently that mannerism crossed borders. Larissa wished they were a bit quieter so she could sleep, but she knew she wouldn't be able to sleep with strangers next to her. Maybe she shouldn't have made space for them.

She crossed her arms tighter over her chest, leaning her head back against her seat, pulling her coat higher over her, before extending her legs across the imaginary line on the compartment floor. She was sharing her space. Ira would have to share hers too.

The couple laughed harder. Larissa could understand most of what they were saying. She wished she couldn't. It would be better if she couldn't. They were making fun of the two Americans, wondering whether the rich one was kind to give up the seats or just scared of them. She looked scared, they said. They laughed again.

The rich one. The words ran over her, feeling false. But Larissa remembered the massive diamond on her hand. It caught the few lights that shone in the window. She hadn't even considered leaving it at home.

"Scared as mouse." She felt the blood rush through her body. Her skin prickled, but she didn't move. She didn't dare on the train, in the dark, in their tiny compartment, where the moonlight twisted its inhabitants' features into childhood playground nightmares.

The boy stretched out his legs, this time tapping into Ira's feet. Even in the blackness, Larissa saw the growl rising in her sister's belly.

"*Proshu,*" Ira said, startling them with her language choice, her voice through gritted teeth. "*Ya khochu spaty. Budte tykho.*"

Larissa suppressed a laugh. Ira had never been so polite, nor had she ever been the one to use those words. I want to go to sleep. Please be quiet.

"And get your damn feet off me," she added, jerking herself up to a sitting position. "Or we'll see who's as scared as *mysh.*"

The couple shifted and met each other's eyes. The boy lowered his feet.

Outside their windows, streetlights blinked as they passed them by. Ira's hair was full of static. Her soft nose and chin had turned razor-sharp in the shadows. She narrowed her eyes that were almost lost in the crevasses of her face. Her barely parted lips revealed teeth that reflected the moonlight. She leaned forward, elbows on her knees.

A high-pitched whine joined the hum of the rails as the train slowed. The couple used that momentum to push to their feet. They linked hands.

They retreated silently, sliding open and shut the compartment door without looking back.

Ira closed her eyes, again throwing her arms over her head.

"Lie down and stretch out, Lyalya. If you don't take up space in your world, someone else will take it from you."

Moving herself to put her purse with its flashlight, medical kit, and talismans from her kids under her head, Larissa stretched herself out obediently. She fought the urge to curl herself up tightly. She wished the compartment had a lock.

"Your alarm set?"

Larissa nodded.

"Okay." Ira rolled over on her bed of red fabric seats, turning her back toward her sister. Larissa hugged her lumpy purse pillow and took a deep breath, forcing herself to close her eyes.

"And with Baba Yaga's help, Prince Ivan found the source of Koschei the Deathless's power under a giant oak, inside a cave, inside a hare, inside a duck, inside an egg, and once he stole it, his beautiful bride was freed, and he held the reign over Koschei's vast kingdom."

The train had come to a stop, and the lights of the new station glared inside their window.

"How did Baba do this?" Larissa whispered to her sister. Her jacket was pulled up over her again, but she still was cold.

"She's got guts, Lyalya." Ira's voice was muffled by the seatback she talked into. "She's where we get them from."

"You maybe." She swallowed. Was her throat getting scratchy? She didn't have time for getting sick.

"Both of us." Without turning around, Ira threw an empty water bottle at her sister but it was far from on target. Larissa guessed that was on purpose. "Go to sleep."

28

Ira

The smell of croissants and mustard confused her exhausted senses as Ira followed her sister into the main area of the small train station. Outside, the world was still dark. She was sleep-walking, her senses confused by every stimulation, the jetlag hitting her harder than she expected. She had fallen asleep only to wake to Larissa's jarring alarm that sounded a full twenty minutes before their arrival. Ira's head felt like she'd been drinking. Her body's dull motions seemed disconnected.

"Let's wait outside on the right platform," Larissa said, walking toward the station doors, away from the wooden benches that were long enough for them to prop up their legs, to rest their heads, to put down their bags and close their eyes for the time they had before their next train.

"Here's fine, Lyalya."

"It's too smoky in here."

Ira ignored her sister, letting her body crumple onto the nearest bench, tucked into the shadows of a corner. She peeled her bag off her shoulder and dropped it at her side. For a moment she wondered if she had been drunk with Stefa and had forgotten. When she closed her eyes, the world spun around her, pulling her toward sleep, seducing her toward a blanket of mindless darkness.

"Did you hear me?"

"No," Ira answered. She cracked her eyes open. Streetlights outside illuminated the stained-glass scenes above the humble doors. Painted people gathered in traditional peasant dress with chickens, geese, and sheep by their feet. A man held an accordion outstretched. Children danced around a pole strung with colorful ribbons. The skin tones varied from pale to various darker shades. Were the scenes in glass capturing the Roma people celebrating something with the Slovakians?

She let her eyes fall shut, but the characters in the glass stuck in her muddled mind. Ira always guessed Baba Vira had had a Roma lover during the war, someone who'd taught her about Sight and palm reading—someone Noncia probably knew all about. There were so many stories Ira knew she'd never heard. Baba Vira had fled to Czechoslovakia during the war years. She had fled there with Noncia. Who else had she escaped with then? Who else had she escaped with now?

Someone slouched down on the bench buttressed up against her own, and she appreciated the camaraderie. She leaned on her bag turned pillow, and the other passenger did the same in sleepy symmetry. She could smell him, his exhaustion and his body odor. His sweat mingled with the smell of the dirt and maybe fertilizer. She imaged throwing her hands back and catching his, uniting in their resolution to not move a single step more.

"Our train was late, so we only have twenty minutes here," Larissa pressed. She stood over her sister, shifting her weight back and forth. Her two bags were slung on her shoulders, and her rolling suitcase pulled up beside her like a dog told to heel. Her sister was the type who would train her suitcase. It made sense.

"Twenty minutes, sure."

She stretched out her legs as Larissa took a single step toward the door, her suitcase rolling obediently by her side. Larissa examined every face that walked by, every shadowy corner, every exit.

She coughed.

"This is too much. I'm going outside."

"Don't let Baba Yaga get you." Ira didn't see Larissa's glare, but she sensed it through her closed eyelids.

Her sister's footfalls became fainter as she walked away. The station became surprisingly silent, but it was the middle of the night. The man on the other side of the bench cleared his throat behind her. She reached her hands above her in a stretch, yawning as she bent her elbows down, tracing the bag behind her head. Her hair had splayed across it, its loose tendrils falling in every direction.

She opened her eyes to confirm that Larissa had gone but pressed them shut again to slow the dizziness. Her head pulsed. Even a few minutes of sleep would help.

Fingers brushed against her own, interlocking with her languid hand.

"Mmmmm," she voiced, just barely louder than the dream she was starting to have.

A deeper voice answered, but she didn't really hear it. The hand entangled with her own squeezed softly, tenderly, tracing the skin of her fingers with its thumb. The big hand was thick and meaty. The man on the other side of the bench shifted, and the wood creaked.

She blinked and saw the stained-glass peasants looking down over her, smiling as they danced, smiling as they delivered their loaves of bread to their neighbors. Her eyelids fell again when the stranger's hand released her own, and sleep washed over her body in waves. She didn't want to fight it, so she didn't try.

A deep, scratchy voice sounded in her ear, as her imagination took over her reality. Dancing girls, flowers in their hair, dancing men kicking their feet high, jumping and flipping in acrobatic feats. A hand touched her cheek as the strange voice sounded again. Not English or Ukrainian. The words were something thick that filled the mouth of the speaker.

The hand traced down her cheek to the side of her neck, brushing her hair aside on her shoulders to feel its way down the top of her arm, moving to her right breast, cupping it, squeezing it, kneading it like dough.

"Mmmmm..." she voiced again sleepily, her dreamy mind on the Ukrainian boys of Baba Vira's tales, the men who courted by dancing, by song, by poetry, the men who bravely marched off to war.

A second hand moved across her stomach and down toward her navel before tracing up to her other breast. A bearded faced pressed into the skin exposed in the dip of her deep v-neck shirt.

The world spun. She danced. She was being eyed by a man. Her head ached but she twirled, ribbons extending from the flowered headdress in her hair. The stranger came closer, taking her hand, intertwining his thick fingers with her own.

They reclined in a field of sunflowers, his eyes full of love, his hands full of mischief, and she let him play with her body. She arched her back and leaned into his touch.

The man's hands were calloused at the fingertips. He was a musician, a guitarist.

But the words he whispered into her skin weren't Ukrainian. They weren't what she imagined the Roma language to be. A hand rubbed down her side, fingers tracing into the waistline of her jeans. Jeans weren't right in this dream.

Ira twitched, tripping over a fallen sunflower stalk and jerking out of her own head. Fast breaths warmed the skin on her neck. A strong hand kneaded her breast. This wasn't right. The man's face was out of focus. She wanted to go back to the dream, to the guitar-playing boy. She wanted to give herself to him. She had been ready to give herself to him. Ira's vision blurred, and she pressed her eyes shut, looking for that dream, for that field of sunflowers. But it was gone. And a heaving stranger was in its place. The stranger was real.

The man looked at her barely open eyes, his hand full of her breast, his mouth open against her skin, his chin pulling down the neckline of her shirt, exposing the lace of her bra underneath. He tried to shift away the soft fabric with his nose and then his teeth. His second hand pulled against her jeans.

Her body jerked again, arms pushing against the shoulders of this man with his smells of sickening manure. He only retreated lower on her body, not giving up the hand on her breast, but moving his face past her navel, toward the button of her jeans now undone.

"Stop," she pushed at him with her leg. "Stop!" she said a bit more urgently, realizing there was no one within earshot in this darkened section of the station.

He mumbled something to her, but the language was wrong, too wrong.

"Shhhh..." he said. He shifted to move his body on top of hers, one hand at his pants and one awkward leg hanging off the side of the bench, supporting most of his weight.

She raised her leg just slightly to come in contact with his crotch. He groaned at her motion, as if she was teasing him.

"Hell no." She raised her leg again more forcefully, connecting her knee with its intended target.

He rolled off her onto the floor, and she stood fast, grabbing her bags, running under the stained-glass peasants and their dance, away from their music, away from the man. Larissa had gone outside to wait on the platform, hadn't she? What kind of mother hen was she to abandon Ira?

Outside, the nearly full moon shone down on her. Cutting around the corner toward the tracks, she bumped into an old woman who turned to scowl at her. Her hair was as stiff and as wild as straw. The skin beneath her neck sagged, a waddle to match her chicken bone legs that poked out from her long black coat. Her fingers reached out like wrinkly twigs. Her eyes were swathed in wrinkles. Her nose came to a point so sharp it was an accusatory finger.

The woman shrieked words at Ira so fast and plentiful, but they were in a language she couldn't comprehend. Maybe they matched the language of the stranger inside. Or maybe they were something else, something more medieval, more connected with the moon and a magic hut and mortar and pestle that she rode through the sky.

Ira's entire body shuddered, but her feet wouldn't move. They woman shrieked something else at her, waving her twiggy hands.

When a hand rested on Ira's shoulder, she flinched to run away. Larissa tightened her hold.

"*Ospravedl te nás,*" she said to the yelling woman, wearing the polished expression reserved for smoothing over minor calamities. Dear God, she was acting like she was in a PTA meeting. But what had she just said? Was it something in the woman's own language? Did Larissa know the language of witches? Was she still dreaming? Larissa yanked her sister's arm, pulling her away, forcing her feet to move.

Ira didn't answer. She couldn't match her sister's composure. Was it her heartbeat or the rumble of the approaching train vibrating her core? The ground shook under her feet. Where was the man with his beard and his heavy breathing?

"Our train's pulling in, Ira," Larissa added. "Are you okay?"

Ira nodded. The thunder was the train. Its engine lights rumbled toward them. She needed to get on it and away as quickly as possible. Would that man be on this train? The platform only held a few people. The witch had walked away. The bearded stranger wasn't in sight.

"We'll be in Spišská Nová Ves just after dawn." Larissa picked up both of their bags, not taking her eyes off her sister. And then we'll find Baba, okay?" Larissa looked down to the tracks, letting go of her sister's eyes. "She was always good at *Obman*," she said as the train screeched to a stop in front of them, the wind blowing back the sisters' hair. "She loved to scare us, but she always let us find her."

Hiding from the moon and the man and the witch, Ira ran onto the train as fast as she could. Being found was the last thing she wanted. Her body shuddered. As the cool air of the train compartment hit her, for the first time, she wondered what her grandmother was running away from.

29

Vira (August 1941)

The nesting dolls sat on the windowsill overlooking the thin park that stretched for blocks in the middle of the small Czechoslovakian town. Vira next to their mother, Lesya next to Vira, Helena next to Lesya, Halya next to Helena. Helena held a favorite doll. Halya held a cookie. Lesya held a braided loaf of bread. Vira held a Baba Yaga mask.

Their mother's matryoshka had tiny sunflowers woven into her hair. Vira stared at those sunflowers every single day. There were no sunflowers in this town. Sunflowers would give it some life. Sunflowers in the green park with its brick walkways weaving between the trees, sunflowers tied to the black metal lampposts, sunflowers at the café with its sculpted cement arches underneath their small one-bedroom apartment. Someone their father once knew let them use the apartment, but Vira had never cared to ask more about it.

Groans from the building's stairs seeped under their door. Vira straightened her posture and moved away from the nesting dolls. She tucked her stone necklace under the neckline of her blouse and twirled her wedding band as the twins played on the thin rug.

They had turned three last week. Vira had been sure they wouldn't be in this place for so long—nearly two months now. Summer showed the first signs of fading into fall. The cool air crept into the apartment at night when they forgot to latch every shutter. There were no glass windows here like home. They'd left this front window open last night, as if allowing the matryoshka the opportunity for their escape, rolling off the windowsill to the slanted rooftop, bumping their way past the chiseled cornices and the weathered frieze, sliding down a waterspout and fleeing into the green park beyond, a park that would feel like the expansive fields of home to such little dolls. Maybe a bird would pick one up, and holding the painted wood in its beak, simply fly far, far away.

"I have letters." Vira's mother said instead of hello. "*Proshu*, help me with these things." Her arms were heavy with food from the market—potatoes, onions, flour, and eggs.

"From Tato?" Lesya asked, coming out of the small bedroom, a rag tied around her hair. She had been doing their ironing plus the tablecloths for the café. The steam of the heavy metal iron had moistened her face. She put a hand to her wrist self-consciously as she spoke, covering up the burn she had given herself the week before when Halya had hugged her by surprise from under the ironing table.

"Not this time, Lesya, but one from Panya Darka, who said that our bees found a home in her barn. They stung her cat, and—"

"Anything about Uncle Oleh?" Vira stood and approached, wanting to tear the letters from her hands, her mother spoke so slowly. Everything about this place moved slowly—the people, the words, the wind.

"No." Her mother's thin lips puckered before she pretended to spit three times over her shoulder after the mention of her husband's brother. She dropped the potatoes into a wooden bowl, crashing them down like missiles, before squeezing her long fingers together, a mimic of a child in deep prayer. "And nothing yet from Mykhail, but I'm sure you'll hear something from him soon." These last words became almost melodic, the familiar refrain, as if trying to get the song of him into Vira's head.

There hadn't yet been a letter from Mykhail. They said the Ukrainian volunteers weren't just protecting their own people and land anymore. They'd become the human shields to the Germans. She'd heard it just the other day from the butcher. The Nazis sent the Ukrainian volunteers to the front lines of worst battles or to the work camps if they refused go—the camps where her Uncle Oleh was imprisoned, where they kept threatening to send her father.

"Panya Darka said the cat fought the bees with its claws and teeth. And in the end, it was as swollen as old Panya Vanda. Do you remember Panya Vanda?"

Vira put a hand to her brow. She took two steps back toward her chair by the window, heel, toe, heel, toe. There were no red boots in this place, no flowers blooming to string through the braid twisted over the crown of her head. The open window let in a drowsy breeze that combed through the few loose wisps of her long hair. She didn't care about the stung cat. She hoped it died and the bees at least had a victory.

Their house had been destroyed too, turned to ash like the sunflowers beyond.

"And at the market, I heard there's people making camps on the outskirts of town now. They're in the fields and in the woods, living in caves and trees. People not lucky enough to have good housing." Her mother narrowed her eyes at Vira.

"I doubt they're living in trees." Vira reached up to tuck the loose hairs back into her braid.

Lesya untied the scarf around her head and ran her fingers through her once-shiny hair. It had become drab in this place.

Somewhere in the back of Vira's mind, worries for Dmytro and Noncia tried to surface, but they were obstructed by a barrier of death and blood and fire and the dust that rested over their new home. If it could be called a home. She knew she didn't have one anymore.

Their mother pulled the last of the food out of her bags. She had forgotten the steamed buns, the *parené buchty*, and the twins' whining began. The one pleasure of this place, they said. Lesya swooped up Helena, the louder of the two. Still on the floor, Halya cried.

"I'll get them." Vira patted the twins on the head as she moved toward the door. Her mother scowled but handed her a change-purse.

"Only the *parené buchty*, Vira." The Slovakian syllables were too heavy in her mother's mouth, spilling out with a disgust Vira almost thought was directed at her.

"Only the *parené buchty*," Vira repeated, knowing that the foreign sounds were truer on her own tongue. She lifted her chin and slipped out the door, down the creaky steps, past the afternoon patrons of the café below their small apartment, and across the cobblestone road into the grassy park.

Her boots were worn and tired, but they still carried her where she needed to go. Wood-smoke and something else from the café filled the air. Lentils maybe or beans. Her nose was still learning the scents of this place. She couldn't wander in this town as she wanted to. She couldn't escape to hide in the sun-flowers or to lean against a hive of bees.

Vira closed her eyes and tried to remember that feeling, the hum that swept up her entire body. The vibration to her core. The memory connected itself with Mykhail, like he was a character in a story she once read. A face she'd seen a picture of once. A man she'd heard of but never really known.

On the other side of the thin park, a guitar played. A mustached man moved one hand over the neck of the instrument, while the other plucked the strings faster than anything she'd heard in months. The rhythm matched her heartbeat and quickened breath. The frantic pace brought heat to her skin.

Her limbs moved, not in a dance, but in a run.

30

Larissa

Larissa cracked open her eyes as the sun rose over the mountains outside their train. Snow-capped summits, flowering fields below covered in yellow buds, a mountain lake so still it reflected the towering peaks above. Was that a deer drinking water at its side? Larissa blinked to make sure she wasn't dreaming a Walt Disney-inspired dream.

"They call it Slovak Paradise, right?" Ira stood up and stretched her legs, sighing dramatically, clearly happy her sister had finally opened her eyes. She crossed the compartment and slid open the glass door to the aisle of the train. The view was better on that side.

Larissa grabbed her purse and fumbled through the face powder, lipstick, and hand-sanitizer until she found her cell phone. She put it on video as she stepped to her sister's side, catching the long shadows of the sunrise falling over the patches of forests, bloom-filled fields, and mountains so majestic they looked like they'd been painted by a hand far more skilled than her own that specialized in stick figures and cartoon butterflies.

"Anna and Alex," she whispered into her phone as the video continued, "you're still sleeping, cuddled up with Mama Kitty and Max the Monkey, but this morning, I woke up inside a fairy tale. I think every bedtime story I ever told you takes place here." She knew she would miss her kids, but this was absurd. Her voice cracked. Larissa took a deep breath in through her mouth and out through her nose. "Auntie Ira and I are on our way to a little town in Slovakia called Spišská Nová Ves. We think your great-baba is playing a great game of hide-and-go-seek, but you know what?" She spoke with a twinkle in her voice that she forced into place. "We're going to catch her. Then we're going to come right home to you."

Ira pulled on her sister's hand to turn the camera on herself.

Her hair stood askew. Her shirt was rumpled. Lord, she wasn't even wearing a bra. "Be good, little buggers."

She reached out and turned the camera on Larissa. "They'll want to see you," she whispered, and Larissa brushed her messy hair behind her ears, blinked repeatedly, and wished she had a better way to send her love across six time zones.

"I love you kids so much."

Ira nodded and ended the video.

"Was that so hard?"

"I look like...."

"Like you've been sleeping on a train? Sure. But your kids won't care."

The rails hummed and rattled underneath them, slowing as they went into a turn. The woods were dense at the base of the mountains, thick with knots of branches and shadows. Baba Vira had told stories about hiding in the forest. Was she a child? Was it during the war? Why hadn't she paid attention?

Larissa looked at her watch. If time-tables were to be trusted, they were nearly there. Not that they were to be trusted. She was pretty sure they had gone in the reverse direction for a portion of their ride. She crossed back to her bag, retrieved a brush and a tiny mirror. Yikes, she looked ghastly. Ira was probably right that the kids wouldn't care, but Greg would see that.

"When we get to our station, we need to find a map," she said, zipping and unzipping pockets in her bag. "I think we can walk to our hotel to drop off our bags. And we need to find an internet café if I don't have a signal so I can send Greg that video. Maybe we can get breakfast there too." Ira didn't answer, still entranced by the view outside. "I have the number of the local police station, though I don't know if they speak English. Or Ukrainian...."

Their train reduced speed again. They were entering the outskirts of a small town. Small solid houses in yellows, reds, and browns—painted shutters, ceramic tile roofs, red geraniums in window-boxes. No graffiti marred the old beauty of this place. She closed her makeup case and slid it back into her bag.

"How close are we to Ukraine here, Lyalya?"

"I don't know exactly. A few hours, I think."

"From where Baba grew up?"

"She grew up in the far west of Ukraine." She brushed her hair behind her ears and ran a finger underneath both eyes to tidy up any stray eyeliner. "Galicia was where the independence movement was rooted, where they had two weeks of Ukrainian independence just before Germany took over during World War II, Stefa told me." She pressed her lips together and looked back out the window. "I didn't know that. Did you?"

Ira shook her head.

An announcement over the train loudspeaker was unintelligible except for what sounded like "Spišská Nová Ves."

"I think we're here." Larissa crossed her ankles below her, with her purse in her lap and her bag at her side, waiting for them to come to a complete stop.

Ira wove her fingers through her hair, fastening it into a messy braid as she stood, bracing herself on their compartment door.

When they exited the train, Larissa went straight for the map inside the small station. No familiar star said, "You Are Here." Or maybe she just couldn't find it. A web of lines ran over peach rectangles and green circles. Solid lines, broken lines, dotted lines. There were numbered markers she couldn't decode. Their hotel was there somewhere. Baba Vira was there somewhere. Maybe Waldo was even hiding there with his books and his binoculars, his walking stick and his striped-shirt-wearing dog Woof.

Ira hovered by her side, watching other travelers come and go. She shifted her feet back and forth, and her new leather sandals squeaked with the movement. She stayed oddly close.

"How's your ankle?"

"What?" She looked down to her feet. Her body shivered. Her hands tapped her thighs, speeding up whenever anyone else neared them. Larissa lowered her eyebrows. "Oh, feeling okay." Ira stilled her body and balled her fists together when her sister stared at her hands.

"Are you up for walking or should we call a cab?"

Larissa didn't care about her sister's drama right now. She traced her finger on the glass covering the map. She thought she found their station. And if that were the case, their hotel should be only a few blocks away. Yes, she found the right street. So they had to walk three blocks, turn left and walk two more.

Outside the window, cars parked on the street. Most people were on foot. A few on bikes.

"I can walk." Ira said, moving toward the doors, waiting for Larissa before she swung the door open.

They walked quickly across the street, dodging the few cars leaving the station. When Ira froze at the curb, Larissa reached back to grab her arm and pull her onward. She was ready to drop their bags at their hotel, connect with the police....

Then she noticed it too, a bright yellow sunflower tied to the rusting silver bike rack. The ribbon that held it in place was bright blue with a pattern of golden tryzubs—ancient tridents, representations of the trinity, symbols of Ukrainian identity.

Ira untied the flower and twirled the stem in her fingers.

"Baba," Larissa whispered. The song of Stefa's girls on stage in Warsaw filled her mind, the haunting harmonies, the rebellious Ukrainian pride.

"She's not planning on being some revolutionary in Ukrainian politics, right?" Ira voiced Larissa's thoughts before she could get them to her mouth. "That's too crazy, even for Baba, right?"

Ira lifted her eyebrows and handed Larissa the flower. She kept the ribbon and tied it into her braid. The gold thread of the tryzubs caught the sun like they'd been woven by Rumpelstiltskin. That's what Anna had said months ago.

Larissa remembered that ribbon. It arrived in the mail, and Baba Vira had taken it to her room and not opened the door. Larissa had asked who sent it, but her grandmother had launched into a story of German officers on a train and batting her once-beautiful eyelashes. Anna and Alex had been enamored, and Larissa never got her answer.

"She left this here for us." Ira tied off her braid and left the ribbon ends dangling in the breeze.

"Baba doesn't know we're looking for her."

"Maybe she's recruiting us as soldiers in whatever revolution she's planning."

Larissa swallowed. She wanted to retort how absurd that was, but with their grandmother, she really didn't know. And she knew what was happening in Ukraine right now.

Stefa's girls had let their voices fill the Polish hall, their tones shaping a hymn, their song a serene battlecry—echoing the passion in Maidan Square in Kyiv, where tents housing protestors had burned only a few years ago, where tires had been set aflame as a protective wall, where people had died wanting change in their country. Larissa shook her head.

"She's leaving breadcrumbs for someone. It can't just be decorations, can it?"

A car flew by close to the curb, causing both sisters to jump back. Larissa tightened her hold on her bag and looked down the street toward their hotel. No, Baba Vira couldn't be involving herself in politics. It was absurd. A block away, another yellow sunflower caught her eye. Her rolling suitcase clattered over the sidewalk as she jogged in its direction. Ira stayed right by her side, her smaller dufflebag slung easily over her shoulder.

Tied to a street sign outside a stone courtyard, the second sunflower looked just as fresh as the first. It hadn't been there long. Its matching tryzub ribbon blew in the wind against a sign for *Černá Hora, a* beer apparently brewed since 1298.

Larissa untied the ribbon, almost wanting to stop in for a beer, and clutched the new sunflower stem tightly in her hand.

"There!" Ira pointed down the street, past a thick green cross that marked a doctor's office and an over-pruned tree with amputated branches jutting out with steadfast determination. Larissa's bag jostled and rattled on the ground as she tried to keep up, passing façades of stone and smooth cement, white and yellow and brown and light blue. Dormers poked out of a slanted roof. A flat-fronted brown building showed off white wooden leaves intricately carved into swags over every window. There were no spaces between these structures that seemed built by different architects in different centuries, sharing walls, sharing secrets.

The third stem was fastened to a mailbox on the street corner.

Ira's head turned quickly from side to side. Cars passed by, and people behind them still trickled out of the train station.

"But how would she know we were following her?"

"It's Baba. She knows." A cyclist rode by them, and Larissa followed his path with her eyes. He swerved around moving vehicles and parked ones without a second thought. "The fourth!" Ira ran, her hurt ankle apparently forgotten. Larissa examined the smooth sidewalk under their feet and Ira's just-too-big sandals but didn't say a word as she hurried to catch up.

At the end of the next block, bars covered a first-floor window. The yellow flower petals contrasted with the black metal, the tryzub ribbon tickling the protected window panes. Ira's fingers untied it quickly. She handed the stem to Larissa, keeping the ribbon for herself. This, Larissa realized, was their system.

"So Baba travels with bouquets," said Ira, less of a question than an acknowledgement.

"She's done weirder things. Remember the time she gave all of the moms at Anna's soccer games poppies and vodka?"

"She said it was for celebrating the team."

"And I had to talk down the parents who thought the poppies were an opium reference."

The streets weren't crowded. Only the occasional passerby came in their direction. Larissa worried about the determined, bordering-on-crazed look in her sister's eye. She wondered if they had seen the same in Baba Vira's.

"If Baba got off her train here—which apparently she did—she arrived fourteen hours ago. Where would she go?"

Ira brought the new ribbon to her hair, fiddling with the braid, loosening it, letting it fall, separating out the locks once again, a ribbon fastened around each one.

"Number five," she said instead of answering. She pointed across the street before taking off, once again, leaving Larissa standing still behind her.

Clinging to the lower branches of a young tree at the edge of a park, the yellow flower hung like a forgotten party decoration. Larissa caught up as Ira untied it.

"Number six!" Larissa chirped, bumping her sister's shoulder to, for once, leave her behind. She picked up her rolling suitcase, holding it awkwardly off the ground, but no more awkwardly than she'd held Alex in his three-year-old tackling-hug phase. She cut through the grass, over the sidewalk, weaving between flower beds and manicured hedges. The sixth flower was tied to the leg of a statue, a soldier wearing a long winter coat.

Ira huffed to catch up behind her but stilled her heavy breathing when she thought she was in earshot. She always forgot about Larissa's hear-all, see-all mother abilities.

Bells from a nearby church rang, calling parishioners or maybe just marking the time. When she turned from the church spires toward the other buildings around them, she spotted their hotel, its cursive script signage almost matching her own handwriting on the notes about their reservation.

"Oh my god, Baba's at our hotel!" She was sure of it. The sunflowers led them right here. She exhaled and put down her bag, allowing herself a moment of reprieve. A bird sang over-head, and a nearby fountain trickled.

"I don't think so," Ira said by her side. She lifted an arm, and Larissa was terrified to look. "Seven," she continued. Ira didn't run this time, but she still walked away. Larissa stared at their hotel with a longing almost as bad as that of wanting to run her fingers through her children's soft hair.

The sunflower was affixed to a metal bench across the street along a wide sidewalk. Behind the bench, a café stood next to a museum, shops, and offices of one sort or another. In another life, Larissa would want to take a stroll here, to read the inscriptions on every metal marker, to take in the spires of that church and the bas-relief carvings on the buildings' facades.

Ira handed Larissa the seventh flower, leaving the ribbons twisted in her fingers. She yanked out her tied-up hair, letting it fall in a mess around her shoulders, and Larissa wondered if she was thinking about Baba Vira or just how to style herself.

A man sweeping up at the café watched them. She forced herself to stand straighter, to clutch the seven flowers in her hands like a wedding bouquet before her, a game of make-believe with Anna if Anna only knew.

The buildings were nestled tightly together here too. She couldn't see any more flowers upon them, nor down the street, nor back in the thin stretch of greenspace they had just come from.

No more ribbons swaying in the wind. No pops of yellow petals.

"I have Noncia's Slovakia address." Ira wove the last of her hair in a braid across the crown of her head, seven long ribbons tied along its length. "Panya Stefa gave it to me while you were with the police. Maybe we should just go straight there."

Larissa lowered the sunflowers to her side.

"Noncia?"

Ira's hands went back to her hair, touching it tenderly, making sure each piece lay just where it should, as if this is how she wore her hair every day.

"Why do you have Noncia's address?" Larissa repeated, speaking through gritted teeth.

"Baba's old friend, Noncia? I've been meaning to mention it."

Larissa was overcome by a sudden urge to smack her sister across the face with the bouquet of sunflowers, but the man at the café still watched. He narrowed his eyes at them. She wanted to snarl.

"What the hell, Ira?"

Her sister laughed.

"I love it when you curse. It's so unnatural, like a kitten spitting fire."

She didn't hesitate. She raised the bouquet high and brought it down on Ira's perfect tryzub ribbon braid. She smacked her again and again, until Ira ducked and threw her hands over her head, laughing harder and harder until tears came out of her eyes. Petals fell around them in the aftermath.

Larissa breathed hard as Ira wiped away the water from her eyes. A nearby fountain, a sculpture whose centerpiece was a bulky bloom somewhere between a rose and a crushing boulder, trickled, and a single car drove by. Larissa lowered the battered bouquet to her side.

"*Ospravedlnte ma!*" The call came from the café.

When Ira looked up, the grin she wore, like she hadn't just been pummeled with sunflowers, fell from her face. The loose petals had tucked themselves into her braid and a sprinkle of yellow pollen sat like gold dust upon her skin. But Larissa couldn't recognize her sister's expression.

"Yes?" she answered in Ira's silence, pushing her own hair behind her ear.

"Oh, English... English, yes." He leaned his broom against a table and stepped out onto the sidewalk. Ira took a step back by her side. "Do you know old woman?"

Larissa's heartbeat raced inside her own pollen-coated skin.

The old woman. Baba Vira. Yes!

"Do you know where she is?"

"Yes. *Áno*. Yes." He approached the sisters slowly, almost cautiously. "Don't you?"

At the entrance of the café, the door opened as someone walked in. Inside, Larissa could see a big vase of sunflowers, sunflowers that matched the battered stems in her hand.

"Where is she?" Her voice lowered.

"Why do you look for her?" He smiled. Larissa had initially trusted that smile. Should she trust that smile?

"She's our grandmother ..." Why was she defending her intentions to this stranger?

"I can take you to her."

"Let's go." Ira tugged on her sister's arm.

"No, now I have job." He lifted his broom. "Later. *Popoludnie*. Afternoon?"

"No, now." Larissa didn't know what was going on with her sister, but she was ready to force this lanky man to bring her to her grandmother. If he really knew where she was. If he was a good Samaritan and didn't want something in return. Oh God, was Baba Vira okay?

"Today, I have work. I cannot give up work," he said with a shrug. "Be done by two. Come back, and I take you to her. She is with my *babička*."

Larissa put a hand to her head. She rooted her feet. She was a tree. She was a mountain. She was dizzy and confused.

"Noncia?" whispered Ira. He nodded. "Your grandmother is Noncia?"

Across the street, their hotel leaned toward them, or maybe she was just tired. It had a place to put their bags down, a clean bathroom to splash her face, beds. She desperately wanted a bed.

"Let's go now," Larissa pressed again.

"I work now," he repeated. "Two. Come back at two."

Ira took Larissa by the elbow and led her away from this man, across the street through the long thin park with its monuments and fountains and across another street to their hotel.

"I have the address. We don't have to wait," she repeated again and again to Larissa, as they entered and checked in. The process was simple and smooth, and they were upstairs before Larissa had gotten past the shock of this man and the café's collection of sunflowers, of his grandmother, of Baba Vira together with Noncia. She knew that name. How hadn't Noncia's name come up before this moment?

Baba Vira was safe, though, she told herself. She was nearby, with an old friend, and safe. They'd be with her soon.

They unlocked their door, and the lights flicked on with their movement. Two twin mattresses were tucked together snugly in a king bed frame, individual fitted sheets drawing a line for a clean divide.

"Beds," Larissa heard herself whisper, before letting go of her suitcase's handle and collapsing onto the not-so-soft but exquisitely wonderful bed. Its crisp white sheets were more starched than one of Greg's dress shirts. She kicked off her shoes and nestled down, pulling the slightly stiff fabric over her while thinking of her husband's arms.

"Beds," Ira echoed. Nodding, walking around to the other side, dropping her bag and bending down to remove her shoes. She flexed her left ankle back and forth with a calculated look on her face. Larissa thought it couldn't be that bad if her sister was so determined to run from sunflower to sunflower. She wanted to think of her sister's fear, but it was too much for her head.

She knew she should put the battered stems in water. They'd wilt if she didn't. But she'd wilt if she didn't close her eyes, this very second, before she thought any more of her sister's ankle, or Baba Vira running away from them, or her husband's starched shirtsleeves.

31

Ira

The alarm buzzed, and Ira swatted away something tickling her check. Only when her hand touched the loose ribbon resting there did she remember where they were, what they were doing, the man they were meeting soon, and the language he spoke that filled his whole mouth and made her body tense all over.

Baba, she reminded herself. We have to find Baba.

On the bed beside her, Larissa rolled over and smacked her cell phone. Her hand tangled in its cord, making it tumble between the bed and the nightstand, banging hard back and forth along the way.

Ira sat up slowly, the world coming into focus. Their hotel room's nightstands, dressers, and headboards were smooth and angular, without a single hint of flourish. There was nothing plush here, nothing warm or inviting. Even the pillows were thin, flat, and beaten down.

At least, she felt better. Rested. Somewhat back to normal. She put a hand to her hair. The ribbons were still woven into her braid. She must have passed out on her flat pillow and not even shifted in her sleep.

A few loose strands of hair were revealed in the mirror on the bathroom wall, but nothing too bad, nothing worth redesigning the entire effort over.

Ready?" Larissa said after applying lipstick and foundation. Her beauty routine was down to two minutes, and she looked good. Hair smooth. Face refreshed. Pretty even. Creases of the pillow still streaked like scars across Ira's cheek.

"We don't need the help. I have the address." She reached over toward her bag, and she fumbled inside it. Her balls of clothes and wads of underwear were easy to run her fingers through. Her wrist slid against her brush. Her short life-line touched her toothpaste. But she couldn't find any paper.

Ira flipped her bag upside down and let its contents pour onto the bed.

"We have a guide, Ira," Larissa whispered, wrinkling her nose at the disorganized jumble now lumped onto the sheets. "What's his name again?"

Ira's muscles tensed. But this was Noncia's grandson. He wasn't... she bit her lip hard, pushing away the thought.

"Brodny," she whispered.

Her hands plunged into her small pile of belongings, no saved envelope to be found.

"Just leave it. I don't want to be late." Larissa took her arm, guiding her toward the door. She yanked away.

"But we don't need him." Ira dropped to the floor to crouch under the bed. She ran her fingers under the nightstand then crawled toward the bathroom, retracing any movement she'd made in the room before they had passed out.

"Someone who has seen Baba here wants to help us." Larissa grabbed her sister's arm tighter this time and yanked her to her feet. "Let's let him help us."

"I don't think—"

"You're not thinking." Larissa swallowed. "Every dancer needs a partner." Ira quit her squirming at Baba Vira's familiar words.

"You're a good enough partner."

"Let's bring one more into this dance."

"I doubt Brodny knows the Hopak."

Larissa curved one of her arms over her head and extended the other outward. Ira batted the closer hand away, but she walked past her out the door. Heel. Toe. Heel. Toe. Feeling the rhythm of her steps but refusing to give them any music.

Down the interior hallway toward the hotel's stairs, lights flicked on one by one as they moved down the corridor, their energy efficiency allowing for the sisters' entrance on an imaginary stage.

"Noncia lives on the edges of this town. She has children in Warsaw and here, Panya Stefa said." Ira spoke to drown out the prickle rising on her skin and the music Larissa hummed. "Some government actions in the eighties scared her two daughters into moving to Poland, but her son stayed here. Brodny is an only child, I think." Her voice sped. Her footsteps slowed.

"What was the government doing?"

Ira swallowed.

"I don't know."

Larissa's forehead wrinkled as she walked. Exiting their hotel, they crossed into the park, a manicured thin strip of a town square. She could see it more clearly now that they weren't scanning for sunflower stems. A massive church stood at one end, its dark Gothic spires reaching toward the few white clouds in the sky. The sisters stuck to the sidewalks this time, wending their way past a fountain carved with rose blooms the size of small boulders, past a sculpted monument where stone men and women were frozen in time—soldiers clutching guns, monks garbed in robes, women hand in hand, a group seated around a campfire.

"Brodny," Larissa repeated like she was prepping for a social gathering and needed to remember the host's name. She put a hand to her sister's back to keep their rhythms aligned.

Ira's feet dragged. The dark green leaves of the trees overhead looked perfect for hiding in. She had to remind herself they were looking for their baba. With her borscht-stained hands, her wild stories, and her endless determination. Knobby branches extended over their heads. A bird's nest seemed laced with string. Two narrowed eyes.

Ira jumped back, grabbing onto her sister.

"What is wrong with you?"

She exhaled. Another mask had been wedged between the lower branches of the tree, straight-lipped and wild-eyed, scraggly hair entwined with the leaves.

Larissa stepped forward to reach for it, but Ira didn't let go of her.

"No," she whispered. "Leave that one there."

Her sister nodded and blew air out of her pursed lips.

Arm-in-arm, they kept walking to the little café on the other side of the park with its white canopy and open-air seating. More tables could be seen inside, past the tall arches that stretched toward the second floor and its wide-open windows. Geraniums bloomed in flower boxes there, and shadows moved just out of sight.

Larissa marched beside her sister with authority. Her getting-shit-done walk. Ira had seen it before—the time Anna had been encouraged not to join the Lego Robotics team because she was the only girl, the time in fourth grade Jon Shoul had told her she couldn't beat him in a race across the playground.

A shadow inside the open windows above the café flickered, stealing her attention beyond long white curtains that blew in the wind. But Larissa stopped walking. Seated on a wooden bench at the edge of the green space, their guide was as still as one of the statues. He wore a baseball cap on his head and a t-shirt with something scrawled across its entire front. His pants were mended at the knees.

"*Dobrý deň.*" Brodny looked from one sister to the other.

"Hi, *dobrý deň,*" Larissa answered, her intensity ebbing. She brushed her hair behind her ear and lifted her chin. "When did you meet our baba?"

"When she tied up flower in front of café." Brodny leaned his elbows on his knees as he looked up at them. "She looked almost lost but reminded me of my grandmother. Old. Slow. Wild spark in eye." He tilted his head at the two sisters. "Then I saw them together. Made sense. Is she running away from you two?"

"Well, she's leaving us a trail." Larissa clasped her hands together and then released them.

"Your *babička* was with my *babička*. Will she be mad if I bring you to her?"

"We'd appreciate it so much."

His head tilted to the side again, his eyes narrowing as he examined them. Ira's heartbeat become steadier. He was as wary of them as she was of him.

Brodny clapped his hands together and stood from his bench.

"Let's go find our babas. Mine always says I get into trouble, but I think she is worse than me."

He motioned for them to follow him across the street. On the buildings next to the café, bold keystones topped archways and window frames. Bas relief carvings covered the exterior walls: a sun with rays so long they nearly touched the rooftops of a tiny sculpted town, a medieval knight resting upon rolling hills with his flag held high in the breeze, a Slovakian lady justice with unbalanced scales stretched out in one arm. Brodny walked quickly. Ira hurried to catch up.

There were no alleyways here. The buildings were siblings conjoined at the hips—individualized but unable to escape each other. A plain yellow stucco storefront connected to a white structure with ironwork detailing between its first and second story. A blue building in the shape of a barn came next, followed by a squat one-story that reminded her of a bunker.

A grand domed roof rose through the treetops across the street at the end of the thin, green park that had spanned for blocks. A giant metal eagle perched atop its basilica.

"Will we all fit into your car?" Larissa looked around expectantly.

"Now you sound like the Americans in my textbooks. No desire to walk, only want car."

Ira crossed her arms.

"In your textbooks?"

"Sure. Americans like fast-food. Don't like exercise. Are fat."

Beside her, Larissa grimaced and looked down toward her belly—not a flat belly after two babies but nowhere near fat. It was a battle-scarred belly. She wanted to pick up her sister's chin for her.

Someone yelled at Brodny through a nearby window. Larissa jumped away from the sound. She bumped into Ira, who fought the urge to bump her back. Brody didn't even turn his head in the yeller's direction.

"How long's the walk?" Ira's feet slipped in Panya Stefa's just-too-big sandals.

"Fifteen minutes." He took off his hat and fanned himself with it before putting it back on his head. The skin on his hands was rough. They were working hands, weathered and worn. He stretched out his fingers before tucking them into his pockets. Another man came around the corner and scowled when he saw Brodny. Ira wouldn't have noticed if Brodny hadn't slowed.

The tall, unshaved man called out something, waving his hands, and Brodny took off his hat and shrugged. His eyes lowered as the stranger continued, hands flying to accent his irritation. Brodny shook his head. The sisters froze two steps behind him. The man yelled something else, and Brodny stepped back.

Larissa moved out of his way, but he bumped right into Ira.

"*Ospravedlňte ma,*" he whispered apologetically, so quietly Ira almost didn't hear.

When she looked back to the angry man, he turned his glare from Brodny to her. The heat of his anger shifted on his face, red-cheeked rage and hatred to something else, something like the train station leer. Noncia's grandson took another step back, then another, not turning, not taking his eyes off the stranger.

"Believe me, I did nothing to this man." His voice cracked.

"I believe you," she whispered back.

The stranger lowered his eyebrows at Ira, making her shiver. He spit out more indecipherable words, punching a fist through the air in their direction, and Brodny turned to run. Ira's stomach twisted at the mouthfuls of syllables, at the deep voice, at the unshaven face. She took off with Brodny.

"Ira!" Larissa yelled, but she couldn't stop. It couldn't be the same man. That didn't make sense, she knew. But his narrowed eyes, his anger, and his curious leer made her entire body tense, every muscle straining to get away.

Her feet slipped in her sandals, but she followed Brodny as he cut down the street and turned a corner. Why weren't there alleyways to hide in here? Or alcoves? Or ladders to climb onto second story balconies, or....

Larissa's footfalls sounded behind them.

The stranger's voice yelled again, closer. He was following them. Her breath heaved. She tripped on a crack in the sidewalk but pushed herself forward, putting a hand to a street sign, not allowing herself to fall.

She made herself run faster, gaining on Brodny who cut into an open garden gate and pressed himself against a wall so as not to be seen from the street. Graffiti scarred the entrance, swirls of black and red paint, accents like daggers. Ira didn't think. She darted in after him, listening for heavy footfalls.

"Ira!" Larissa called again.

Her back against the cool cement wall hid her from the street, but Ira had lost her sister. Larissa was out there with that man, that man with the hairy eyebrows and the pale scruffy face.

"Lyalya!" she screamed, moving to stick her head back out the arched entryway, but Brodny grabbed her arm.

"She'll be fine," he whispered, pulling her back, his breath warming her skin, giving her goosebumps. "His hate is for me."

Ira jerked her arm free of his grasp, stepping back, deeper into the garden. Her feet slipped on wet garden stones. She kicked a garden pail, and Brodny widened his eyes. He turned toward the garden entrance as slow footsteps sounded.

Larissa moved into the space, exhaling when she saw her

sister, before peering around at the back of the house.

"Why did you... Who did you think...?" She whispered incomplete questions one after the other until she put herself out of breath, but as soon as she fell quiet, Ira rushed to her, throwing her arms around her.

"What is wrong with you?" she said, wiggling free from Ira's grasp.

Tomato plants and carrot stems tickled their ankles, and Larissa pulled them both away from the emerging sprouts.

"Is he gone?" Brodny cleared his throat and replaced his hat on his head.

"Who was that? What did you do to him?"

Brodny didn't shift his place in the wall's shadows.

"Nothing," he answered, his voice flat, not defensive. He whistled softly to himself before stepping back to the gated entrance, looking from side to side until he was sure the stranger was nowhere near. "Let me take you to babas." He tilted his head in the direction they would go—a different path than before, off the busier streets.

Brodny didn't speak as he led them onto a side street, past a market with baskets of potatoes and peppers in the windows and a bus station without a bus to be seen. Larissa shot her sister questioning glances, and Ira shook her head, shook her hands out, shook off the touch of last night's stranger on her skin.

The roads shifted from paved to dirt, and the sidewalks ended. A small red and green flag with a wagon wheel on it hung inside a cracked window. A cat splayed itself in the sunshine by a nearby front door. Another crouched in the shade between the wheels of a battered motorbike.

Here, outside the center of the town, the small houses stood independent of one another, plywood and sheet metal construction buffering the supports of older, cracked plaster walls. The farther they walked, the more the dirt settled over everything, window frames and laundry lines and the fur of a dog that trotted between homes.

Flower boxes full of bright red geraniums surrounded the front door of another house. A woman walked out speaking rapidly to Brodny. The Slovakian was as melodic as Ukrainian but softer somehow, full of more vowels. She silenced herself when Ira and Larissa stepped forward.

"Pani Vira's granddaughters," he said to her.

"Oh!" the woman put down the watering can she held. Without anything in her hands, Ira could see her round belly. She kissed them both on the cheeks, rattling off again so quickly in a language that wasn't quite as offensive as it had been minutes ago. The words were almost understandable to Ira's Ukrainian-tuned ears if she only slowed down.

"English," huffed Brodny. "They don't understand you."

"Oh!" she said again, closing her mouth and pushing out her lips. She rubbed her belly as she contemplated the right words.

"My wife, Darina," he added to the sisters. He didn't give their names in return. Ira didn't think he remembered them.

"The babas left," she said, clasping her hands on her belly absentmindedly the way pregnant women do. Ira remembered when Larissa did that. She just hoped this woman wouldn't ask her to feel any kicking. Or hiccups. Something about fetus hiccups creeped her out.

"They left?" Ira was fairly sure Larissa hadn't meant to yell.

"I gave car." Her words tumbled out of her mouth in bite-sized pieces, one by one, as if she tried to find the complex recipe for every one. "They went to wartime home."

"*Jaskyňa?*" Brodny took off his hat and scratched at his head.

"*Myslím fontána mladosti.*"

"No, *jaskyňa.*" Brodny's quick Slovakian made Ira's brain trip over itself. He looked up to the sun still hanging high in the sky and nodded. "We will walk, *sestry*. We will be back before dark."

32

Every day, Vira waited for the guitar player to enter the sliver of park that cut through her new town. She'd settle herself with mending right by the window so that the music would sneak inside and overtake her.

Vira's body turned to wood in this place, unmovable, indefinable—a doll tucked within a doll, a doll holding her sisters safely—but the rapid melody of the guitar plucked at her insides.

Words about more soap for their laundry tumbled from her lips, and she rose and crossed the room.

The stairs at the back of the café had become familiar, as had the weave between the vase-topped tables, the exchange of words between the waitress who never met her eye, the steps out of the shade of the open-air arches onto the sidewalk, the cobblestone street, and the park beyond.

The strummed music became louder with every step she took. She tried to inhale it, to hold it inside her body, to let it play in her veins and bones. With the first of the park's trees behind her, blocking her from the view of their unshuttered apartment window, she threw out her arms before arching one over her head, tapping her heel then her toe, and turning in a narrow circle. The sun fell down on her in bursts of light through the thinning autumn leaves.

Heel, toe, heel, toe. She outstretched both arms again and searched for the smile that always went along with these steps, but she still couldn't find it. Arms akimbo at her sides, she lifted one knee, then tapped her toe behind her to the unfamiliar melody. Deeper into the park, sunlight could barely find her under the canopy of leaves, but maybe that meant no one else could either.

The weight of the stone around her neck lifted and fell against her breastbone. The music became faster and so did she, twirling and twirling so quickly tears moistened her eyes. She closed them, less willing to be caught crying than making a fool of her herself dancing like a madwoman. The neat braid she had folded over the crown of her head this morning had loosened. Strands fell, flying wildly in the wind she created.

The music stopped, and so did Vira. Her breath heaved, and she clutched the iron back of a nearby park bench. Not so far away, the Roma guitar player shifted the hat on the sidewalk before him as two women walked by, neither acknowledging him but for a kicked pebble that flew up and hit the leg of his ripped pants.

Vira had heard that the Germans might pay the Slovakians for every Jew they deported to the Poland camps. She didn't know if there was a price for each Roma here too. She clutched her arms around herself. None of it seemed real. She didn't know if they were sent to the same place as her Uncle Oleh, who wasn't Jewish, who wasn't Roma, who only dared to write words and dream of Ukrainian freedom.

A brown-tinged leaf fell from the tree over her head. She needed to go get the soap. Her mother's tight lips turned into a Baba Yaga scowl whenever she was gone for too long. Her bulbous nose, her chin that had become more pointed in their time here. They'd all become a bit thinner.

Vira crossed out of the park straight toward the guitar player, pulling a few coins from her apron pocket and dropping them in his empty hat. He spoke to her rapidly, thanking her, offering her his assistance with handiwork, with ironwork, with roofing. She shook her head before walking away.

Vira put a hand to her stone necklace, tucking it back under the neckline of her blouse as she walked through the door of the market.

"Is that vagrant still harassing people out there?" asked the shopkeeper. She held chicken eggs up to the light of the window, peering at the shadows inside, before placing each gently in a basket beside a stack of onions. "I can't put my trotle out on the sidewalk, because it'll disappear as soon as those thieves come around the corner."

Vira walked to a nearby table and picked up a potato, examining the eye where a thick root had popped though. She pushed on it with her fingernail until it flung across the counter and landed on a pyramid of bread.

"He's playing his music."

"Oh, it's you, Pani Vira." The shopkeeper moved her basket of eggs to the other side of the counter.

Vira dropped the potato she held. It fell back into its pile, causing a small avalanche of dirt-flecked roots to the floor.

"*Vybachte*," she apologized, bending over to retrieve them, one by one.

The shopkeeper had stopped inspecting eggs. She leaned on the counter before her and drummed her fingers on its surface, nothing rhythmic, nothing musical, nothing more than spit and venom.

"I keep telling myself that my son is out there fighting to get rid of that garbage, the cheaters and the thieves." The shopkeeper moved toward her, but it wasn't to help. Her eyes scanned the folds of Vira's skirt, the pockets of her apron. "That garbage and everyone who speaks up for them."

Vira's hands were dirty by the time she returned the last potato to its place. She wiped them on her apron and didn't meet the shopkeeper's eyes. She crossed past the carrots and onions. She pinched tiny spears of dried dill, stealing only its familiar smell on her fingertips.

"I didn't like that he volunteered," the woman continued. "He didn't have to fight. But he's in Kyiv now. I got a new letter." The woman took up a rag and crossed to the shelves near Vira.

She dusted where no dust had settled. "Maybe your husband is fighting with my son, eh?"

Vira didn't know why she emphasized the word "husband" like it was a reprimand. The bars of soap were wrapped in off-white paper that looked in need of scrubbing. Vira picked up one bar, trying to read the German words on the wrapper before quickly giving up. There was only so much she could pretend that she knew. This woman had so many German products in her shop. Her stomach twisted. But maybe Czechoslovakia always had lots of German things.

After Vira paid the woman, she put the soap in her pocket and swallowed hard before wishing her best for her son. Outside, the sunshine made Vira squint, but she turned to face it without shielding her eyes. A train whistled at the station, and she walked toward the sound. She needed to get back soon. She was probably already taking too long, but she couldn't force herself to return to their cramped apartment where she would sit, where she would feel herself turning into wood, where she would watch the twins giggle and play because they didn't know any better.

The houses, built close together on the street, reminded her of the huddled, whispering, jealous girls of her childhood. Their white and tan exteriors were so plain but for a sculpted cornice tucked under the eaves of the roofline, like a ruffle partially hidden under a skirt.

She didn't know where those girls were now, and she didn't really care. She didn't know if they had war husbands or lovers or if they still danced somewhere, flowers tucked into their hair.

Past the last house in the row, the fields on the edge of town came into sight, the fields that buttressed the forest, and people there huddled around campfires and makeshift tents. She'd never wandered that far before, but there was no reason not to—except her mother's scorn, but she'd get that anyway.

Faces looked up at her for only a moment before resuming their work. A man banged a red-hot metal bar with a hammer on an anvil. Sparks flew into the grass beyond him where a horse shifted its feet. They were unshod. The man shifted the glowing metal and hammered again to make it not break but bend.

"*Aké vašej šťastie?*" a voice called out. A woman sitting on a nearby stool braiding the hair of a small child, reached into her pocket to retrieve playing cards. She dropped the child's half-finished plait and shuffled them between her thick fingers. The hearts and spades, the clubs and diamonds.

"What?" Vira's Ukrainian gave away her foreignness in this place.

"What's your fortune?" the woman repeated in a more familiar tongue. She patted the child on the head. The girl moved away to the side of the man with the glowing metal. Sparks flew again, landing on the ground near her feet, but she didn't flinch.

"You have questions about what will happen next to you," the woman continued. She straightened her hunched-over body but didn't stand from the short wooden stool she sat upon. "I can give you answers."

Vira had never had her fortune read. Her mother had always scoffed at the idea whenever she or Lesya had brought it up. Vira didn't mean to stop walking. She didn't know when she had. The horse neighed. The blankets upon its back danced as it shook its head. The cards leapt between the woman's hands.

"Okay, *tak.*"

The woman moved from the stool to the ground beside it, spreading out her long skirts and tucking her feet inside them. She waved her arm to the grass on the opposite side of the stool.

"How much?" Vira asked, not moving to sit, feet as heavy and immobile as wood.

The woman stared at her, taking in the worn dress she wore, her empty ears, the wedding ring on her finger, then her neckline. Her stone necklace had slipped from inside her collar again and rested on top of her blouse.

"How much money is your future worth to you?"

The cards leapt between her long fingers, hearts, spades,

clubs, diamonds. Her brown eyes looked away after the child who now hugged the man's leg as he hammered, as fire leapt into the air, as the horse shuffled and stirred.

"My ring?" Vira twirled the thin gold on her finger.

"Okay, *tak*," the woman repeated Vira's own cadence and reached out her hand. The necklaces around her neck jangled with the movement in a way they hadn't when she'd been shuffling the cards. The hammer banged at their side.

"After the reading."

"How do I know you'll pay me?" The woman stopped shuffling and placed the cards down on the wooden stool.

"How do I know you won't just tell me what I want to hear?"

"You want to hear about your lost love."

Vira twisted the ring.

"You want to hear if he's alive."

Fire fluttered into the air. The horse neighed. The child moved to a massive wooden wheel resting flat on the ground, tip-toing between the spokes, around and around.

"You want to know if you'll ever have to tell your husband."

Vira pulled the gold band from her finger. It slipped off easier than she expected—no godly attachment to her skin. She set it on the round stool between them next to the cards.

"It's only yours if you don't lie to me."

"I don't lie." The woman reached for the gold band, but Vira covered it with her own hand first.

"I'll decide. The ring stays here."

When the woman agreed, her necklaces jingled again.

"Think about what it is you want to know," said the woman. The child at the wagon wheel behind her marched over each spoke with high knees, arms extended beside her. "Cut the cards."

Vira reached for the deck, placing her hand on top of it. She breathed in the smell of metal and grass, of sweat and horse. Her fingers traced down the stack of cards until she settled on a spot, far more than halfway down. She placed the cut deck side by side.

The woman didn't blink. Her necklace remained silent around her neck.

"The first card is for your past," she said, flipping the top card from the cut deck. A three of hearts. Its red matched the glow of the metalwork beside them. "You couldn't make up your mind, which emotion to follow." The hammer beat down on the metal. The child skipped and fell, but the woman didn't look away. "Who to love."

A voice sang something low, warbling in a way Vira remembered from parties, where she'd sing with friends. But this voice howled and ached.

"The second card is for your present." She flipped over a seven of spades. "Someone has been giving you advice. It's not good advice. You shouldn't follow it." Vira shifted herself in the grass to ease the stiff blades poking at her legs. "Perhaps it's advice to yourself," the woman added.

The singer's voice fluctuated between notes, reminding her of the best of Ivan's performances on his viola.

"The third card is for your future." She flipped over a two of spades. "A broken relationship." She frowned, looking away to the child, who continued her play on the wheel. "A choice you will make that could haunt you for the rest of your life."

The hammer banged, and the metalsmith lifted up the glowing metal. The wind blew fallen strands of Vira's hair.

"Yes, you will see him again," the woman continued, reaching for the wedding band. Vira blocked her.

"Who?

The woman moved her ringed fingers to the deck and shuffled it once again.

"Cut the deck," she said when she finished, setting the stack of cards on the wooden stool.

Vira didn't hesitate this time. She split the deck quickly, holding the woman's gaze, lifting her chin.

The woman flipped over a king of clubs, her lips upturning for only a moment before the expression disappeared.

"A dark-haired man. You're going to see him very soon. He thinks of you every day."

Vira narrowed her eyes at the woman, not moving her hand from her wedding ring on the stool.

"His sister needs you," she continued.

Vira released her grip on the ring.

"Do you know them?"

"No."

The woman took it up and slipped it on her finger. She craned her neck toward the sun, and Vira did the same. Thunder rolled in the hills. She didn't know if it was a rainstorm or gunfire.

33

Larissa

Larissa's face flushed. She wasn't sure if it was the heat or the memory of the summertime she was pregnant with Anna. In front of her, Brodny's wife Darina shined with perspiration. Tendrils of her own hair had always escaped her ponytail too, curling as they touched her neck, adding a layer of warmth and dishevelment. Darina's dark hair hadn't been ready for visitors. It had been recently slept on and swept back haphazardly. Wisps rebelled. Larissa's hand went to smooth down her own hair, which was miraculously behaving.

She pushed breath out of her mouth between clenched teeth as she spoke.

"*Nemyslím si,*" she began, but her voice died as if it gave up out of exhaustion. "Come back soon."

"Their war cave." Brodny adjusted his hat on his head an inch forward and inch back.

Larissa shifted her weight from side to side as she stared out to the mountains beyond. She brushed her hand through her hair again. She knew her face looked as sweaty as Darina's. Today she had planned to go home—the day they found Baba Vira in Spišská Nová Ves, the day they met her long-lost wartime friend, the day that ended with stepping into the cool dry air of an airplane that would take her back across the ocean.

"How do we get there?" Ira addressed Darina instead of her husband.

"The path..." She wobbled her hand back and forth then up and down. "Tricky."

"We can handle tricky." Larissa heard her voice come out flat and flustered. She always tried to catch herself before she sounded that way, before the kids heard her mounting frustration, her lack of caring about anything but the task at hand.

"They might be back soon," Brodny added, stepping close to his wife.

Wind blew through the trees of the street and the hanging clothes on their neighbor's line, tickling roofs and electric wires.

"Will you take us there?" Larissa forced the words out of her mouth.

Brodny looked to his wife and her belly. The wind rattled the metal sheet that patched the far wall of his small house.

"My baba was to stay with Darina. If she is not here, I cannot go."

Darina rubbed her belly, looking at the sisters. The wind settled. So did the sound of the metal wall. She shook her head and waved her hands.

"*Nie*, you go," she said to Brodny. "Not baby's time. I told them too old to go alone."

"You told them they were too old?" A smirk cracked through Ira's hard expression. Larissa knew what she was thinking. No one told Baba Vira she was too old for something. That always made whatever it was she wanted to do more appealing to her. That was what got them into this entire mess. Wasn't it just four months ago that Baba Vira came to her while she cooked spaghetti and miniature meatballs, put a hand on her arm, and declared she was going back to the old country before she died? Larissa had laughed. Why the hell had she laughed?

"You go. You go now." She looked up at the sun that had already passed its peak in the sky.

"We won't be home before dark."

"Use car to come home."

Darina moved one hand from her belly to her husband's scrawny arm. She squeezed it, and after a moment, he bent down to kiss her cheek. "*Pod*." He gestured them forward. "Come."

"*Počkať.*" Darina waddled inside. The sisters exchanged glances, unsure if that was her goodbye.

"Bye?" Larissa offered just as the pregnant woman reemerged from the doorway, a small bag in her hand. She offered it not to her husband but to Larissa. A canteen of water. Bread. Apricots. She would be a wonderful mother.

"Are we borrowing a friend's car?" Ira asked, taking a step back when Brodny walked close to Larissa.

"No." He put a finger to the bag, pulling slightly to peer inside. "They have already once-borrowed car. No *pálenka*?"

Darina pressed her lips together, giving her husband a single-raised-eyebrow expression Larissa knew would translate well into motherhood.

Brodny shrugged.

"We walk," he answered Larissa.

"Walk?" She tried not to make her internal groan apparent in her voice.

"Yes." He touched his hands to his lips as he looked at his wife before turning to walk down the road.

"How far is this cave?" Larissa hurried to match his stride. Ira's footsteps sounded behind her.

"Too many questions."

They walked past more houses resembling Brodny's—water spouts disconnected, plaster cracked, fallen walls replaced with sheet metal, plywood, or branches woven like the most extraordinary of baskets. Brilliantly metallic flower pots glinted in the sunlight, but soon tall grasses tickled their ankles. The dirt street turned into a narrow footpath. Larissa wondered if anyone mowed out here or if shepherds brought in goats or sheep.

Across the field, they saw a man herding a small flock of geese, directing them down another nearly parallel dirt path with a stick.

Mountains rose before them, green and dense—a place to pick a spot and sit still, thought Larissa. Maybe Baba Vira was sitting on a tree stump, waiting for someone to find her.

"Is this the forest of Slovak Paradise?" Ira whispered.

"Yes." Brodny answered, walking faster.

The roads weren't straight. They wound like they were designed by a drunkard, leaning just a bit this way and then that. Past the outskirts of town, houses arose here and there, but they became fewer and fewer. Larissa saw the geese herder kept pace with them across the field. They angled together, as if they had the same destination.

"How long is this walk?" she asked again.

"You Americans are funny."

She adjusted the bag Darina had given her tighter against her shoulder. Its weight was heavy. Maybe that's why she'd chosen Larissa. She spared her husband the burden.

"Twenty minutes? An hour? Two?" she pressed.

"Depends on how fast you walk." Brodny looked at the sisters. "With you two, maybe we get there tomorrow."

"Tomorrow?"

"He was kidding, Lyalya." Ira walked up beside her and fell into step with her stride. Brodny grinned at them under his crooked hat.

"Your sister understands me." He fell back and threw an arm over her shoulder as they walked, and Ira winced, shrugging off the arm.

"What? I took shower today." He laughed. "Married man. No concern for you."

"Where are you taking us?" Ira asked, her voice low.

"To the babas' cave."

It sounded too much like a story Baba Vira would tell her kids for Larissa not to smile. Did she ever remember Baba Yaga having a cave? A hut with chicken legs that disappeared into the woods and turned away its door unless you knew the right words to say, sure. A cave? She didn't think so.

Ira shifted herself to Larissa's other side, away from Brodny. He laughed as he said something else to her. He didn't sense her discomfort. He smacked his forehead and said something to himself in Slovakian.

Larissa shifted the bag on her shoulder again. She fought reaching for Ira's hand but held back the motion.

The goose-herder across the field was getting closer. He led his little flock to a wide pond, a pond that sat right next to the dirt road they now walked upon. The water stretched as long and thin as one of his bird's slender necks. Wind rippled its surface.

A thin dock extended into one side. It ached for a lounge chair and for her children to hang their little fishing poles off the edges, leaning over far to see some sort of small fish living in the water, making Larissa put her hands on their shoulders so they could stare down with fascination without falling in. Though Alex would still find a way to fall in.

The path wove to the water, and the man prodding his large white birds turned toward them. It wasn't a stick but a long ski pole in his hands. Gripping it tightly, he examined them like they were new features on the landscape.

"Our babas and their cave. What are we going to do when we get there?" Brodny mocked and winked at Ira, and her face fell. It shattered. The pained expression appeared out of nowhere and made Larissa's heart ache.

Ira leaned toward her sister then leaned away. Larissa shadowed her frozen steps. Brodny had kept walking.

Ira took off. She ran as fast as she could in her too-big sandals, feet kicking up dirt with every stomp. She darted down the dock and stood with her toes hanging over the edge. She teetered and looked back. Larissa tried to ask her what was wrong just with her eyes. They were sisters. They could reach each other like this. They could always connect—for better or for worse.

The water splashed as Ira cannon-balled in.

"Ira!" Larissa darted toward the ripples in the water. Her face felt hot, but it wasn't the heat or exhaustion. Her sister was infuriating. Ira was just being her Ira-self, spontaneous and nonsensical. Both her grandmother and her sister had gone mad, and she was stuck in a foreign country where she didn't understand the language, cleaning up the pieces of them both. She'd be the one to drag them both kicking and screaming home. She crossed her arms as she waited for Ira to surface.

The water ripples spread out farther and farther. Larissa wondered where her sister would arise, ribbons trailing out of her braids and behind her in the water. Across the way, the geese herder stared after her bemused.

"Ira!" Brodny echoed, repeating the name as if he was sloshing it around in his mouth. He hadn't known their names. Larissa was sure of it. He probably still didn't know hers.

The water's ripples began to still.

"Ira?" Her arms uncrossed and fell to her sides.

She pictured her sister amid long water weeds, holding her breath, cheeks puffed out. She imagined her with a cartoon straw poking out, disguising itself among the reeds.

"Ira!" Brodny stepped out onto the dock, taking off his hat. He squatted low, staring into the water, palms pushed against the boards underneath him. She pictured Ira tangled in the stems, skin nipped by fish, eyes open and unresponsive.

Larissa kicked off her shoes and dropped the bag to the dock beside her. She couldn't jump in after her if she didn't know where she was. She didn't want to land on top of her and crush her. She sat down and dropped her legs into the water.

"Ira!" she spit out, lowering herself slowly into the cold, stretching her feet into the pond's murky depths. She wasn't even waist deep and hadn't released her hold on the wooden boards, when a gasp across the pond made her twirl around.

The geese honked, and the geese herder yelled something as Ira emerged within feet of his flock. A pond-monster with tryzub ribbons trailing behind her. She glided toward the edge of the pond, water licking her shoulders then trailing downward as she moved toward the edge.

"What the hell, Ira?"

Ira turned and shrugged her shoulders, sidestepping around

the geese and yelling man. Larissa thought she was about to be impaled with the ski pole. But Ira just beamed, and the geese-herder fell silent. Soaking wet, Ira had charmed him.

"Your sister is crazier than your baba."

She wanted to argue with him but she couldn't. Larissa pressed her hands onto the creaking wooden dock, pulling herself out of the pond. Her jeans were saturated, but her shirt was barely wet. Her sunglasses were tucked into her shoes. She didn't even remember doing that.

Ira's return to them was audible with the squish-squish-squish of her every step.

"Think we can help our babas with whatever they're scheming?" she said, as if their conversation hadn't been broken. As if she hadn't turned into a crazy woman diving into the water to escape who-knows-what.

"You're unbelievable."

The wet denim clung to Larissa's legs as she walked off the dock and into the grass beside the road. She dug her fingers into her bag to find a rolled-up sundress. Ira squish-squish-squished to her side.

"You're a cartoon. That's why my kids love you so much."

"They love me because I'm original." She walked down the road ahead of Brodny and Larissa. "Come on, already."

Brodny returned his hat to his head and trailed after her. He didn't quite come to her side but remained a few steps behind.

Larissa clutched the sundress, staring at her sister whose t-shirt left little to the imagination. She knew that body—thin waist, perfect chest. Years ago, that same body had been her own. Brodny tilted his head to the side as he took a step closer to her. Something inside her shivered.

"Here!" she yelled, running after them. "At least put this on."

34

Ira

Ira found a nearby clump of pines before changing into the sundress. Larissa stood guard over Brodny, ensuring he was turned in the opposite direction. Cotton material over her head, arms through the holes, Ira shook out her hair. Pond water and anxiety flicked away.

She had slipped off her shoes—Stefa's gorgeous strappy leather sandals—and let them dangle in her hand as she continued barefoot. Barefoot was better. She needed to root herself. Good Lord, she sounded like Larissa.

"Okay." She let her voice go sing-songy. "I'm ready."

Brodny turned around, clearly amused.

"You are crazy," he said again, taking off his hat and scratching his head before replacing it. He led the way, but he gave a wide buffer when she stepped up even with him.

The forest closed in over the path ahead of them, a tunnel of entwined tree branches, intimate white-bark birch trunks, and shadows.

"Welcome to Slovak Paradise, *sestry*."

Sisters, he called them. They were less individuals and more characters now, entering the woods, seeking Baba Yaga, Baba Vira. Was there a difference?

The mountains rose before them, pine-covered giants, tucked all together, sleeping off a magic spell. These were the forests of her grandmother's stories, she knew. They were made for fairytales and heroics. Wind brought the sweet, deep scent of leaves, moss, and dirt. Ira was ready to reclaim her position as heroine of the adventure.

She led the way down the trail that cut through the forest as if she knew the way, over knobby roots that stretched into the dirt-path trail, around bends where oak leaves brushed against her shoulders and tangled vines dangled spider webs. Brodny would stop her if she was wrong, wouldn't he? She plunged forward. Bugs chirped around her. The shadows embraced her, and her heart beat more steadily than it had for days.

Dirt caked her feet. Rocks poked her bare soles, pressing against her toes, but none had drawn blood yet. Her feet were tough. She'd always been proud of them.

A river whispered in the gulley they approached, where the land dropped off like it had been carved away as a punishment. A pound of flesh, an acre of land. The trail ended at a cliff, at a raw face of rock that offered a staircase over the ravine, wire mesh shelves affixed to the vertical stone by skinny metal brackets. The thin shelves hung one after another, fastened to the rock face, each step little more than a foot wide. A weather-worn chain also attached to the rock wall hung as a railing.

"This way," Brodny said, passing by the place where she had frozen. He stepped onto the first metal shelf. It held him. The chain rattled against the mountain as he moved forward with it as his guide. He stepped from one shelf to the next as if it was the most natural of pathways.

A hand touched her shoulder, and she remembered that her sister was here too.

"Are you okay?" The anger had drained out of Larissa's voice, replaced by a slight tremor.

"If Baba did this, so can we." Ira filled her lungs. The air was cool.

"Do you really think Baba did this?" Larissa scrunched up her nose.

Ira put a hand on the chain and pulled hard to check its hold before lifting her foot off the solid ground. Sure, it might have made more sense for the chain-link railing to act as a guard against a fall rather than to be attached to the face of the rock wall beside them, but if that wasn't the way of Slovak Paradise, she'd have to make do.

"She's always said people underestimate her." Ira put her foot down on the first metal shelf. The metal mesh grid of the platform made an impression on her bare foot.

"She's an octogenarian, or no, a..." She felt her sister search for the word for a ninety-something. She stuck out her tongue as if she could find it in the air.

"Knowing Baba, she found someone to help her get what she wanted." Ira brought her second foot to the platform, wondering if she should sprint across them before they fell. The wind blew through her hair, around her body, and under her toes. The river trickled across its rocks over twenty feet below. She gripped the metal chain hard with one hand. "Okay?" Ira stuck out her other behind her, reaching for Larissa's. When they clasped onto each other, the heartbeat in their lifelines pressed together.

"Okay," Larissa repeated.

Ira pointed her feet as she took each step forward, letting her toes grope into the air before her. Then she felt the metal under her feet. A second shelf. A third. Rust clung to their edges. They creaked, each tiny groan echoing in the valley below them. She gripped the chain harder, and it clanged against the rock face as she moved forward, as Larissa moved behind her. Neither said a word.

The sundress she wore blew in the breeze. They were at least twenty-five feet in the air now. Ferns clung to the cliff-side. Water tumbled over smooth river-stones. Wind blew the oak and birch leaves, one of which broke loose from its bough and tumbled down, down, down.

"Are you coming, *sestry*? I don't want to leave Darina for too long."

Brodny was far ahead of them now, walking on the thin metal shelves as casually as he'd walk up any other non-life-threatening staircase. She could do that. She puffed her hair out of her eyes. She was the heroine.

"Just enjoying the sights," she called back to him. She squeezed Larissa's hand, and her sister squeezed back. They were off-balance holding onto each other. Their two hands were better served on the metal chain railing. Her sister must have sensed it too, because they released each other in the same moment.

Hand over hand on the chain, step by step on the metal, they made it to solid ground on the other side.

"Does Noncia walk this by herself?" Larissa worked to keep her voice steady. Her heartbeat in her shaky voice betrayed her.

A tiny chitter was followed by a movement in the nearby undergrowth. The sisters both jerked their heads around. A yellowish-gray squirrel jumped through the brush at the edge of the mountain.

"No." Brodny laughed but tried to clear the amusement on his face when he was met with a double-scowl. "I can't remember the last time she went to her cave. Are you sisters scared of squirrel?"

The animal darted across their path, which now wove away from the river. Tree roots were entangled in the dirt, and Brodny stepped over them without looking. Leaves rustled at their side, and for a moment, Ira wished Baba Yaga would jump out at them. She puffed out her chest. Goosebumps tickled her arms. She had refused the matching mommy-cardigan Larissa had offered with the borrowed dress.

Brodny disappeared around a hairpin turn. Larissa stepped to Ira's side, taking her hand this time to propel her forward. The shadows stretched here. They spread themselves out to relax in this strange pocket of forest. Ira bit her lip before plunging into them. Brodny waited for them at the base of a boulder, where thin metal footholds were fastened as a ladder up its side. Her sister scanned the ground for any other option to the trail.

Their guide scampered up it not so differently from the squirrel. Ira put a hand to one of the metal rungs but didn't move farther. Larissa stepped up to the boulder, squeezing between her sister and the rock face, and climbed.

"I don't think our grandmothers did this," Larissa called out above her. The words came out between puffs of breath. "And where was the car?"

"They probably used other way."

The ladder's bars were slick, but Ira's loose shoes would have been worse than the bare feet she now climbed with. The ladder kept going up, allowing them to step off at the top of one boulder and feel the security of a platform, only to discover another ladder affixed to another rock. Brodny was far above them now.

"There's another way?" Ira couldn't see her sister, but she could imagine her face as she said these words. All the power of all the Ukrainian women in history was held in that one expression of hers.

"They've been going to cave decades before trail built. But trail faster."

Ira climbed rung to rung to rung, foothold to foothold, past clinging lichens, beetles, and ants, until she joined the others at the top of the hill. She expected a moment to catch her breath, but Brodny kept moving, stepping into a ditch, a miniature ravine that probably filled with water every time it rained. Tree roots broke free of the soil and plunged out into the open air across it, pale white arms trying to ensnare a passerby.

Her own arms outspread, Ira took baby steps into the ditch. Her feet pressed into the damp mud and slid, gravity on the side of the reaching roots.

"Are we going off the trail?" Larissa called as she fumbled into line behind him. They had to march single-file up the narrow ditch, lifting their knees high with every step.

"No. This is trail."

"Oh," Larissa replied, filling the gap of the silence as if etiquette required an answer of some sort. The branches of trees stretched out ahead of them, a pine needle wall. Ira's thighs ached from the high-steps. Her feet were so caked in mud, she could no longer see her toes. Brodny didn't slow as he approached the massive pines. He pulled off his hat and wiped his hand over his brow before replacing it on his head. She wondered if he would just part the curtain of sticky tree boughs and keep walking through. Then he turned to the right and stepped out of the ditch. Massive gray stones jutted out of the landscape, and a clear trail began again.

"We go down now. Almost there." Brodny's footfalls crunched over the dead leaves covering the ground. The sound of rushing water grew as they followed the path. The trail jackknifed back and forth, switchback after switchback until their guide stopped at the edge of a ravine staring out at a tumbling waterfall.

He lowered to a squat while the sisters approached him. Larissa reached for Ira's hand like she was a child getting too close to the edge, but Ira let her have it.

The mist of the waterfall blew into their faces, swirling up from the falls below. The sun cut through the trees, creating rainbows in the mist.

"Their cave," Brodny said pointing through the spray.

Just after the waterfall, there was a crack in the mountain, a seam that became wider and wider until a craggy mouth opened up. The shadows inside the cave were indecipherable—rocks or people, their grandmothers or the long-lost hiding place of Koschei the Deathless's mortality stored inside a needle inside an egg inside a chest buried under a massive oak. Ira scanned the trees clinging to the cliff above the cave. Swirls of wind were captured in the movement of the water droplets in the air.

Ira waited for her sister to again say that their grandmothers couldn't have come this far, that they were too old, too feeble, but Larissa had taken out her phone and had pressed record. The kids would love this place, Ira knew. She loved this place. She let the moist rainbow-filled air fill her lungs. The breeze carried the smell of grass and trees and childhood crushes on boy scouts.

Beyond where Brodny squatted, more metal platforms attached to the steep cliffs. Another rusty metal chain acted as a handrail against the rock. These platforms walked them down around a corner from the cave. They'd have to step off the trail into a nook of ferns and moss. It didn't look so bad, though. She craned her neck toward the cave to see if her grandmother was inside. The waterfall crashed against rock after rock on its way down the mountain. If they called out, no one within the yawning, potentially-enchanted cave mouth would ever hear them.

"Let's go," Larissa said, putting away her phone. Ira laughed when her sister's mommy-voice made Brodny stiffen and stand beside them.

"We will collect babas and take car home. Much faster." He moved forward onto the first platform, slick with the mist. He gripped the chain by his side with his right hand. "No more healthy exercise in the fresh air. You American girls will be happy."

Brodny turned back toward them, not watching his footing. When his shoe slid, his eyes widened and his teeth clenched. His one-handed hold on the rust-covered chain strained as he flailed. His body banged hard as his feet slipped past thin platform. His legs dangled in the waterlogged air, no railing on the exposed side blocking his fall.

The cascades crashed around them as if calling him down, welcoming him to the craggy river below. The branches of the ancient forest swayed. With his empty hand, Brodny grasped at one of the thin metal braces that secured his platform to the rock.

Ira wobbled when Larissa pushed her away from the ravine before rushing toward him in a single inexplicable motion. She hooked one arm around the chain and reached for Brodny's free hand. He looked from her to the brace, unsure which would be stronger. The waterfall roared. Brodny yelped and spat words that were indecipherable.

"Help, Ira!"

Ira remembered that she could move and rushed to mirror her sister's movements, hooking her arm around the rusty chain with her elbow and reaching a hand to Brodny. They each grabbed him by an arm. The single narrow platform creaked under their weight. The water and rocks and mist and ravine made her dizzy. She pulled back her reaching hand to secure both on the chain, to see if she could help while standing on a farther away metal shelf.

"You've got to help me with this." Larissa's calm voice somehow rose about the crashing water. Her sister's eyebrows were bunched. Eyeliner smeared under her eyes. Why was she wearing eye-liner? "Ready?" Her sister continued. "We're pulling him up on three."

Brodny whimpered while Larissa counted. The mist shifted toward them with a strong breeze. It almost clouded Ira's vision. She blinked away the water droplets that hung on her eyelashes.

"Pull!" Larissa yelled, and Ira tried to be obedient. She reached out for Brodny's arm that was hairy and slick. Ira tried to lean back, to throw her entire body into the pull, but the side of the rock wall was so close. It pressed into her back, tiny knuckles of rock. "Pull harder," Larissa shouted.

Ira could feel Brodny slipping from her grasp. His awkwardly bent body was yanked higher on her sister's side. But she couldn't adjust her grip without letting go.

"Ira, you've got this!" Larissa shouted.

Brodny's eyes were wide. His arm had grown cold, but Ira didn't know if it was from the water or from fear. He pleaded with them in Slovakian, in some other language she couldn't decipher. He seemed to be pleading with the sky, with the spirits of the forest, with God. Wait, was he cursing them?

"Big pull again on three," Larissa yelled. "Keep your elbow hooked." Larissa spoke loudly over the water crashing around them, but her voice was steady. "Dig in your fingernails if you have to." Brodny's body moved as he kicked at the rock underneath the shelf.

Ira wished they could be nesting dolls, hopping inside each other for strength. The metal, never meant to hold three people, groaned again underneath their feet.

"Now!" Larissa screamed. How had she missed the counting? Ira tightened her grip. The jagged knuckles of stone pressed into her. She closed her eyes and leaned back, a misplaced game of trust. She prayed that the platform would hold, that the rusty chain would hold, that they were strong and brave and true and that the magic of Baba Yaga would help them.

Brodny's body scraped against the metal shelf as he was hauled upward, and with a gasp, he reached the chain. The narrow shelf that held them all creaked and shifted. Larissa took a quick step onto the next platform toward the cave.

Ira panted while she scrambled on all fours back to the mossy land in the opposite direction.

Brodny didn't say a word. His knuckles were white as he clutched the chain hand over hand as he followed Larissa.

Ira's hands felt empty when Brodny's arm was let go. She was light-headed. Larissa moved toward the cave. She looked back to check on Ira only for a moment before ducking her head down and disappearing inside. Ira's legs shook too much for her to move. She didn't trust herself. She didn't trust the metal platforms. She blew out a deep breath and straightened her neck, lifting her chin.

The mist shifted its direction in the wind, easing its drizzle upon her body. Brodny stepped off the metal stairs three platforms ahead of her. He was about to disappear into the mouth of the cave just as Larissa came out.

"They're not here." Her arms were akimbo upon her hips. Ira knew that posture well. Brodny scratched the stubble under his chin. "Of course they're not here. I don't know why I ever believed they would be. Baba couldn't have navigated this hike."

"I thought maybe Andrej had carried her," Brodny mumbled.

"Who?" Larissa narrowed her eyes at him.

"The goose-herder." He nodded toward Ira. "The one who watched crazy sister jump into pond. He helps my baba go places. He...."

Ira raised her chin and swallowed, but she didn't move. She strained her ear in their direction to hear their conversation.

"Why the hell did you think they were here?"

"They said they were going where they waited out the war."

"They didn't wait out the war in a cave."

"They did...."

Ira couldn't hear everything he said. Water droplets covered her skin like a cold blanket. The sun barely broke through the tangle of branches over her head. The shadows danced over her, magical underlings to a higher being. A bright beam of light struck her in the face.

"Hungary," Ira said as loud as she could muster.

"Seriously not the time, Ira." Larissa called over to her. "Your stomach is worse than my kids'."

"No," she said. "The country. Hungary." She pressed her hands into the thick green moss, pushing herself to an unsteady stand. Her hand reached to a thin tree trunk for balance. "Before Baba immigrated to Canada, she spent the end of the war years at a hot spring in Hungary. She had some sort of job there."

Larissa frowned at her. Her entire face leant itself to the expression.

"Er... my baba was there too." From the look on Larissa's face when Brodny spoke, Ira wondered if she was about to smack him on the side of the head.

"Where is this hot spring?" Larissa pushed her messy hair out of her face and crossed her arms over her chest. Her feet were rooted into the ground, and if the cave behind her held any magic powers, there was a good chance the man who stood next to her was about to go up in flames.

"Heviz." Brodny took a step away from her as he answered, though he didn't yet dare to cross back across the slick metal platforms. "People call it the fountain of youth."

35

Vira (October 1941)

Gunfire murmured in the not-so-distant hills beyond the make-shift camps. The sound woke up Vira in the middle of the night. Next to her, she could feel Lesya stirring too. Her sister's breath was quick, matching her own. Vira pulled the covers up higher. The war wasn't supposed to be anywhere near them.

Lesya shifted so that their shoulders touched. Vira reached out a hand and found her sister's fingers, entwining them with her own. Their shutters were closed, but the air around them had cooled. There were no glass window panes here. Yellow sunflowers and multicolored bee boxes had reflected in the panes she remembered. Vira's nose was cold, and she pulled it under one of the thick goose-down blankets they'd recently finished making to layer atop their bed.

"Are we safe here?" Lesya whispered so softly Vira wasn't sure she'd spoken.

Vira squeezed her sister's hand, and Lesya squeezed Vira's back.

"I think so."

"What have you seen those times you've disappeared?"

"I haven't disappeared."

"When you go out to help mama, you do more than help mama."

Someone in the other bed rolled over, one of the twins by the sound of it, a small tumbling under the covers.

"Just don't disappear, okay?"

Lesya pressed her shoulder into her sister's, her warmth

familiar and reassuring against the shots that rang out again.

Vira whispered, "Okay," but the sound barely came out.

Her sister's breath slowed and evened as she fell back into sleep, but Vira's mind wouldn't let her go, moving from memory to fear, from hope to desperation. She stretched out her body, pointing her toes and stretching her arms out from under the warm covers, feeling the prickle of autumn in the air.

Their big trunk sat in the corner closed, with clean clothes folded on top of it. The shadows of those clothes stretched across the wall, a monster of her childhood dreams—she wondered if she preferred monsters. At least it would just eat her and be done with it, pain without the agony, death without the suspense.

Vira's eyes were just beginning to fall as dawn crept through a crack in one of the shutters. The twins stirred simultaneously, as always. Vira's mother groaned and sat up as Halya crawled on top of her. Helena giggled. Lesya closed her eyes tighter, unwilling to part from her night's sleep. Vira clasped her hands together, the absence of the wedding band on her finger surprising her once again.

"We're leaving today, *divchynky*," their mother said through tight lips. She grabbed onto Halya, who tried to stand up on her uneven lap, and hugged her. She pulled in Helena too when she came within her reach.

"What?" Lesya's eyes were wide open now. She sat up next to Vira, neither of them removing the covers pulled up around their shoulders. Back home, they'd covered goose down in silk. The cotton was heavy and rough.

"Your father's been moved to one of the camps in Poland." Their mother's pale face was pressed with the lines of the frayed pillow. Her voice sounded equally bedraggled, wavering on every word. "Bad connections, they said. Collaboration in Ukrainian independence with the Underground."

"But he never—" When their mother shook her head, Lesya didn't finish her sentence.

"How long have you known?" Vira pulled her hands out from under the covers and crossed her arms over her chest. The cool air prickled her skin. "What are those camps?" she rephrased, knowing her mother would never answer the first question.

"You've heard the same rumors I have." She said it like a swat of a wooden spoon would follow. "I don't know if it's true." The twins wiggled in her hold, but she didn't release them. She kissed the tops of their heads. "Too many people know we're here. I don't want anyone coming looking for...."

She trailed off but looked straight at Vira.

"Me?"

"You married a member of the Underground. You've openly supported your uncle." Her eyes rested on the nesting dolls sitting on the windowsill. On Vira's doll. On the Baba Yaga mask in its hands. "You've made choices people have seen."

"Never anything political."

"Everything is political."

"But Tato... and Mykhail," Lesya whispered. "How will they know where we are?"

"I don't know." Their mother's straight lips matched the line of her doll's across the room. "I've been trading letters with Panya Darka. She's moved to Budapest. She has room there for us."

She pushed off her covers and immediately grabbed for sweaters and slippers atop the big trunk.

"Vira, I need you to go to the market for me." Her mother didn't look her in the eye. She remained focused on the trunk before her, the pile of clothes, the small knapsack of Ivan's that Lesya had worn on her back for their last journey, the one Vira supposed she'd wear again now.

Vira rubbed her hands together and blew into them.

"What do we need to do?"

Her mother unlatched the shutter on the bedroom window and let the cold air burst into the room.

234

"We need food for the train ride. Wear your winter coat." Halya and Helena both hugged a leg of their mother before rushing out of the small bedroom toward their breakfast at the mention of food. Lesya followed them but paused in the doorway. "When you go," their mother continued, clasping her hands together less in warmth than in prayer, "when you go, take as much time as you need."

"I'll be quick, Mama."

She pulled on her clothes, tied a scarf around her messy hair, and topped it with her winter coat. The cool morning would warm as the sun rose higher. She probably wouldn't even need this heavy coat, but her mother encouraged her to take it, so she did.

After having a bite of cheese and a thin slice of bread, Vira went down the stairs, through the café with its empty metal chairs, out into the sunshine, the cobbled street, and the shade of the narrow park where more leaves were missing from the trees. She couldn't dance in privacy now. She couldn't talk to the guitar player unseen.

Vira moved in the opposite direction from the market. Her mother had said she could take her time. Had she grasped that she needed to find peace with this? Had her mother for once in her life understood her completely?

The dirt road led through the town but it also led toward the forest, toward the cover of trees so thick she could hide just for a moment. She put her hand to the stone necklace, ran her fingers along the string that held it, then reached behind her neck. The worn knot held as she tried to cajole it into loosening. Her fingernails dug into the string. She yanked it hard, but it only became tighter, the string pressing into her neck almost magically bound as she pulled it one way then used both hands to yank, tug, and wrench it apart.

Vira lifted the string necklace to her teeth. She had to be done with this. The gritty fibers of the string tasted foul in her mouth, but the strands frayed. She chewed harder, gnawing until a snap broke through the air, until the tension broke, until the stone fell to the ground at her feet.

She should have traded it away instead of Mykhail's wedding band, but it was worthless. It had always been worthless. Maybe she was worthless. She knew her mother had noticed the ring's absence. If she ever saw her husband again... But the thought was just as ludicrous as the dream of returning to Ukraine.

No, Ivan was gone. Uncle Oleh was gone. Her father was imprisoned. Mykhail was....

A rustle of a footstep on nearby leaves made her close her eyes. She didn't wince. She just waited. All the worst had already happened. Another step came closer. If hands came down to grab at her or a gun poked into her back, she was ready. The shrubs shifted behind her.

"My sister said you were in this town, but I didn't believe her."

A hand gripped her arm, turning her around. She forced her eyes open. But she didn't see. She couldn't see. Unsteady, light-headed, she must have been confusing her day with her dreams.

Dmytro was thinner than her memory of him, as sinewy as a line-drawing of himself.

Pieces of thoughts tried to arrange themselves in her mind. Dizziness swept over her, and she grabbed for a thin tree trunk growing up by her side, unsure if it had always been there or if it had somehow just appeared. Like he had.

"How are you here?"

Dmytro bent to pick up the stone at her feet. Her trembling hand mingled with the leaves of the thin tree and shook a leaf from a low branch. The flash of yellow fell in the narrow space between them, reminding her of their night shadowed by camp-fire light.

"Noncia needs you."

"How could she—?"

"Come."

He didn't kiss her or pull his body close to hers. She didn't feel his breath on her skin. He just held her arm and pulled her deeper into the forest.

"I have a train to catch. My family is leaving...."

"And my family needs you...."

Her feet followed him before her mind or her mouth thought to argue. They stepped over rocks and roots. Ferns tickled her ankles. Brambles snagged on her long skirt, threatening to slow her down, to stop her. As the terrain became steep, he let go of her arm to climb on all fours.

"Where are we going?"

She tried to mimic his form, stepping on the rocks that jutted out of the hill, using branches and vines for balance, ducking under low-hanging limbs. Her heart beat so fast it silenced her tongue. She had to go back. There was no way she could just follow him. She barely knew him anymore. Maybe she never did. Her boot slipped in a patch of mud, and she landed on her belly, winter coat caked in muck and moss.

"This is *smishno*. I can't. There's no reason...."

"Please." For the first time, he stopped and held her eyes. They were as dark as ever, darker than the dirt she lay in, darker than the shadows under the trees, darker than the ashes of her old home that filled her dreams.

"Please," he repeated. "Noncia's baby is coming."

Vira's fingers grasped in the mud.

"Baby?"

"And it's too soon."

She reached for a rock on the hill to steady herself, to push herself out of the damp mossy leaves. Dmytro stepped back to help her. His pulse beat inside her hand.

"I don't know why you were at the edge of Slovak Paradise," he said, his voice heavy, "but I think it was a sign. You are here to help us." He pulled her up to a stand and tightened his grasp on her hand. "Our *cim'ï* separated when we moved out of Ukraine through southern Poland." He broke the hold on her eyes and stared out into the forest. "They had told us to stay out of Poland."

"You should have stayed in Ukraine, in Galicia."

He frowned but didn't answer. Far off, a train whistle cut through the woods. It couldn't be her train. She had time before her train.

"Where is Noncia?"

He leaned over and pressed his lips to hers. Everything went silent but her heartbeat. She swore she heard the buzz of bees.

"This way."

And she followed.

From the top of the hill, she could see a river winding through the mountains. Dmytro crouched down and pointed to a bend where the mist blanketed the gulley in a veil of white.

"There," he whispered, reaching for her hand again, steadying himself against the tree branches and boulders that acted as makeshift railings for their steep descent.

Vira heard the deep moan before she saw the cave or Dmytro's sister. The relief in Noncia's eyes flashed for only a moment before the pain ripped through her body once again—her body that was not nearly as round as Vira had been expecting. She was clearly with child, but the pregnancy appeared nowhere near its end.

Noncia stood in a squat, leaning against the wall of the cave, a shallow puddle of red underneath her. Vira rushed to her side and put an arm around her back while Dmytro stood just outside the opening, mist beading on his dark skin.

Vira shook, but she tore off her muddy coat. Two piles of blankets were nestled deep in the cave. Two bundles of clothing. Some cookingware, some tools, a familiar pouch full of buttons.

Another contraction seized Noncia. She rocked and groaned. There had barely been two minutes since the last one. Vira held her eyes, forcing her to breathe. She needed to breathe. That was the only thing she knew for sure.

When the pain passed, Vira wanted to mop up the puddle

of blood so Noncia wouldn't see. She wanted to sweep the dirty rock ground and give her goose-down pillows to ease down upon. She reached down to brush off a thick stick on the cave floor. When the next one came, she told Dmytro's sister to bit into it.

Far away, past Noncia's moans, past the splash of the waterfall outside the cave, a train whistle tore through the valley like it ripped it open. Vira's head shot up and away from the woman in her arms and away from the blood now mingled in her own fingers. The echo of the train tore through her too. She knew she had taken too long.

36

Larissa

The shadows had grown and blanketed the world around them in night before Larissa, Ira, and Brodny emerged from the edge of the Slovak Paradise forest. The semi-circle moon hung high in the sky—shaped like a D, Alex liked to say. He'd been so proud of his letter discovery, a D-for-Daddy-moon. Larissa's skin warmed at the thought of her little boy, a better feeling than the lingering fretfulness on her mind.

She didn't know where they were. They didn't have flash-lights or water or scrub-brushes to clean the caked mud from their shoes. Larissa used the moon's reflection off the golden thread of the tryzybs in Ira's hair as her guide. She had barely noticed those strands of gold in the daytime. Her eyes had adjusted to the darkness now, but its shapes were driven from her children's imaginations. Trees stretched out their limbs reaching for her. The low houses were merely crouching, waiting until the right moment to straighten, stretch, and shuffle forward. Were wolves native to Slovakia? Were their nearly silent footfalls pacing through the fields around them?

"You sisters can spend night with us," Brodny said from ahead of her. He'd been nearly silent since they'd pulled him up from the creaky metal shelf, since they'd found the cave empty of people, of everything but an etching of a girl's first name she didn't recognize, a cross, and a jagged engraving of "1941."

"So you stay?" Brodny walked faster. They had to be getting close.

"No, thanks. We have our hotel," Ira answered before Larissa had a chance to properly consider it. A clean floor to curl up on didn't really seem that bad. She took refuge in similar spaces in the bedrooms of her kids after they'd had a nightmare. A dream about reaching trees and crouching giants. Darina looked like the type to have a clean floor.

The stars hovered over them as they trekked onward, stuck in a bedtime story that wouldn't end. Maybe she needed a purple crayon like Harold. She needed to draw her house, her window, her bed.

The homes nestled tighter together now. Larissa couldn't tell if they looked familiar. They might have been on Brodny's street, only houses away from his own. That's what she told herself as she tried to keep up with Ira's flashing hair ribbon, ignoring the human or animal shadows that moved between the most haphazard of the structures.

Brodny threw an arm out behind him, motioning for them to be still.

"You hear?"

Larissa stopped her tired feet, listening for witch cackles or a wolf's howl.

"No," she started to say, but then she did, the noise at once a howl, a groan, and a gasp of pain.

"Darina," Brodny whispered, breaking into a run.

The sisters followed, falling into step with one another. She hadn't noticed how dark the other houses had been until she saw the candlelight that shone out of the windows of Brodny's. None of the houses seemed lit by electricity, even if they all had wires tangling the spaces between them.

They all tore in the front door. Larissa squinted in the brightness. Darina squatted on the floor, holding her belly, eyes pressed shut in pain.

Brodny exclaimed something she was pretty sure was a curse at the babas as he took his wife in his arms.

"You are home," Darina whispered in a moment of reprieve.

Brodny kissed her forehead and looked anxiously at the sisters. His face contorted almost as badly as his wife's when the next contraction hit.

The groan filled the house, shuddering over Larissa's skin. She knew that feeling where your body left your control, where you had to give into it. She had fought it the first time when in labor with Anna. She hadn't won.

"Breathe," she insisted, coming closer. She put one hand on Brodny's knee and another tentatively on Darina's damp head. The woman inhaled, and Larissa's own breaths came fast. She remembered the focused patterns. She locked eyes with Darina.

"Have you called the doctor?" she whispered when the pain had passed.

"No doctor. My babcia was going to..."

A necklace hung around Darina's neck, twisted almost too tight from the contorting forward and back. Larissa's own forehead became damp.

She reached over to loosen it. At the end of the twisted leather strap, a small stone with a hole at its center dangled like a talisman. She shifted it forward and allowed it to fall back into place on Darina's chest.

"Old stone. Old story. For luck," Darina whispered.

The creamy white stone stood out against the light brown of her skin.

"How far apart are the pains?"

"Close," Darina whispered.

Larissa nodded. She moved her hands to Darina's temples and massaged them.

"What should she do?" Brodny's words were lost to another yell as Darina curled into herself.

A thin purple vein stood out at her hairline as she contorted, flexing her wrists backward and her knees and elbows inward toward her round belly. She silenced herself only for a gasp of air before wailing out again.

Larissa bit her lip. Her sister still hovered by the doorway.

Her arms were crossed over her chest.

"Ira boil some water!"

Ira didn't answer but she moved toward the small kitchen space. She banged open cupboards looking for pans. Darina winced at the noises.

"Quietly!" Larissa added. She nestled onto her knees at Darina's side. She ran her hand over the woman's long dark hair. "I can take care of you," she whispered, feeling her face warm. She could do this. She could do this. She had to do this.

How many times had Larissa told Anna she could do anything? Hundreds of times. Thousands of times.

She was the little engine that could. She breathed hard. Puff, puff, puff. Chug, chug, chug. The little engine was originally a girl, after all, capable of anything, no room for doubt.

She shifted behind Darina and rubbed her neck. These moments between pain were short but she had to relax the woman as much as possible, make her think Larissa knew what the hell she was doing.

"The baby will be in your arms soon," she cooed in Darina's ear. "You're a strong mama already. This is just your first adventure with your little one. You're in it together."

Brodny shifted his weight as he sat next to his wife. He wanted to go. He started to stand.

"You're staying," Larissa grabbed the collar of his shirt, pulling him back down.

"I need...."

"You need to be with your wife." She ripped off the hat still perched on his head, throwing it across the room. Larissa breathed at an increased pace through her mouth, inhaling quietly, exhaling with an audible blow. In, out, in, out, a metronome. Brodny mimicked her. Darina pursed her lips.

"The baby needs your breath," she said, calmly. "When it gets bad, focus on your breath." She reached out again for Brodny's shirt. She gave it another tug to make sure she had his attention. "This is your job. Keep her breathing. Keep her focused on her breathing."

She released Brodny and guided Darina's hand to the stone that now nestled between her swollen breasts.

"For luck," she repeated. "I need you to focus your eyes here and to breathe. Brodny will help you breathe. Let him help you."

One more contraction, she told herself. Then she'd examine the woman. She had to. Her face blushed, and her hands were clammy.

Darina stared at the stone as if it would save her. She nodded at it, as if it understood.

By the time the next jolt of pain struck Darina, the plan was set and practiced. The initial scream diverted into patterned breathing. Her wild eyes sought out the stone bouncing on her breasts.

"You're doing wonderfully. Keep breathing." Larissa shifted in front of Darina to take up the stone, holding it higher so she could see it clearly. "Through your mouth." She tapped her mouth. "In, out, in, out. The baby needs your breath."

Ira clanged something in the kitchen, and Larissa winced.

"Ira, bring her water." Her sister froze next to the pot she had put on to boil. "Not the boiling water! Drinking water!"

Ira nodded quickly and opened and shut more cabinet doors, looking for a glass. They squeaked and banged.

Darina's eyes still locked on the stone. Wife and husband breathed hard together, on the downhill side of the pain. The tension in Darina's face relaxed, bit by bit, blood vessel by blood vessel. She didn't notice Ira's clatter.

"You're doing great. A good mama already," Larissa said to her, when the pain passed. Darina pointed weakly to a fabric pouch on a nearby table. Larissa stretched out her arm to take it into her hands then opened up the clasp. Metal instruments were inside—long scissors, tweezers, forceps, a miniature turkey baster, various old cloths. Larissa brought them across the small room to Ira, still immobile at the counter next to the almost boiling pot of water.

"Boil these," she said to her sister, as gently as she could. She put an arm to her shoulder, without any response to her touch. "The metal ones. Please, Ira."

Her sister picked up the metal tools like they were dirty diapers, and Larissa washed her hands in the wide basin sink.

She swallowed when she returned to Darina's side.

"I have two babies," she explained when she knelt again at Darina's knees, as if this statement would justify her looking between the woman's legs. Her face reddened, she knew. She wiped her hands on one of the rags from the medical bag. Her hands needed to stay clean, and Darina shouldn't see them shaking. The laboring woman's eyes were huge. Larissa was all she had.

Ira appeared at their side with glasses of water for everyone, an awkward waitress.

"Ira, tell us a story." Larissa composed her face then folded up the layers of skirt over the woman's knees.

37

Ira

Ira's forehead sweated from standing so close to the boiling water, but where else could she be? The air inside the small house was muggy and oppressive. There wasn't much difference on the other side of the room, the living area—only separated from the small kitchen area by a few long strides.

Ira scooped up the collection of metal tools and dropped them one by one into the boiling water as her sister instructed. She wasn't sure how she'd get them out. Not her hands. Spoons of some sort? Tongs? Chop sticks?

"Let them boil for a minute," Larissa called out to her. "She needs one of your stories."

Ira fisted her empty hands as she approached the three nestled onto the floor, but she stayed on the outskirts. She shifted a few steps more to the side, not wanting to see under Darina's skirt folded up over her knees. Larissa crouched between her open legs with an expression pained and full of awe.

"Once upon a time." She paused, drifting over the stories to tell in her mind. The metal instruments were surely sanitized by now. Would they hear her if she told her tale from across the room by the stovetop? "Once upon a time, there was a warrior princess named Marya Morevna." Ira forced herself not to move, planting her feet into the floor like a creature cursed by Baba Yaga. She cleared her throat. "She was as gorgeous as Vasilisa the beautiful and more fierce than Koschei the Deathless, the old cranky wizard who had discovered the secret to eternal life."

Nestled next to Darina, helping her into a better position,

Larissa nodded at her sister's choice, just as the woman's body tensed again. Her posture broke as if her skin just sprouted thorns.

"And Marya Morevna..." Ira whispered.

"Wait," Larissa snapped. "Wait for the contraction to pass. Then keep going."

Ira closed her mouth and retreated across the room, her roots ripping up from the floor, the medical tools her excuse. A knife. Scissors. Various clamps. Forceps. Tweezers. No, the tools weren't much better.

Baba Vira was probably at the fountain of youth in western Hungary by now. Darina had growled to Brodny about it between her pains. She'd mentioned it before their trek into the forest too. Ira didn't know why she hadn't really listened. She hadn't translated the words in her head until later. Maybe Baba Vira would meet with Koschei the Deathless at the fountain of youth, steal his egg, take his power. Or maybe she just caked herself in medicinal mud, letting it drip from her bony body in globs, making her messy mark on her surroundings. Ira wanted to chase her, to track her down, to join her and Noncia on whatever crazy scheme they were up to. Noncia fled this birth, so why couldn't she?

The pain seemed to have passed. Larissa knelt in front of Darina, coaching her on a new way to breathe. Ira didn't know if truly helped or just distracted. But air was good. She took a deep breath, feeling her chest rise. She exhaled deeply, feeling the heat of the steam from her boiling pot.

Larissa, Darina, and even Brodny were totally absorbed in their repetition of "hee, hee, whoo..." Ira just heard demented laughing owls.

She shifted her weight back and forth.

"Okay," Larissa called over to her. "The story again."

"Okay," she echoed, turning off the heat and staring at the hot metal pieces inside. Digging them out was going to be tricky. Did she have to use sterilized utensils so she didn't contaminate the tools? She fingered a nearby dishtowel before using it to pick up the pot. Ira held it out far from her body and poured the boiling water into the sink, terrified one of the metal pieces inside would clang out and she'd have to begin all over.

"Come back over here so we can hear you. Just pause every contraction, okay?"

"Okay," she repeated.

Brodny's face was white. He kept looking at the door, but Larissa wouldn't let him leave his wife's side. The air became somehow more moist ten steps closer to them. Ira fought a gag.

"So Marya Morevna was a powerful warrior. She led her army and conquered anyone who dared to go up against her. She'd defeated kings and tyrants, and one day, when she discovered Koschei the Deathless, she captured him and brought him home to the dungeon in her castle."

"I know this," Brodny said, lifting his head, but Larissa's hand moved quickly to shift his face back toward his panting wife. Ira tried to slow her own breaths.

"Marya Morevna fell in love with a prince named Ivan," Ira continued. Brodny held onto his wife's hand. His face was almost as damp as hers, his shirt maybe more so. Darina's face tightened. "And after she married him, when she went off to her next battle, she told him he could go anywhere in her castle except for the dungeon, which he was not allowed to open. Well, the idiot—"

"Shut up, Ira!" Larissa's words barked out. Darina's face contorted. Brodny breathed hard at her side, following the practiced patterns like his life depended on it. Like his wife's depended on it. Ira didn't know if it did or not. Larissa joined them both while holding up the stone as if it were a sacred relic between them.

Ira's hands tapped a rhythm on her leg when the puffing stopped and she dared to continue.

"But when Marya Morevna was away in battle, Prince Ivan opened the dungeon door. Koschei the Deathless swept away to the battlefield, and the wizard took Marya Morevna away to his far-off kingdom."

The poor pregnant woman before her stared helplessly at the ceiling. Ira swallowed and pretended she was just telling the story to herself.

"Prince Ivan waited until Koschei the Deathless left his kingdom and tried to free his wife. But Koshchei heard of the escape and caught up to them on one of his fastest horses. He threatened Ivan, telling him that if he tried to save Marya Morevna again, he would be killed.

"But Marya Morevna stole a magic handkerchief from the old wizard and gave it to her husband, telling him that Baba Yaga had horses faster than even Koshchei's best steed. That's actually where he got his fastest horses, I think. He had married Baba Yaga at one point....

"Story, Ira." Larissa turned over her shoulder to glare at her sister. Apparently, someone was listening. "No, wait."

Darina folded in on herself, and Ira again thought of thorns poking out from every pore, a curse from an immortal wizard, an ancient witch. She didn't know what any woman had ever done to be punished like this.

"So," she continued, when Darina gasped for air, letting her body collapse against her husband. "So, Prince Ivan rode his horse deep into the woods for days and days, coming across birds, bees, and a lioness. When he didn't kill them, they promised to help him. He waved Koshchei's magic handkerchief at the River of Fire, and a magical crystal bridge appeared to take him to the house of Baba Yaga."

When the contraction came next, she closed her mouth before Darina or Larissa could send her death glares. How long did a birth take? Maybe she needed to stretch out the story. She'd be Shahrazad, weaving her tale for as long as it took to survive.

Darina grunted a sound that vibrated Ira's skin. Larissa moved to look under the woman's skirts again when the contraction passed. She wiped her forehead with the back of her hand and tilted her head to one side and the another like she was stretching before a track meet. She'd forgotten that Larissa used to be a runner. She'd been fast too. No one could catch her. Not unless she let them.

Her sister pointed to her bulging mommy purse that she had dropped by the door.

"Ira, get me a rubber band for my hair."

Ira obeyed and dug through the bag, not knowing why Larissa had half the things in there. Did she think she'd need to entertain Ira with crayons? She dug past makeup and Larissa's wallet and passport. Underneath the eye-liner and tangled around a pen taken from their hotel was the hair tie.

Larissa practiced the demented owl breathing again. The three in the middle of the floor spoke in whispers. Brodny repeatedly leaned away from the women, and Larissa put a hand on his back every time, bringing him closer.

Ira wanted to just throw the hair tie at her, but she inched nearer, keeping her eyes focused anywhere but under Darina's skirts. She fixated on her sister's hair. It had a few grays. They were stiff and haphazard, as if rebelling against Larissa's endless regulation. She finger-combed her sister's hair before pulling it back into a neat ponytail.

Darina opened her eyes and gazed into Ira's. She forced herself to blink and turn away, taking a few steps back before she continued.

"Baba Yaga's house was surrounded by a fence made of bones, and it stood upon chicken legs that scratched at the dirt underneath it. When Prince Ivan neared, Baba Yaga herself stepped out and demanded what he wanted. She told him she could help if he first helped her."

Darina's wails filled the small house as the next contraction hit her hard. The screams filled Ira's head, and she closed her eyes. She echoed the breath pattern softly, as if this would be over sooner if they all got it right.

Larissa held up the small stone at the end of Darina's necklace. The pregnant woman squirmed, and Larissa moved herself between the woman's legs again. Brodny supported his wife as she shifted. Ira closed her eyes again as her sister became more intimate with Darina than, Ira guessed, she'd ever been with herself.

"*Diet'a, Diet'a!*" Darina gasped, and Ira wished she understood.

"I think she's ready to push," Larissa called over her shoulder. She whispered to Darina, tapping her chin and touching her chest, tucking her head down as if preparing for a somersault. Darina nodded. The stone had dropped back down upon her chest. Sweat covered her face. Larissa wiped the hair off her forehead.

"On the first day, Baba Yaga told Prince Ivan to mind the stables," Ira continued through the groans and grunts and pants. "The horses broke free, but the birds he had spared helped him herd them all back to their stalls by the end of the day. The bees helped the second day, and the lions helped the third day, until he was granted Baba Yaga's fastest steed, and he raced off to find Marya Morevna."

"Here we go," Larissa whispered. Darina gritted her teeth, and Brodny looked one last time at the door. Larissa didn't have to guide him back this time, though. He clutched one of his wife's bent knees, as Larissa put herself into the same position on the other.

Ira closed her eyes as Darina yelled out something primeval.

"And Prince Ivan reached Marya Morevna within the day, and on their horse, together they raced away faster than Koschei the Deathless could go," she whispered to herself. "And they lived happily ever after, Marya Morevna kicking ass until the day she died, and Prince Ivan never doubting her advice again."

Ira tried to block out the smell of sweat and salty sour birth. She tried to focus on her grandmother. On the fountain of youth. And how they'd get there. Then a baby's wail cut through the moist air.

38

Vira (October 1941)

Vira couldn't walk away when the lifeless baby left her hands. She couldn't leave as the almost-mother sobbed and clutched the too-tiny, pale body. She couldn't leave after she washed her hands and the dirty rags in the stream, giving Noncia space to scream and wail and beat her fists on the ground. Only when Noncia's sobs turned to whimpers and exhaustion, when she'd folded the too tiny baby girl into blankets like she was sleeping, and when Dmytro turned away from the cross he'd etched into the cave wall and opened his mouth to speak was she able to get away.

She didn't let herself hear his words. Instead, Vira retrieved her heavy coat from the rock floor near Noncia's sleeping body. She took a blanket from their strewn pile of belongings and draped it over her.

"Do you have enough food?"

"Will you come back?" Dmytro reached for her hand, but she didn't offer it. She walked away, forcing his face to slip into the shadows of the forest behind her. The craggy hillside dotted with patches of moss and ferns gave her footing. There were vines to wrap around her grasp. Her boots caked in mud. It oozed inside them, squishing between her toes and stockings, but she climbed, reaching for limbs of trees in lieu of arms of family to draw her forward.

Vira didn't process anything but her balance and her way out until she stepped into the slant of sun at the edge of the woods. The stone with the hole at its center lay amid the brown leaves and pine needles on the ground. She stepped on it hard as she walked away, but it didn't break. Her mother was going to unleash a fury beyond a Baba Yaga's.

A wisp of a campfire's smoke trailed through the air like the trail of a steam engine. Where was the rest of their family? How were Dmytro and Noncia all alone? And why did they choose the woods over the strange camp that had formed? Had it been a man in a camp like this that had done this to Noncia?

Vira stamped her feet hard on the dirt road to release the caked mud from her boots and ran toward the train station. White geese scattered ahead of her. The closely tucked houses of the village came into view. People widened their eyes at the sight of her. She knew she confirmed every doubt they'd ever had about her—the woman from the market with her narrowed stare, the butcher who averted his eyes as if conversation with her was somehow indecent—but she had to get to the train station. Her mother had said to take her time. If the train had been in the morning, she wouldn't have said to take her time.

Vira's wet skirts beat her legs as she moved. The mud squished inside of her boots, making her slip and slide with every step. The skin on her calves rubbed painfully with every stride.

At the ticket booth, she bent over to catch her breath. There were only a few passengers lingering, no sign of her mother or sisters. They were probably still at the tiny apartment, packing, annoyed she'd disappeared so long. Her mother probably spit on the ground, cursing about her, spittle Lesya would try to clean up before they abandoned their rooms.

The ticket seller called something out to her she didn't understand. After months, she knew she should understand more Slovakian, but she'd never really tried.

"The train to Budapest?" she tried, hoping at least the city name would be understood.

He shook his head, saying something incomprehensible, as he examined her.

"What?"

He pulled out a calendar and pointed to a day, and Vira tried to figure out what he meant, what today was, and if he pointed to tomorrow like she thought.

"Tomorrow?" she ventured.

"*Zavtra*," he answered nodding.

Vira bent over again, resting her hands on her knees, bending over to catch her breath and hold up her body. "I didn't miss them," she whispered, half to herself.

"Miss who?"

A woman stood beyond her holding a schedule. Her Ukrainian was so welcome Vira fought the urge to hug her.

"My family. I guess, I had misunderstood...."

The woman squinted at her.

"Did you ask about Budapest?" When Vira nodded, she continued, "A train to Budapest left two hours ago. The next one's not until tomorrow."

The woman pointed to a schedule she held. Bold black ink covered the page indecipherably, line by line

"A mother and three girls boarded the Budapest train," she added.

Vira's heartbeat hammered, choking any words that tried to escape.

The station's clock read two thirty-eight, its graceful metal arms pointing in opposing directions.

Vira ran her fingers through her hair—her messy hair, flecked with leaves and sticky tree sap. She backed away from the woman and turned back to the road, her body moving in painful, squishy steps past more houses so close together, past their shingled roofs, flower pots, and yellow stucco stains. Through the park and its changing leaves. To the café under their small apartment.

The owner was placing candles on the tables.

Vira rushed past him toward the back stairs.

"Pani Vira," the owner said, taking her by the arm. "What

are you doing back here? I thought your train left."

She rushed past him, up the creaky wooden steps. She fumbled in her pockets, not having a clue when the key might have slipped from her possession. She pushed on the door, finding it unlocked. But the apartment was bare. No trunk, no coats, no food on the counter, no clothes draped over Lesya's ironing board. No iron. No wooden spoons forgotten by the twins on the floor.

On the window sill, the dolls were gone, escaped, fled... all but one. Vira's doll stared back at her, all alone, clutching its Baba Yaga mask, smiling as if it had everyone else figured out.

"Pani Vira," the café owner called from the bottom of the stairs. "Did you forget something? Are you all right?"

"No," she whispered. Her steps tracked dirt across the swept wooden floor. Lesya would have made sure to sweep that floor.

Her doll was light, but something rattled inside as if her sisters hid there, as if it was all a disappearing game. She twisted the painted wood halves, and the matryoshka popped open. A roll of money was twisted inside, held by a rubber band.

The café owner appeared in the door behind her. She didn't hear his heavy footsteps or smell the apricot brandy scent that accompanied him like a perfume.

"Can I help with something?"

She closed her matryoshka and picked up the light doll in her hands. She cradled it and didn't meet their old landlord's eyes. A small knapsack had been tucked into the corner. Ivan's. The smallest one they had owned. The goose-down blanket sat folded underneath it. Vira snatched at the knapsack with her free hand and embraced the blanket as best she could, fleeing past him out of the apartment and down the creaking, narrow stairs.

In the green park beyond the café, she allowed her body to crumple onto a metal bench, her load falling onto the brick sidewalk at her feet. A small boy, not much older than the twins, pointed at her and laughed. His big brother turned and caught sight of her, covered in mud, leaves, maybe even in blood.

She scowled and glared. "Get away from me, or I'll eat you up!"

They quieted but didn't move away. The older one picked up a stone and threw it at her. She stood up and spit at them, using the Ukrainian words of her father's men that she'd never before spoken aloud.

The boys ran, and the matryoshka fell from her gasp, its Baba Yaga mask staring at her from where it sat in the grass. She stared at it. It stared back at her.

Vira picked up the small knapsack and opened it in her lap. Clothes. Soap. A brush. A tin drinking cup.

Another train whistle rolled through the small town. The smoke from the far-off campfires rose over the hills toward the clouds. She picked up her matryoshka, brushing the dirt from its side. She tucked it into the knapsack and closed it tight.

39

Larissa

The hum in Larissa's body felt as audible as the train rails underneath her. Holding Darina and Brodny's new baby girl in her arms, all she wanted to do was introduce the newborn to her children. Look what Mommy helped bring into the world. Look at the tiny new person grown inside another woman, delivered into her new family by Larissa—through blood, through sweat, through miracle. She knew she couldn't explain it to them, but something had settled over her. It prickled at her fingertips and filled her veins.

Her own children had been puffy and red-faced, and she'd been exhausted but euphoric after their long labors. They had been wrapped in the white hospital blankets striped with rose pink and cornflower blue. Anna's dimpled chin had already been set in stubborn determination. Two years later, Alex's ears were like complex little seashells.

Now, their long bodies were tucked into twin beds, cribs packed away. When she had called Greg, Larissa hadn't told her husband much more than their updated destination, but she had forced him to hold up the phone to her kids' sleeping heads. Alex's breathing was soft and even. Anna had a little snore. Larissa had covered her mouth, but she'd been sure the hum that tickled her skin could be transferred via a phone line, from the resonance of her breath to the timbre of the air filling their lungs.

They had named the baby Sinfi after Darina's aunt, a woman who never had children of her own.

Tears wet Larissa's eyes, and the hum traveled across her skin in swells as the train rattled around her. She was the Little Engine That Could. The Hungry Caterpillar emerging out of her cocoon as a butterfly. No, her chrysalis. She'd always wished Eric Carle had gotten that one right. Only moths have cocoons.

Across from her, Ira slept, passed out with her mouth open and her long hair falling over half her face. Larissa fought the urge to tidy her.

After miles of open fields, they rolled through the outskirts of a town. A glassy-still lake appeared out her window. She checked her watch. Probably Lake Balaton. Their destination, Keszthely, was on the lake, the nearest town to Heviz with a train station. They'd have to catch a bus from here. She hoped there weren't any pictures of local attractions in the train station. If Ira found out they were ignoring the centuries-old palace, it would be a battle. She didn't know who wanted to be a kick-ass princess more, Anna or Ira.

Larissa nudged her sister with her foot, and Ira jumped up, ready to run like Baba Yaga chased her.

"I think we're almost at our station."

Ira grunted in reply, relaxing her body from her false start and pushing her hair out of her face. She reached into her bag and pulled out the tryzub ribbons, their long thin length wound into a neat coil. She placed them on her lap while she ran her fingers through her messy tendrils and tried to work out the tangles.

Larissa reached for her purse to lend her sister a brush.

"Think there will be more sunflowers?" Outside her window, two white geese flew low against the sky like they were looking for landmarks.

"I don't know." Ira wove the blue and yellow ribbons through her new braid, folding it over the crown of her head, not needing to check her reflection in the train windows. Larissa licked her lips and bit down on them to redden them, too tired for makeup.

The train's speaker crackled before it announced their

arrival. Larissa reached around her to collect her things, but there wasn't much to collect—her purse in her lap, her bag by her feet, the odd stone with a hole in it around her neck that Darina had pressed into her hands as an exhausted thank-you and good luck.

The language tossed between the few passengers lugging bags over shoulders was thick and heavy in the open-air train station, the words fully foreign now—Hungarian not at all related to Polish, Slovakian, or Ukrainian. Tiny gray birds settled in the eaves of the covered platform. They watched the sisters without a song.

Across the street from the station, pedestals and stone sculptures dotted across a park. The houses beyond were a graceful mishmash of Romanesque balustrades next to dark Gothic angularity next to Tudor beams. And there wasn't a sunflower in sight.

Roses climbed up the houses' railings. Fresh paint emboldened their facades that only showed occasional cracks and crumbles. The small yards cherished their privacy with tall wrought-iron fences acting as dividers.

"Heviz," Larissa whispered, not letting the absence of golden petals intimidate her. "Darina was convinced that they'd be at the spa in Heviz. Did you know that's where they waited out the war?"

"Sure, at the real fountain of youth," said Ira. Larissa's lips pressed into a line. She kept her mouth shut. "What? It's what Baba always told me. I never knew where it was though, or if it was real."

Larissa exhaled and refocused on the humming under her skin. She moved forward, and it crescendoed. Her arms swung to its song. It drowned out the squeal of releasing train brakes and loudspeaker announcements that barely registered in her ears.

Ira pulled her out of the way of a courier laden with packages.

"Let's go this way," she said, clutching Larissa's arm. Larissa followed, feeling the bounce of Ira's step to another rhythm but not altering her own footfalls to match. She tired of matching. Their shoulders bumped. Their bags jostled each other. They stepped out of the station's covered breezeway, past the silent gray birds into the sunlight.

The small paved lot that separated the sisters from the park held the bus stop. Tiny folded schedules were tucked into a plastic box, and Larissa plucked one out, checking her watch again. They had just missed the bus to Heviz. The buzz on her skin didn't mind.

A nearby bench was perfect to settle upon, to bask in the day, in the feeling of being alive, in the knowledge that they were about to finally find Baba Vira—she absolutely knew it. But Ira didn't take a second glance at the bench.

She released Larissa's arm and walked across the street toward one of the park's pebbled paths that wove under a canopy of trees.

A glimmer of a thought passed through Larissa, a hope that the centuries-old palace wasn't within walking distance, a fear they'd lose time, but then it was gone. She scanned over the rooftops and the park's tall trees. She folded away the bus schedule and tucked it into her purse, before she noticed Ira waiting for her across the street.

Her sister's tryzub ribbons blew in the breeze, making her look ready for an entrance onto a Ukrainian folkdance stage, even with her jeans and American version of a peasant blouse. Ira held out a hand, and Larissa darted across the street. If she was going home to her family soon, she needed to collect at least one more story for them. She needed to collect it for herself.

"Let's explore," she said to Ira.

Ira raised an eyebrow. "How much time do we have?"

Larissa bit her makeup-free lips to redden them again. "We've got time."

She clutched her sister's hand and ran. They were kids again, and she pulled along her little sister because she really, really wanted to see around the next bend. Ira, an inch taller now, still had to pick up her speed to keep up.

A white stone statue greeted them around the second curve. The woman towered over the sisters on her etched pedestal. One hand held a lyre and another arched above her. A chiseled braid folded over the crown of her head, and only a loose hint of a long skirt hid her nude form. Her arms were thick, and her curves were rounded. The expression on her face wasn't the fierce countenance of the Warsaw mermaid, nor the romantic gaze of a classical nude. This woman was a force—a confident, friendly, daring, dancing, uncompromising, naked force.

Ira looked down to her loose top and fingered its hem.

"I'll keep it on."

"Thanks for that."

They walked past the statue and crossed over to the brick sidewalk that led them deeper into the town, away from the cool breeze that sent the chill of Lake Balaton in their direction.

The sun warmed Larissa's face.

"I think there's this palace...."

40

Ira

Stepping off the bus, Ira breathed in the warm and humid fresh air and moved toward the entrance of the Heviz hot spring, imagining herself as Vasilisa the Beautiful, as the warrior queen Moira, as the seeker of Baba Yaga. Squared spires on either side of the arched gateway reached toward the treetops and beyond into the puffy white clouds in the sky. Ira puffed out her chest like it was a magical quest. Larissa walked beside her and took her hand. Ira squeezed her sister's palm, feeling their life-lines press together. Ira's life-line was short and her love-line fractured, but her family-line was deep and unbroken. Her sister's was the same.

Shaded under the wooden structure, they could see the grounds of the spa beyond. A pointed gray roof looked stolen from a fable, and soft green lily pads and pink water lilies stippled the surrounding water. Water lilies. Ira was fairly confident she'd never actually seen real water lilies. A paved path led along the storied fountain of youth and into the shadows of the forest.

"This way," Larissa urged, pulling them inside.

"Did you see something?"

"No, I just have a feeling."

"Mother's intuition?"

"Granddaughter's."

Willows arched over their heads. The reflection of the nearby water cast a speckled light upon the world around them, making everything flicker. The humid haze of glimmers and darkness practically held droplets in the air. Larissa's hand was warm in her own.

Two musicians played their instruments where tightly knit birch trees opened to a clearing no larger than a good-sized picnic blanket. The violinist, a woman, pulled her bow brisk then fluid on the strings as she led her partner on guitar. Her eyes were closed, and her expression told the saddest story in the world.

A white-haired couple sat on nearby bench by the water, enjoying the trills of the Hungarian folk song. Ira examined their features, debating if they might know of her grandmother, if she would have made herself known here somehow—tirading, terrifying, or taking strangers into her arms and letting them cry against her bony frame.

"I think she's here." Larissa kept moving but slower now.

Ira closed her eyes, trying to feel her grandmother's location, but instead her mind filled with images. The last time Baba Vira had been here, these waters had been filled with broken soldiers, broken families, and broken lives.

She took a step backward as if to dodge the sadness that swelled in the music. Baba Vira had lost her brother, her sisters, and her mother to the war. She'd lost her favorite uncle, her father, and seen the hanging body of a friend. Ira had known the stories as long as she could remember, but they had just been stories. Not her grandmother's life. Not anything really connected to hers. Ira's breathing matched the rapid-fire pace of the nearby violin.

"You okay?" Larissa stopped.

The tree branches above her reached out like arms and she imagined bodies hanging there, bodies with stars of David, bodies with inverted brown triangles, bodies of family and friends. Ira pulled air into her body in a shudder.

A whirring sound approached behind her, and she pulled back, opening her eyes and stepping off the path onto the mossy waterside bank as quickly as she could.

A biker passed, pedaling hard. The water lilies' soft scent filled the air and her lungs.

Larissa guided her sister's hands to the back of another nearby bench along the water's edge.

"She saw her brother murdered," Ira whispered. "And her father...."

Larissa pushed Ira's long hair behind one of her ears.

"I'm not sure if she saw either."

"But they were killed—why?"

"You know the stories." Larissa's low voice was well trained to deal with sudden outburst of panic. "The intelligentsia was among the first to be wiped out. The teachers, the writers, the musicians, the educated..." Ira's arms had goosebumps. She didn't know when they'd gotten goosebumps. "Anyone who might lead an opposition." Bullets echoed, drums in Ira's ears. Soviet guns. German guns. Did they sound different from each other? She swallowed. Her mouth had become dry and sticky. The smooth black metal bench was cool under her fingers. She imagined the lines of its back multiplying and rising before her, bars in a prison. "Hey," Larissa interrupted herself. Her voice was distant, outside of their great-grandfather's labor camp cell, beyond their great-uncle's underground hideaways after the Resistance in Galicia had fallen. "Um, so do you know any Baba Yaga stories about a fountain of youth?"

Ira blinked, still walled in by soldiers and blood and the depth of the hunger in Baba Vira's once young bones. Birds warbled nearby. The violinist and her accompanist had stopped playing.

"What's the oldest Baba Yaga story you know?" Larissa prodded, putting a hand on her sister's back. "How'd she become Baba Yaga?" Beyond the birds, a sound of humming or far-off singing rustled in the leaves deeper in the woods—she imagined squirrels, chipmunks, mice, hedgehogs... Her knowledge of European woodland creatures was based in fairytales.

"Wasn't she something before she was a witch?" Larissa

rubbed a hand in a circular motion across her sister's back. Ira realized that her kids were so incredibly lucky.

The taste of the water lilies still hung in the humid air when she parted her lips to speak.

"She came from an old fertility goddess, a patron saint of women." Larissa nodded encouragingly, her circles a lethargic pendulum. Ira took a deep breath before continuing. "But my favorites were the later stories," Ira continued, feeling her mind climbing out of the blitzkrieg of memories in their family blood. "The ones where she's sometimes kind and sometimes a terror, depending on the worthiness of the person she's with."

"Why are old men always wizards and old ladies always witches?"

Ira shrugged. She swallowed. It was true.

In the spring beside them, only a step or two away, a turtle's head emerged from the water. A jogger passed on the path behind them, and Ira imagined the young man as an old grand-father who'd just emerged from the magic waters with decades shed off his life. A stray cat nestled into the roots of a leaning tree, its dappled fur shining and glossy, and Ira wondered how many years, decades, or centuries it had lived.

"Maybe I'm being crazy, convinced she's here somewhere." Larissa shifted her weight, removing her hand from Ira's back.

"No." Ira took another deep breath. "I think you're right."

Another turtle slipped from a jagged rock, splashing into the smooth water to join its friend, its little head surfacing amidst the ripples and reeds a moment later.

"There aren't any sunflowers this time."

"We'll find her." Ira released the bench back she hadn't real-ized she still clutched.

The dappled cat slinked along the path toward them then abruptly shifted its direction toward the spring at the sound of more bike wheels. A teenage girl rode along the curved trail. The wind blew back her long brown hair, and the sun sneaked through the leaves of the overhanging tree branches to dance across her face.

Ira didn't know why she looked behind them as the girl approached. She didn't hear the sound of the other bike's wheels or any coos from the baby strapped into the bucket-seat. The pedaling mom had one hand reached back to her infant, her eyes scanning the ground directly ahead of her for sticks or rocks that would jostle their ride.

The teenager threw out both arms and closed her eyes, a smile growing on her tanned face.

"Watch out!" Larissa shouted just as the girl whizzed past them and toward the other bike. Her handlebars clipped the mother in the side. Their knees collided. Ira ran toward them.

The mother's bike wobbled into the moss-patched grass toward the spring. Its wheels kicked pebbles into the water. The woman leaned against gravity, but she wasn't winning. Ira reached out her hands to her, and the woman twisted in her seat, one hand stretching to Ira and the other reaching out again toward her baby. Her eyes were wide as she missed Ira's fingers. She tumbled toward the water, and the bike fell toward the grass.

Larissa caught the falling baby, somehow maneuvering her hand to brace its little head before it collided with the ground. Ira dove for the mother. The woman's head was in line with the turtle's jagged rock. Ira's arms wrapped around the woman, shifting them both away from the harshly angled stone, but not enough to keep them both from falling in. They landed with a splash with Ira underneath, being pressed into the water, water deeper than she'd thought. Or maybe not so deep, but deep enough when held down. Her cheek pressed into the fuzzy bottom, tickled with algae and organic mud. Her hip banged into something pointed and heavy when she tried to shift toward the surface. Her fingers flailed through the water grasses, her hand stinging when it connected with something sharp, as the woman's weight remained on her chest.

Bubbles escaped Ira's mouth, and she kicked against the

woman's weight. The water was too cloudy to see through, flecked with tiny plants like motes of brown and green dust. Like gun-smoke after a battle. Like incomprehensible ash muddying up the air.

The mother moved above her, slowly then rapidly, reaching for Ira's arms and yanking her to the surface.

Ira gasped as she emerged. Larissa knelt at the water's side, handing the baby over to the mother shaking with fear and adrenaline. Far beyond them now, the teenager wobbled and zig-zagged away on the thin path. She didn't look over her shoulder or apologize, but rode on, hair tangling in the wind behind her. Ira knew that feeling of being lost in the wind and the sunshine. But now she dripped and panted. And the baby cooed. And the mother spoke thankful words they didn't understand. And the sun fell on her face in speckled warmth.

"Your hand!" Larissa twisted to open her purse before Ira saw the slice of skin on her palm. Her sister pressed gauze to the bloody wound, sprayed anti-bacterial ointment onto it, and debated the right bandaid size. "It's deep."

Larissa refolded the gauze, holding it again to the stinging cut. Blood flashed every time she released her pressure on it.

"Wait," Ira grabbed her sister's wrist with her good hand. She held her cut palm upward, the slash a smooth line that curved from the center of her hand to the side between her thumb and pointer. Blood rose to the surface of the new line. Her life line—her too-short life life—had just been extended.

"That's going to leave a scar," her sister mumbled.

"If I'm lucky," Ira whispered.

She didn't know if she should believe the magical properties of these waters, if they could extend lives or restore you to a version of yourself better than ever before, if this spa advertised an ancient secret that few took seriously enough to believe.

"Did you hear that?" Larissa straightened.

Ira tried to listen through the water in her ears, through the distraction of the blood and the extension of her life. She didn't hear anything.

"Listen."

Larissa stood so still Ira thought she could become a part of the mythos of the place.

Ira tapped the water out of her ears. When she froze and hugged herself in the breeze, she heard it too. Singing. Far off, there was Ukrainian singing, their baba's warbling voice unmistakable among the others.

41

Vira

(MARCH 1942)

They'd moved their sleeping pallets together months ago, taking turns with the middle spot, away from the dampness of the rock walls and the chill of the winter air that seeped into the cave mouth. Early in the winter, Dmytro let Noncia and Vira take turns in the center cocoon of body heat under the goose-down blanket, but somewhere in late December, he too entered into the rotation, a middle of the night roll that they'd perfected, body over body, limb over limb every few hours until daytime broke and they tried again to figure out their plan.

Though Dmytro had his plan, now. He'd been waiting for the first signs of spring, and yesterday, they'd spotted tiny red buds on the trees at the edge of the forest.

He pushed himself up, perching on his toes and straight arms without letting the blankets lift up too far. Vira rolled herself underneath him, toward Noncia's sleeping body. But Dmytro didn't lift his arms to let her all the way through. He didn't lower himself onto her but hovered, face as unreadable as the rock that surrounded them.

His breath warmed her chilly face, the tip of her nose that felt like ice, like the crag of a baba yaga's profile, for that's the destiny her mother had left her, hadn't she? She hadn't meant Vira to buy herself her own train ticket and to chase her family down, wherever in Budapest they might be. She cast off her oldest daughter like a spell that no longer choked her. And Vira refused to go begging back.

"Can you survive by yourself?" she whispered when she realized Dmytro wasn't moving. She didn't want to know the answer if the same question was turned on herself.

His lips tightened.

"I think so."

She wished his answer was more confident. He didn't move from above her. Instead he lowered his body that smelled of dirt and moss and spice on top of hers.

"Kiss me," he whispered. "I'll be gone tomorrow."

She moved her chin down, away, like she had ever since she had joined them.

"My sister is asleep."

He reached toward her mouth with his, nudging her nose with his own. Vira didn't tell him to stop, she didn't tell him to go, she didn't say a word—neither did her limbs or her heart have any warmth left to pull him closer or push him away.

Dmytro's lips were cracked and rough, but she knew her own were too. She wanted to feel something, anything, her own heartbeat in her skin or his where they touched. Yet even his body on top of hers didn't thaw her. He moved his hands into her dirtied hair, but they only snagged in its tangles. She closed her eyes, and her mind wandered to the time she'd woven the flowered crown, how she'd warmed when his face was close enough to kiss her and how her skin prickled when he'd wrapped his arms around her. How the buzz of the bees also had stirred inside her with Mykhail.

An involuntary shiver ripped through her, but Dmytro took it as a stir of pleasure as her wall finally broke down. He kissed her harder, shifting himself to free a hand to rub over her body, down her neck and under the neckline of the multiple shirts she wore.

The crown of flowers had reeked of smoke and ash. Lesya had known about her midnight escapes all along. She'd said she'd wished she could be more like Vira. Vira hoped wherever she was that she was anything but. She didn't blame her sister for leaving. She was always the good girl to their mother, always the listener. But Vira knew she'd protested getting on that train. She often imagined that argument between mother and second-eldest daughter. She only hated her mother the more for it.

Dmytro's movements stilled when Vira's head fell to the side.

His face turned again to stone.

"You regret your choice of us."

But Vira knew it was never a choice. Her family hadn't given her a choice. She knew he wanted to hear her say no, but she couldn't.

"I..." She tried to force something out of her mouth. "Please be careful," she whispered, as he rolled over and away, allowing her the warm cocoon, surrounded by the siblings, the warmth that wiped away any thoughts from her head except for the relief of sleep.

When she woke up, she was pressed close into Noncia's side. Vira's back was cool, not exposed by forgotten blankets, but lacking from body heat behind her. She rolled over.

Dmytro's sleeping pallet that had been tucked so close to hers for months had been wrapped up and taken away. His bundle of clothes and blacksmithing tools and a small portion of food were gone.

The mouth of the cave showed a hint of morning light. She didn't move only because she didn't want to take her own warmth away from Noncia. Noncia's loss had been as bad as her own. She never looked to the spot on the cave floor where the blood hadn't completely washed away.

Noncia's eyes flickered, and Vira held her breath, hoping she hadn't woken her friend, but the blink turned into a stretch and a slow roll until the two women met exhausted eyes.

"I'm going into town today," Noncia said instead of good morning. She understood without looking that her brother was already gone. "We need a plan too."

"I have a little money left," Vira whispered. The cave ceiling above her head dripped with condensation. The droplets had formed a puddle not far from their heads.

"Not enough. We need to get out of these woods. To a city somewhere."

"But cities aren't safe."

"Neither is a haunted cave."

Not having a mirror, they wiped sleep from each other's faces with a damp cloth and pulled at their clothing as if the wrinkles only needed a tug to be released. Vira no longer stumbled on their path through the woods. For months, she'd told herself the tree branches were the fine railings of her staircase. The patchy grasses her fine rugs. She swallowed the tears that wanted to fall. She refused to messy her face with them.

On the sidewalk outside the market, the shopkeeper scowled at her, and Vira didn't blame her. She only stopped in a few times all winter, emptying shelves, each time purchasing as much as she could carry, and today again, she was filthy. But she'd save her shopping for later. First, she walked on to the café under their old apartment. The owner was the one person in this town who remained kind to her.

"Good morning," she called to him, seeing him with a broom by the open door.

"Ah, Pani Vira," he answered, seeing her, seeing everything she had become, but he didn't scowl or retreat. "You are here. You are okay."

"You said in the spring you would have more customers, that you might be in need of a waitress."

She raised her chin through her grime, her wrinkled clothing, and her desperation.

"I'm hoping I have something better for you. Wait here."

He leaned the broom against the doorframe and retreated inside. The morning was cool, but a promise of warmth hung in the air. Big white puffy clouds only partially hid a blue sky, bright blue, like the skies she remembered over their sunflower fields. She would give anything to go back to those fields, to dance among the tall stalks as if they were suitors surrounding her, to be a younger girl hiding beneath their brilliant yellow faces.

"Pina Vira," the café owner said, returning, putting a hand on her thin shoulder. "This came for you."

A letter with her name on it appeared before her.

She gasped and blinked, staring at the stamp, attempting to decipher the blurred ink that wasn't from Budapest, that didn't seem like Lesya's script. Was it simply a rushed version of Lesya's handwriting? Had she convinced their mother to take her back? She swallowed as she took it into her hands, wincing at the dirt in her fingernails against the crisp white paper.

"It came over a month ago," the café owner said, keeping his hand on her shoulder, as if preparing to catch her if she were to wobble and fall.

She tore it open, looking for her sister's fine handwriting, always so much better than her own.

The café owner tightened his steadying hand on her. She could feel him holding his breath for her too. Yet the handwriting wasn't familiar. It wrote her name, of trying to find her for so long, of being so far away, of hoping this note would reach her. Only at the bottom of the letter did she understand. The signature made her entire being ache. "With your faithful husband's love, Mykhail."

She repeated her husband's name on her tongue. Her body felt weak, unnourished, detached from herself. She didn't know if this letter was real or if the past winter had been. Her muscles ached from the cold of the cave. She thought of the warmth of Dmytro, the warmth of her husband's strong arms, the buzzing of the bees inside of her. Vira tried not to shudder because she knew if she shuddered, the quake of her body would turn her to pebbles, then sand, then silt no different from what she knew in the cave.

"Is it from your husband?" the café owner repeated, squeezing her shoulder. "He's alive, thank God!" He crossed himself.

"Thank God," Vira repeated, hearing another name she had-n't spoken or thought of for so long. She read the letter again, understanding its contents this time. Mykhail was alive. The Germans had taken over his Ukrainian regiment, but there was a hint of hope, of determination, of emotion she couldn't find in herself. He prayed to see her again. He told her he and two friends had a plan to make sure they would survive.

He shared an address in Western Hungary, a resort town the war hadn't yet touched, a town looking for women, for multi-lingual hostesses who could help its international guests, for women interested in training in medicine. He wrote of spon-sorship for going to Canada, to start their life anew when the war ended. He wanted to make sure she was safe, to know where he could find her. Vira swallowed. She couldn't take in any of it. In the park across from the café, Noncia sat on a bench, head in her hands.

Medicine. Noncia always wanted to study medicine.

Her Uncle Oleh had told her to preserve her story so it wouldn't be forgotten, but all she wanted was to leave this chap-ter behind. She thanked the café owner and crossed toward the park. A child yelled after her, calling her a witch. Vira scowled and spit at him, only sorry the spittle didn't land square across his face. Someone needed to make sure people got what they deserved. They had no idea how lucky they were. They had no idea what the world could do to you if you weren't ready for it, if you weren't giving it everything in your power, if you were lazy or weak or dumb or vile to the people around you.

She put a hand on Noncia's shoulder.

Together, they would have just enough money for a week or two more of barely enough food. Or maybe, enough for two train tickets. To western Hungary, to the resort town of Heviz. To a new chapter of her story. To a stronger one. To one where she would teach the world how it should be before it crumbled to the ground.

42

Lyalya

The singing wove between the beech trees, bouncing off the firs and oaks, saturating the air around them. The song sounded so much like home to Larissa, but she knew home was nowhere near where she stood. Baba Vira's voice wasn't in the backyard singing to Anna and Alex. Her baba wasn't singing to herself as she cooked or gardened or cross-stitched with fingers stained and shaking but still flawless in every effort.

Baba Vira sang in the middle of Baba Yaga bedtime stories sometimes, in the moment of suspense right before the child was eaten or the young girl was saved.

Larissa lifted her head and pushed her fallen hair behind her ear. Her heart was true. Her body was strong. Her mind was brave. With Ira at her side, she walked, picking out the tune their grandmother had sung to them when they were small, the tune she'd still sing to her children on days when other lullabies weren't quite enough.

"*Cuckoo, cuckoo, ptychka mala. Cuckoo, cuckoo, ptychka mala....*"

The song that mimicked birdsong spread itself out through the forest of this resort known for hundreds of years as the Fountain of Youth. She had a desire to drop breadcrumbs on their path. Or pebbles. That was the lesson of the old story, wasn't it? The birds would eat the bread crumbs.

"It stopped," Ira whispered.

Larissa looked at the path before them that forked and curved both toward and away from the spring, toward eternal youth and away. She didn't know why she felt a substantial life choice ahead of her.

"The singing," Ira pressed. Larissa didn't know when she'd stopped listening, but Ira was right. The lullaby no longer washed over the woods.

"It's a Baba Yaga trap, isn't it?" Ira added at her side.

She nodded, unsurprised that her sister's thoughts mirrored her own.

"She always said the world needed more baba yagas." Larissa tilted her head to listen. Warbles of birdsong like Baba Vira's vibrato met the breeze blowing through the leaves. A small splash sounded as a frog jumped into the water.

"She always told me I needed to help her become Baba Yaga." Ira approached the fork, placing one sandaled foot on either side. Larissa thought, in the right Baba Yaga story, her sister would rip herself into two, with both selves continuing to walk along their separate ways. "She said it was good for the world," Ira continued, "that the world needed baba yagas to get stronger, smarter, kinder."

Larissa shushed her sister at the sound of footsteps, but it was just another jogger.

"To scare people into thinking about their choices more, you know? To scare them into being better." The ribbons tucked into Ira's hair fell flat against her head. She tugged at the wet fabric of her shirt that clung to her shoulders then straightened her arms at her side as she stepped into a splotch of sunshine on the path away from the pond. The stippled light painted her upturned face.

"Are you freezing?"

"I'm okay."

Laughter interrupted the cascading trills of competing birds. Baba Vira's laughter. Close. Larissa never thought she'd be so happy to hear that unnecessarily loud cackle.

They left the path at a break in the trees, choosing away from the spring, a third option Ira had found before Larissa. The leaves overhead were heart-shaped, designed as if cut by a child learning to use her scissors. Mammoth rectangular stones lay nearby, pieces Alex and Anna would love to pick up and position again one by one, maybe building a castle this time, something with stuffed animal catapults and ramps for Hot Wheel attacks.

Hints of a conversation reached them through the woods and the fallen walls, and she wanted to see her children so badly, to swoop up boney-legged Baba Vira and take her home.

They moved past the massive stones through a narrow tunnel of beech trees into a clearing where a single umbrella-shaded table accommodated three women. Their grandmother looked up to see them, her bulbous nose red from the sun.

"Lyalya?" She wove her thick fingers together before her. No stains of blood or borscht today. "Irena?"

"*Dobroho ranku*," said one of the other old women sitting next to their baba.

"*Dobroho ranku*." Ira repeated the Ukrainian greeting, dashing to their baba's side, throwing her arms around her and pressing her wet body against her. "I knew we'd find you!"

Baba Vira returned Ira's embrace, cackling again at her wet state. Before her on the table were two nesting dolls. When she released Ira, her age-spotted hands reached out to hold them. At the edge of the clearing, Larissa's feet wouldn't move. The buzz that snapped across her skin since they'd left Slovakia was stronger, itching deeper toward her bones.

"Irena, how—?"

"She looks just like you," said the darker-haired woman, putting a hand to the long gold necklace that draped a boar's tooth over her chest.

"Noncia," Larissa whispered from the border of the sunshine.

The woman dropped her hand as she twisted to see Larissa more clearly.

Larissa swept her hair away from her face and forced herself to move forward.

"*Dobroho ranku*," she repeated to the women.

"My Sonja's girls," their grandmother said to the other women, who took on expressions that wrinkled their foreheads—wrinkled them more than they already were, mistreated storybook pages, stained and crinkled over time.

"Your baba says you keep her good," the other woman said. She reached over and patted Baba Vira's leg. "That used to be my job. She could always get into such trouble."

Larissa's hands were clammy, and the wind kept blowing her hair back into her eyes. She crossed to kneel next to Baba Vira opposite Ira.

"Why didn't you tell us where you were going?"

"Because you would not have liked."

Flowers surrounded the field in the forest, framing them in shades of blue, green, yellow, and pink. Peonies, daisies, and blue poppies. Any other day, Larissa would not be able to turn away from those buds, but today she wanted to shove their colors away so she could focus.

"Darina had a baby girl," Ira said to Noncia.

"I knew it would be a girl," the old woman answered. Her hand returned to the boar's tooth around her neck. "Did you meet her?"

Larissa nodded, absently, the flower colors a technicolor effect, Dorothy now in the land of Oz. She blinked and faced her grandmother's squinty eyes.

"But why the game of *Obman*?" The birdsong vibrato and accompanying cuckoos wanted to interrupt her, but she wouldn't allow it. "If you wanted to visit Noncia, if you wanted to go to a Hungarian resort, why the game of *Obman*? Why not just tell us?" Larissa heard her accusatory voice, her angry mommy voice. She had had such a nice break from her angry mommy voice.

"*Obman*?" Baba Vira repeated the word, and Larissa swallowed.

"You left us clues, the sunflowers and the ribbons, the masks."

"The Warsaw mermaid statue," Ira interjected. The tryzub ribbon in her hair moved in the breeze. Larissa put a hand to her neck, fingers tracing the cool strength of the stone.

"What is this game, *Obman*? Deception?" The other woman inserted herself again, and Baba Vira reached beyond her granddaughters to take her hand.

"Lyalya, Irena, I need to introduce you—"

"Excuse me, I'm sorry," Larissa interrupted, putting up a hand to the other woman before taking up her grandmother's. It wasn't polite, she knew, but for once in her life, she didn't care about being polite. "You didn't leave us that trail? We only found you because...."

Across the table Noncia sat up straighter. Her long, braided hair was flecked with gray. It fell over her shoulder as she moved.

"Your necklace," she whispered. "Vira, that necklace."

Their baba let go of the other woman's hand to lean toward Larissa's neck. She put a hand to the stone that rested between her collar bones and closed her eyes. When they opened, they were full of tears.

"Dmytro's stone," she whispered. "I never told you... He said he'd come back to us, but he did not, could not. Arrested and sent to Chelmno. So many killed there. I was pregnant with your mother years later before I knew."

"Dmytro was my brother," Noncia added.

"The blacksmith's son?" the third woman asked, looking between them.

Baba Vira closed her eyes again, nodding, clutching the stone at Larissa's neck. Her wild white hair wasn't fully contained by the braid that bent over the crown of her head, but in the sunshine, the loose wisps reflected in her halo. She didn't look mad here, not crazed or senile or out of place, thought Larissa. In this patch of European forest, surrounded by these women, she looked at home.

"My Lyalya, she is much like you," Baba Vira said to the third woman as she opened her wet eyes. "She is a *hospodinia*, polite, generous, always taking care of me and drives me crazy."

Baba Vira tapped the smaller nesting doll on its head. It clutched baked bread in its hands. Its golden curls were tucked under a red floral scarf that matched a red floral apron.

The other doll was slightly bigger, golden locks a shade darker, green eyes, a long-nosed, pointy-chinned mask of some sort in its painted hands.

"I found Lesya," said Noncia, motioning first to the bread-holding doll and then the other woman.

"Lesya?" Larissa repeated, squeezing her grandmother's hands. "Your sister, Lesya? But, Baba, you'd told us Lesya died in the war."

The flowers at the edge of their clearing swayed and danced in the breeze with some petals raised over their beautiful heads, others stretched out in welcome.

"Oh my God, I see it!" Ira exclaimed. "The nose and eyes. They have the exact same nose and eyes. It's your nose and eyes, Lyalya."

"I'm sorry, but..." The familiar refrain slipped out of Larissa's mouth but she stopped it. There was nothing for her to be sorry for here. She wished the flowers would stop distracting her.

"Lyalya, Irena, this," their grandmother looked from the dolls before her to the old woman beside her. "This is my sister. I said I lost her in war, never died."

Ira stood from her kneel to embrace the woman she'd had her back to, but Larissa stayed by Baba Vira's side. Her grandmother's hand was still on the stone. Her feet wouldn't have moved anyway.

"Before war, when we were girls, our Uncle Oleh gave us these dolls," Baba Vira continued. The paint had faded, and a crack ran down the larger one's side. "This was mine, and this," she tapped the second doll, "was Lesya's." The wooden dolls were clearly painted by different hands, one that gave rosebud lips and long eyelashes, the second with wide open eyes and a smile that was not looking for anyone else's idea of perfection.

"I've had your baba's doll for over sixty years," said Noncia.

"She wanted to throw it away, but I kept it. I knew someday she'd want it back." She held her face up to the sun, seeming to soak up its warmth before continuing. "I had never really known Lesya, before or since, but when I found her, and she had the doll to fit inside, I knew it was true."

Baba Vira leaned forward to take the smaller matryoshka in her hand, twisting with trembling fingers to reveal more dolls inside.

"My littlest sisters, the twins, Helena and Halya." She rotated the nesting dolls over in her hands before bringing them one after the other to her lips.

"Both died years ago." Lesya, their baba's sister, their baba's lost-but-not-dead sister seemed so serene, so poised, so beautiful amid her age spots and wrinkles and white-washed hair. "Helena a few years after the war, a fever that never broke, and Halya to pneumonia thirty years after her sister to the day."

Baba Vira's sister tucked one inside the other, inside the other, inside the other, her wrinkled, veined hands well acquainted with the ritual, each sister keeping the other safe, becoming stronger because of their proximity. Then she reached into the bag that sat in her lap.

"A gift," Lesya continued. "I don't know how you are here," she said to Larissa and Ira, "but this is for you too."

From her bag, she pulled out a new brightly colored nesting doll, its gray hair braided over the crown of its head, its eyes fiercely green, a wide sunflower in its hands.

Baba Vira inhaled sharply.

"Did you paint that?" Ira leaned forward.

"Open," Lesya said.

Their grandmother's hands hadn't moved from the stone at Larissa's neck.

"You open, Lyalya."

Larissa and Lesya both leaned forward, but then the older woman grinned, letting Larissa take the gray-haired matryoshka in her hands. She twisted it open to reveal a doll with painted gold curls inside, eyes fiercely green, hair loose without a braid or headscarf, and in her hands was a bird, a messenger from heaven.

"Mom," Ira whispered. Her shoulder touched Larissa's, as she twisted this one open too. Inside was another with blond hair, this time long and wavy, with brown eyes and perfect rosebud lips. "It's you." Ira gently took the doll from her sister's hands and held it up beside her. The eyes and nose were just right.

"How did you do this?" Baba Vira released the stone on Larissa's necklace to accept her sister's wrinkled hand.

"I had help."

Larissa saw the shared squeeze.

"You've always sent me pictures," Noncia added.

Ira lowered the matryoshka from the side of Larissa's face and twisted it again. She gave Larissa both halves of herself and revealed the smaller wooden doll inside, blond hair woven into a braid across the top of her head, long-lashed eyes, and hands empty.

"Why are my hands empty?"

"Mine too," Larissa said, realizing the same absence of detail in the two matryoshka halves in her hands.

Baba Vira's eyes teared as she looked to Lesya, who just nodded.

"For the hands, it's still up to you. You get to decide."

❀

Little reveals the immense strengths and weaknesses of who we are as people more so than the stories of our pasts, yet we don't often take the time to linger there, to question the choices of those who lived and loved before us. I have been fascinated by the stories of my family's history for as long as I can remember, because hiding between the lines are truths more complicated than anything I've ever been able to put into words—and I've been trying to put versions of Ukrainian World War II stories into my own words since a young age. In any given moment, there are so many unique tales to be told. This was one I always found missing in the public narrative, and I've always known I needed to amend that.

While my characters and their journeys are fiction, I have tried to capture the historical events, passions, culture, words, and realities that surround them with as much accuracy as possible. However, because life itself is a subjective experience—one life differing greatly from another in the same time and place—I recognize the variables that may go into capturing historical truths.

The pleasure and challenge of this research led me to seek out relatives, family friends, new acquaintances, university professors across various countries and continents, and more, allowing me to learn so much more about my own cultural heritage and ancestry, as I sought to respect the story I wanted to tell. Yet what has struck me the most about everything I have learned is a thread of my family story I have always understood since my earliest days: there are countless ways that a woman can be strong, no matter where her life might take her, and it is this, especially, that I hope to honor in these pages.

Acknowledgments

The Baba Yaga Mask would not be the story it has become if not for the strong women (younger and older) in my own family, most especially Romi Muzyka Poteryko-Spisak, who repeatedly assisted with accuracy and authenticity questions throughout my writing journey. Others who greatly offered their expertise and insights from Ukrainian culture and history to Romani culture to medical subtleties and beyond include Adriana Helbig, Dr. Angéla Kóczé, Kelly Petroski, and Dr. Maria Myroslava Tanczak-Dycio and her book *My Life's Journey from Ukraine to Maine*. In addition, the book *Kobzar's Children: A Century of Untold Ukrainian Stories*, edited by Marsha Forchuk Skrypuch, was a powerful resource.

In addition, I must thank the creative writing teachers and mentors who guided me in ways they may never have even realized, when I played with the bones of what this story could be in various forms over many, many years, particularly Ms. Leslie Shaffer and Carolivia Herron, Douglas Jones and Clay McLeod Chapman.

The support of my family and friends through this writing project has been endlessly valuable, but I want to give extra recognition to Frank Petroski, who is always game for an off-the-beaten-path journey, which we can sometimes call "book research," as well as Katharine Herndon, Karen A. Chase, Lisa Hagan, Mary Chris Escobar, the James River Writers community, the Women's Fiction Writers Association, and Twitter's #5amwritersclub. In addition, the judges of the Tall Poppies' "Popstars Writing Contest" gave me valuable insights that changed my perspective on my opening pages. Special thanks, as well, to Nancy Cleary and the wonderful, wonderful team at Wyatt-MacKenzie Publishing.

Writing sometimes seems like a solitary endeavor, but every author knows that this is far from the truth.

Kris Spisak is the author of *Get a Grip on Your Grammar* (Career Press, 2017), *The Novel Editing Workbook* (Davro Press, 2020), *The Family Story Workbook* (Davro Press, 2020), and now the novel *The Baba Yaga Mask* (Wyatt-MacKenzie, 2022). In addition to her books, her "Words You Should Know" podcast, Grammartopia® events, and Story Stop Tour programs are designed to help writers of all kinds sharpen their storytelling and empower their communications. Kris lives in Virginia, and when she's not writing, reading, or talking about writing and reading, she can most often be found enjoying the great outdoors with family and friends.

Learn more about Kris and her books at Kris-Spisak.com

Questions and Topics for Discussion

1. How is female strength epitomized in Larissa, Ira, and Vira? How is it shown differently in each of them? How does the country, culture, and story of their youth affect this strength?

2. Vira wants to save the world by becoming a baba yaga, by scaring children into being honest, brave, and true. What is your reaction to her desire to change the world by starting with its youth? What is your reaction to her strategy?

3. What does having a say in your country's future mean to an individual? Vira's father chooses silence and patience, while other family members choose resistance through actions with the underground movement and through art. Why does each choose as they do? What are the driving factors for these decisions?

4. How do the women in this novel act as nesting dolls, protecting one within the other within the next?

5. *The Baba Yaga Mask* is told through three points of view: Larissa, Ira, and Vira. Which of these threads did you connect with the most, and why?

6. Every family has stories—known and unknown—that shape them. What is a story of your family that has influenced future generations? Or what is something about your family that you wish you knew?

For more discussion ideas, as well as a guide to symbols in Ukrainian folk art, please visit:
BabaYagaMask.com